DAYLIGHT HOURS

JON KERSHNER

DEDICATION

To Monique.

ACKNOWLEDGMENTS

CE, as my first editor, I'll never forget your drive and ambition to help me take this first step. I couldn't have done it without you. MD and KD, your advice and guidance pushed me forward. Thank you, CK, for being an exceptional proofreader, and CB for being my first fan and urging me on. A special thanks to all of my friends and family for your support and advice.

PROLOGUE

Sol could smell the blood. It called to him from the bathroom. He wanted to go. He wanted to taste it.

No! Fight it.

The small man sat on the sofa. He kept running his fingers over the gold crucifix hanging on the chain wrapped around his hand. It was a gift from his mother when he was a boy. It felt cold against his burning skin.

Sol said his prayers like he always did when the hunger rose. It clawed its way up through his soul. He tried pushing it down, burying it. How could he though? Every molecule of his body was burning from the hunger. He was starving and fresh meat was so close.

He could hear the sound of bones snapping in the bathroom. He could hear Dave tearing at the flesh and growling from the thrill. Sol knew how exciting it was to feel all that meat between his teeth, taste all the blood pouring out of every chunk. There was nothing like a fresh kill.

Sol kept his eyes closed. He wouldn't give in. He wouldn't eat. Not until he couldn't fight it any longer. If that happened, God help him, *when* that happened, Sol would lose a little more of the man he used to be.

The bathroom door opened. The enticing scent of hot blood rushed through the trailer. It was ecstasy.

Sol squeezed the small cross so tight it almost cut into his palm. *Fight it.*

"You're pathetic," Dave said.

Sol didn't look back. He wouldn't. He didn't want to see all of the blood on Dave from his kill. He shut down his senses. He didn't want to breathe in the sweet metallic scent of blood emanating from the bathroom. He didn't want to see the white tiles stained crimson.

Dave had gone hunting for dinner. He was supposed to bring back food from the nearest gas station. Instead, he brought back a

1

man whose car had broken down on the highway a few miles away. Dave couldn't help himself. There wasn't much game in the area large enough to feed the both of them. But there were humans. One human wouldn't fill their stomachs, but it would satisfy them. At least for a while.

Dave wasn't ashamed of what he was. He welcomed it. Sol couldn't. He didn't want to be a monster. Dave hated him for it.

"Quit praying. It won't help you." Dave ran a hand over his bare chest. The blood was already starting to dry on his flesh.

Sol's leg started twitching. He sat on the edge of the sofa, staring down at the cheap brown shag carpet that ran through the decrepit trailer. The television was playing nothing but static. Sol had turned it up as loud as it would go to try to drown out Dave's feeding. It had helped, but only a little.

Sol stared out through the small window above the television. The curtains were open and he could only see darkness on the other side of the glass. There was nothing but a few other cheap trailers miles away using up acres of land in the area. He considered running out into the wild to escape the urge. But if he did go out, if he did change, what poor soul would *he* hurt just from hunger alone?

Dave was an animal because he chose to be.

Sol was an animal by accident. He could control the change, but he couldn't fight the hunger very well.

"Hey. Did you hear me?" Dave asked from the doorway.

Sol couldn't think. There was only the hunger. It was so strong. The need burned through his chest.

Sol opened his eyes, staring down at his cross. He could feel the tears burning in his eyes. He was giving in. He always gave in. There was no fighting it for long. Sol simply wasn't strong enough and he never would be.

"I'm not praying for help." Sol started to feel hollow inside, broken. "I'm praying for forgiveness."

Dave laughed, heading back into the bathroom. "Come on. He's getting cold."

Sol thought of his wife, Mary. She hadn't even been able to look at him when she found out he'd gotten sick. He went to her, trusted her love for him. She blamed him, said he ruined their lives. As if it was his fault. He thought of Stephanie; she was turning eight soon. He didn't even get to say goodbye to her before he ran. Sol thought of everyone and everything he had to leave behind after he got sick and killed those people. He thought of it all and the hunger started to boil to the surface. His beast started to win the battle like it always did.

"God, forgive me." Sol got to his feet. The hatred for what he was overpowered everything, even the hunger.

Sol always gave in.

The front window shattered.

The bullet pierced Sol's shoulder. He fell back over the couch, screaming as he hit the ground.

Dave heard the gunshot and the glass shatter. He hadn't heard anyone outside before that, not over his own hunger and that damned television. He ran to the doorway of the bathroom. Sol was writhing and twisting on the floor behind the couch. The blood was already pooling underneath him.

"Jesus Christ!" Sol screamed in agony. The first hint of a growl rolled out of his throat.

Dave could hear his friend's flesh sizzling and burning from the bullet wound.

Silver.

Dave's heart was pounding. He was panicked. They'd been found.

Three more shots exploded in the night and into the trailer. One bullet went through the wall and out through the television screen.

Dave stayed in the bathroom with his prey.

Sol didn't dare move. He held his arm and fought against the indescribable pain shooting through his body.

Both of their sensitive ears heard men yelling at one another outside. They heard footsteps on the porch. The television was gone and they could hear it all so clearly now.

Dave growled savagely at Sol. It was his fault they didn't hear anyone coming. The weakling deserved to die.

Sol rolled onto his side and his eyes were fierce, his face red from pain. This was it. "RUN!"

Dave didn't hesitate. He rushed out of the bathroom and towards the small spare bedroom that Sol had been sleeping in. He moved faster than any man could.

The cheap front door flew off its hinges. Gunshots rang out and Dave felt them tear through the air around him as he ran for his life.

Giving into his beast, Dave let out a terrible roar and released his monster.

The wolf trapped inside, burst out. The human body and clothes vaporized, exploding outward in a violent eruption of particles.

The wolf rushed through the trailer moving impossibly fast. Its bulky mass clipped the frame of the doorway of the bedroom and ripped through it. Without stopping, the wolf braced his head and leapt through the bedroom window.

Dave erupted out of the trailer in a spray of glass and wood.

There was a human a few yards in front of the window, a rifle in his hands. Dave flew straight towards him. He plowed into the human and brought him to the ground with devastating force. His sharp fangs crunched down on the man's throat and nearly severed his head with a violent jerk. The hot, fresh blood sprayed into the back of Dave's throat. The excitement surged through him.

Bright lights flared to life. They were blinding, unbearably bright.

Dave didn't know what to do. He instinctively froze, standing his ground. There were six or seven large pick-up trucks and SUVs parked in the clearing around his trailer. Their high beams shined on the lone wolf snarling at them.

Dave could see human silhouettes behind the lights. They stood up in the truck beds and behind the open doors for safety. A few more were closer to the house, like the corpse who'd been too close to the bedroom window.

All of them had weapons. All of them had to die.

Dave's black and silver fur stood on end. His claws curled into the dry, barren earth. He bared his fangs. Blood dripped down his muzzle from the dead man beneath him. The growl that came from his throat petrified most of the humans nearby. Dave could smell the fear on some of them. It only made the wolf more vicious. He barked and snapped his jaws, ready to kill.

One of the humans got brave.

The first shot rang out.

The bullet missed by inches. Dave dashed forward with supernatural speed. He rushed the nearest human in front of him.

He was a thin man, only a few yards away. The human fired his rifle. The silver bullet ripped through Dave's pointed ear. It was the only shot that human got off.

Dave's jaws snapped down on the man's leg and crushed the bone effortlessly. Without even stopping, the wolf thrashed his head, savagely dragging the man through the dirt like a doll. Dave dug his paws into the ground and threw his victim with a sudden jerk.

The man's limp body skidded and tumbled along the ground like a stone. He smashed into one of the truck grills a dozen yards away, shattering one of the headlights.

Dave barked again, even more blood in his mouth. He turned his sharp blue eyes to his next victim.

For a second everyone just marveled at the beast's limitless strength.

Then people started shouting.

Gunfire rained down on the wolf.

Silver bullets tore through Dave's body instantly. He collapsed in the dirt, snapping his jaws and yelping. The gunfire stopped, but Dave couldn't move. Every pant burned like fire. The bullets had severed his spine and decimated his body. His dark coat of fur was thick with blood.

Dave couldn't see anything but headlights. The blinding light became his world.

Someone came running towards him. Dave's mind told him to attack, but his body was broken. He heard shouting and cursing.

Dave looked up at the barrel of the rifle just inches from his eye. It was the only thing he could see other than the bright light.

The shot rang out. The wolf's body exploded into particles.

Dave's naked human form lay dead in the middle of the yard. Half of his skull was shot off.

Sol hadn't moved in the trailer. He listened to everything and kept his eyes shut as the footsteps came closer. He held his mother's cross tighter than ever and did everything he could to keep his beast buried in his flesh. He didn't want to die an animal, but a man.

The silver bullet was killing him. His heart ached more after every beat. The silver was too close; it was spreading.

Sol barely opened his eyes to see two men with guns aimed down at him. They kept their distance. Another man was close to Sol, not afraid at all. He smelled like a human, but Sol knew he was another monster, just a different breed.

The man looked disgusted.

A woman walked in through the trailer to join them. Her dark boots matched her dark hair. Sol looked at her; the look in her eyes and the gun in her hand made him fear *her* more than the others. She was human, but Sol knew that she brought death with her.

"God forgive you," she said with dreadful disdain as she stood over him.

Sol smiled and closed his eyes. He had been praying for just that.

The shotgun shells decimated Sol's chest. He felt no pain as the silver destroyed his heart.

Both of the monsters were dead.

Some of the humans in the trucks came up to the trailer with flamethrowers. They sprayed Sol's body and everything else with streams of fire.

The gold crucifix beside Sol's corpse started to melt in the flames as the trailer burned.

They burned Dave's body in the front yard as well.

The group of humans gathered their dead, turned off the lights on the trucks, and waited.

The trailer went up in flames and Dave's body blazed on. The two fires illuminated the area like a grim bonfire as the humans watched.

They all stared proudly at their work.

There were two less monsters in the world.

1

"Kristopher, I need a favor," Jack said from across his large oak desk.

An old wooden fan clicked overhead and a lamp on the wall illuminated the room. I sat there in the small private office Jack spent most of his time in. The wood paneled walls and hardwood floor gave the place a southern charm.

Jack was the owner of one of my favorite bars on the beach, Mikey's. Jack was also one of the few Weres I've ever met that I can stand to be around. Unfortunately, I was in Mikey's to feed, not talk business. I hate being bothered on my dinner breaks.

"If you need a favor, I have a question," I said as casually as I could, ignoring the human pressing the shotgun to my back.

Jack just looked at me, unimpressed in his old leather chair. Jack wasn't too tall, maybe five ten or eleven, but he was built with solid, dense muscle; not too big, but you wouldn't want to piss him off. He had a head full of salt-and-pepper hair with a matching goatee. Working in the sun for years had turned his skin to leather. His voice was raspy, but not because of the cigars, but because of the animal lying just underneath the surface. Jack wasn't just any Were, he was a Werebear. Sure, he wasn't the most intimidating man I've ever met, but I've seen his bear, his beast. It was enough to make any sane person cautious around him. Too bad I'm not that sane.

All I have to do is imagine him in a hat telling kids how only they can prevent forest fires. It relaxes me.

"What, Kris?"

"Why do you call it 'Mikey's'?" I asked.

Jack just kept his pale green eyes on me, as blank as could be.

"I mean, shouldn't you call it 'Jack's' or 'Jacky's'? Though I guess 'Jacky's' sounds a little feminine. Maybe you should call it Jack—"

"Shut up." The man behind me shoved the barrel of the shotgun into my shoulder.

I smirked at Jack. I'm told I have an irritating smirk.

"Kris, you owe me," Jack said as if he hadn't even heard me talking.

"What are you talking about?"

A growl escaped Jack's lips. "I'm not in the mood to play games right now. You know exactly what I mean."

I knew. Last spring I had been involved in an accident of sorts. The accident being three unruly Werewolves trying to kill me because they thought I was intruding on their territory. They were punks. I took them out and accidentally killed one of them in the process. I hadn't thought much of it. Unfortunately, the one whose heart I ripped out happened to be important. He was the son of the leader of a Werewolf pack trying to do a business deal with Jack. Jack was a businessman, had been for a long time. He owned a lot of land up north and rented it out to Weres who needed some getaway time from humanity. The Werewolf's son dying in Jack's territory could've been quite the deal breaker.

As it turned out, the Werewolf's dear old dad wasn't very dear. His son had been dealing drugs and reprimanded before for pimping out women to other Weres for sex and food. That hadn't sat well with Jack, so he let me slide without any kind of repercussion for slaughtering the little pup. As for dad, he just turned a blind eye on the whole thing. And they say I'm unlucky.

I sat there with Jack looking at me in his dark plaid button-down shirt.

"Jack, I'm here for a snack. Can't business wait until tomorrow?"

"No."

I jerked my thumb at the guy with the shotgun aimed at my spine. "Well, what's this idiot think he's doing?"

Jack's eyes looked up to the man behind me.

The human pushed the gun into my back harder this time. "Watch your mouth."

It made me smirk.

"Jack…" The Werebear just stared back at me. "Is he supposed to be a snack?"

I caught a whiff of the man's fear in the air. God, I love that scent.

"Try it," the man said. I could hear his finger rubbing along the trigger of the shotgun.

If I wanted, I could've gotten up, spun around, snatched that gun, and shoved the barrel down his throat before he even realized I'd moved. I was contemplating wanting to.

"Hey." Jack nodded to the door. I didn't even turn around. I heard the man behind me lower his gun and walk out of the office. Good boy.

I turned around in my seat and watched the door shut, the sound of music spilling into the quiet office for a second before it was silent again. Once the thug left, I turned back to Jack.

"Was that really necessary?"

Jack shrugged, the tension and seriousness on his face vanishing. He grinned at me and reached into his desk drawer. He pulled out a bottle of George T. Stagg and a small shot glass. "I have to make sure the boys know when I mean business. You know how it goes."

"He new?"

Jack nodded as he poured himself a glass. "That's Rick. Just moved out here from Nevada. Worked as a bodyguard for some hot shots in Vegas. He's a good kid, serious as all hell though."

"You going to tell him this is *my* territory?"

Jack shrugged. "Maybe later."

"What happened to Hank?"

Hank had been Jack's previous bodyguard and enforcer.

"Hank is taking some time off in North Carolina." Jack downed his shot of bourbon and winced.

"How come?" I asked.

Jack chuckled. "Said he was getting too old for this. He's been with me for ten years. That's a long time. Needed a break. I told him to join the club. Rick there's his replacement."

"So do you even need a favor, or were you just showing off for your new muscle?"

Jack leaned back in his worn-out leather chair. "I don't need a favor as much as I have a request."

I got up out of the uncomfortable green chair in front of the Were's desk. "I don't need advice, Jack. I need to get a bite to eat. I'm starving."

"That can wait." Jack watched me stand. "Kris, you have to listen to me."

"Do I have to?"

Jack sighed. "I'm told that there's been some recent killings up north."

Killings? That grabbed my attention. There was only one type of killing that mattered to people like Jack and me.

"How many Vampires?" I asked.

"Three, and two Werewolves too. They even managed to take down a Witch. She wasn't even practiced in the arts. Just known because of her kin." Jack looked miserable. He poured himself another glass.

"The killings coming this way?" South Florida was a melting pot or salad bowl or whatever they were calling it these days. Usually there weren't too many rogue Vampire or Were hunting's going on down in good old Florida. If there were, I'd have known about it.

Jack nodded. "A friend of mine in Georgia says that one of her cousins went missing. She's afraid that she's been hunted down."

"Sorry to hear that."

Jack took his second drink and pulled himself to his feet. "It's nothing to fret about. She may turn up."

We both knew it wasn't likely. If you had kin that was the same Were species as you, then it bound you closer than blood. If the girl was gone, she was probably gone for good. I didn't like Jack's optimism.

"I've watched some news on the killings. They're calling whoever's doing it heroes. Funny isn't it? You and me slaughter a few men and women and we're monsters. A group of thugs with guns and flamethrowers do it and they're called heroes." Jack had been around a long time, maybe too long. His eyes seemed to drown as he looked down at his empty glass. "Sick world we live in."

"It's not sick," I said. "You just don't like the rules."

"I forgot. Life's just a game to you."

"It is, Jack. It's a game I'm pretty good at. I know the rules and I know how to bend them and break them, even ignore them if I have to. It doesn't bother me too much when the humans do the same."

"So now that you know that we may have a gang of hunters coming our way soon, you gonna lay low?"

"I always lay low Jack. You know me."

"Three Vampires, Kris. Three." Jack walked around the table and put a hand on my shoulder.

Jack was one of the few men I trusted enough to let touch me. I could almost taste his worry on the tip of my tongue.

I smiled and it made the lines in his brow deepen.

"Thanks for the heads up, Jack."

I turned to walk out of the small back office. Jack cursed under his breath. "Where you going off to tonight?"

"Down to the beach," I said. "I could use a drink."

"Which beach?" Jack asked.

I stopped midway to the door to look at the old bear. "What's it matter?"

"Just curious."

"Uh huh," I said. "Pompano, maybe?"

Jack's face lit up and I didn't like it. "Good. You wouldn't mind checking up on something for me would you? Since you're heading in that direction."

"So you do need a favor." I couldn't hide my grin. Usually Jack wasn't this roundabout with getting me to do a job.

"It's easy." Jack headed back for his desk and plopped down in that old leather chair. He started putting the bottle of whiskey back in the desk drawer.

"You always say it's easy."

"But I mean it this time."

I stepped away from the door and stood behind the ugly green chair I'd been forced to sit in. I didn't sit down this time.

"What do you need?"

"I got a phone call from Gary down at The Hornet," Jack said.

I knew The Hornet. It was a small club down in Pompano. Not really much, but they usually drew a big crowd with cheap drinks and decent music. The food was supposedly decent, but I didn't have the same appetite as most of the regulars who went to The Hornet looking for a meal. I'd been there four times and never picked up anything worth my time. Maybe my standards were too high.

"What's wrong?" I asked.

"Gary said that some guys were asking around, wondering if there's been any Vampire or Were problems that he knew about."

"What did Gary say?"

"Gary's a good guy, Kris. He didn't say a thing. Called me instead."

I didn't know Gary well; hell, I didn't know half of the people that Jack knew. But if Jack trusted him then it meant I did by association.

"I'll go check it out." I turned back for the door.

"Don't go hurting anyone," Jack called to me. "Just see who it is and—"

"I'll handle it, Care Bear." I grinned at Jack and could see the dry iciness in his eyes. "Don't worry about a thing."

"Just don't make yourself a target. Remember what I said about laying low."

"I'll just check it out. I'm not staying long though. I need to feed."

"I know, I know. Just give me a call and let me know what happens. Now get."

I put my hand on the doorknob and stopped. I glanced back at the worried Were watching me from his desk.

"What?" Jack asked.

"Do I just walk out or did you want to throw me out just for the hell of it?"

2

I walked out of Mikey's without getting anything to drink. I'd stopped there for a snack and came out with a job to do instead. Not to mention the lecture about being careful. I wasn't worried yet, but if Jack was, I probably should have been. But worrying isn't something I do. It takes the fun out of everything. If the whole hunter issue were such a big deal then I'd take a look into it later…much, much later.

The cool ocean air glided along my skin. The moon was hidden behind silver clouds and I felt its energies washing down on me. It was close to ten o'clock and I could tell it was going to be a beautiful night. There's nothing like South Florida in mid-February. It's as close to paradise as I've ever felt.

Mikey's was right on the beach. I walked through the packed parking lot in front of the bar and headed south on A1A. The Hornet wasn't too far south. It would be a twenty-minute walk if I kept a good pace. I was doing Jack a favor; missing my feeding time to go check up on Gary. No one was dying so I didn't really have to hurry. I walked along the sidewalk with my hands in my coat pockets, an empty stomach, and a head full of thoughts.

I couldn't get what Jack said out of my head.

Three Vampires. That was tough to do for whoever did it. It meant that they traveled to three different territories looking for trouble. We amazing creatures of the night are more territorial than you'd think. We're also an endangered species these days.

Personally, I've only met a few Vampires. One was the man responsible for turning me into the fine, upstanding supernatural figure I am today. Another was a co-worker of mine for fifteen years. Then there was the Vampire who ran this territory before me. The other two or three were just brief acquaintances I made while travelling and looking for a place to settle.

What can I say? Beaches, fun in the sun, women in bikinis; South Florida was the place to be. You'd have to kill to get real estate like this. Trust me. In all fairness, I did ask nicely, but the

14

Vampire before me was old and stubborn. I might not have been as strong as he was, but I'm creative. Sometimes, that's all it takes.

I had been a little hesitant about becoming Territory Master at first, but once I worked out a deal with Jack, it seemed meant to be. Jack was one of the most laid back people I'd ever met. He was a Werebear, but he was a good man. He kept a majority of the other Weres off my back because of the respect the community had for him. Jack was old too. He said he contracted lycanthropy during the Yukon Gold Rush in Alaska back in 1903. He went out there with his cousin and uncle to get rich and wound up being the only survivor of a bear attack instead.

Jack thought he was cursed at first. He went out after the Were that changed him, found him, and killed him. Too bad lycanthropy doesn't usually work like that. You can be cursed, sure, but lycanthropy itself is just a disease like any other. If you get HIV from somebody and you go out and kill them, it doesn't change a thing. You still have HIV in the morning.

So Jack had become a Were and made the best of it. The rest, he says, is history.

Weres usually age no differently than humans. Jack tells me that he's still aging, it just takes longer than most. According to him, first-generation Weres age slowly, but any of their children born with lycanthropy age normally. He was well over one hundred, but he only looked like he was in his early forties. Not bad if you ask me. But I still look better.

Considering the time when he was changed, Jack became one of the first business bears to open shop down in the Sunshine State. Many Weres went to him for advice or for help in starting their own businesses.

Jack was quite the philanthropist. I couldn't even begin to tell you how many businesses he owned and how much money he had coming in. I knew it was a lot, and it baffled me why he spent most of his time in the back of some cheap bar. I've asked, but he just tells me that it keeps him close to me. Jack cares about a lot of people and he even gets along with me. He may just be a big furry Saint.

That's why I made Jack my business partner after I killed the previous Territory Master. The way things used to work was simple, and by simple, I mean archaic. The Vampire was in charge and everyone had to pay their dues for safety in the territory. He used fear and murder to keep people in line and make sure they paid. It was horrible. Okay, I guess I do it too sometimes, but what can you do?

Now, I'm not really a big fan of responsibility or dictatorships. Jack's the smart one. He's better at running the territory than I am, and he's trustworthy. We made it a partnership. I earn my keep by being the muscle when I have to and making the big decisions with Jack when serious times come.

We'd been running things like that for the last two years and it was going great. It was the reason that I didn't complain that much about going to check on Gary at The Hornet. It was all part of the job. Who knows, I might even find something to eat there. How's that for optimism?

The walk took a little longer than I thought it would. After a forty-minute stroll, I walked up to The Hornet. The club wasn't on the beach like Mikey's. I had to take A1A the whole way down to Pompano and then head west over the Intracoastal to US-1.

The club was a standalone building painted a rich, dark green. There were no windows, just a bit of graffiti covering the bare walls. In a bright electric sign on the roof of the bar were the words, "The Hornet", with a vicious little insect mascot spray-painted at the top of the front entrance. It could've come off as corny as hell, but it…oh wait, it did.

The music inside vibrated off the walls and shook the ground, at least to me. My senses are only about a billion times more sensitive than a human's is. I had to concentrate on lowering my sense of hearing or else I'd go deaf as soon as I walked into the bar. New Vamps sometimes go insane from not being able to control their senses. For me, it's like flicking a switch. I can tune down all of my senses one second, and then crank them up the next if I want to.

I can heighten my sense of smell to the point where I could hunt down or track just about anyone or anything by scent alone.

The same goes for my hearing and sight. In a nightclub with awful heavy metal playing, I'd wind up blowing out my eardrums.

The parking for The Hornet was a little scarce. Other than a small lot in the back and a few roped off patches of gravel nearby, people had to park wherever they could find a place. The front of the building had a cement ramp winding up to the entrance like an amusement park. People were standing in line and an irritated bouncer stood between the hopefuls and the inside of the lousy club.

I recognized the bouncer. He worked the door every time I came and he should've known what and who I was. He was over six and a half feet tall and about eight shades darker than any of the other people waiting in line. The long dreads that came down to his shoulders swayed a bit as his head turned and he saw me walking straight for him.

I ignored the stares and yells from the people in line. The bouncer looked at me and nodded. Good boy.

I patted him on his arm, just about the size of a watermelon, and he gave me a nod that said head on in.

I stepped through the large double door and the sound of music bombarded me. It felt like it was shaking my bones. With my hearing in check, I found the rhythm of the blaring music thumping out of the speakers and kind of liked it.

The Hornet was bigger inside than it looked. I walked in through the dark, dimly lit entrance. At the other end of the building, I saw the countless bodies moving with the music in the middle of the dance floor. The spray of lights on the ceiling flashed in sync with the bass. Still, the humans all danced and partied with one another. Compared to what I'd grown up with, the dancing that kids were doing these days looked like they were having seizures on the dance floor.

Seizures on the Dance Floor; wasn't that a band?

The entire back of the club was devoted to dancing with a platform on the far wall for DJs. That night, the man behind the music equipment seemed devoted to making all of the women in black fishnets and leather leggings shake what they had, to the strange mix of heavy metal and techno.

Wrapped around the dance floor in a semi-circle was a black carpeted and tiled area that led to different areas. On my right was a large lounge with a few tables and benches that matched the décor with black and dark wood. People sat drinking, laughing and carrying on at the large bar that sat in the back of the lounge.

To my left was another similar lounge with matching tables and bar, packed full as well. But just beyond that there was a staircase that led to the second story of The Hornet. I made my way to the stairs and through the people coming down and heading onto the dance floor.

I watched a number of twenty-something girls catch my gaze as they passed. A few of them were gorgeous, dressed in black skin-tight slacks and tops that made it clear they weren't wearing bras. I felt underdressed for this type of scene. In my dark jeans and black coat, I didn't quite match the rough and tumble dominatrix theme going on.

Two bouncers blocked off the stairs. I didn't recognize either of them. Both were dressed in matching black jeans and black dress shirts. On the left was an enormous Hispanic guy who looked like he was all upper-body strength. The other was a more evenly muscle-bound blond with sunglasses on.

"Can't come up here," the blond said to me as I approached. His hair was cut short and the veins on his forearms looked like they were going to pop out any second.

I decided to ignore Corey Hart and talk to the Hispanic guy instead. "I'm here to talk to Gary. He called Jack about a problem."

The Hispanic thug smirked and looked me over. I was only six feet tall and he was close to half a foot taller with thirty pounds more muscle.

"Gary said someone was coming to see him." The Hispanic guard swatted his partner on the arm and they both parted.

"Go ahead."

Mr. Sunglasses kept looking at me as I headed up the stairs as if he didn't trust me. A part of me wanted to knock those glasses off his face, but I behaved. I was there for a job and then to leave and go on with my night. Nothing else.

There was another bouncer at the top of the stairs. He was wearing black jeans, but a white button-down shirt that was more casual than dressy. The top few buttons were open to show of his tanned muscular chest. He had black hair long enough to curl around the back of his neck and he was a man I recognized from every trip I made out there.

"Mark," I came up to stand with the man who was my exact same height.

"Kris," he grinned and waved me up off the stairs. "Where've you been? I haven't seen you in months."

The music was still vibrating the walls of the club so I had to practically shout at him.

"I don't really come out here much. No offense, but this isn't the best place in town."

Mark shrugged and was all smiles. "I know what you mean. Gary told me you were coming out."

"Yeah," I practically screamed. "He up here?"

Mark pointed over my shoulder at the lounge that took up the entire back of the second floor of the club. "He's at the bar."

"Thanks,"

"No problem. Just don't kill anyone while you're here okay?"

It made me laugh. "No promises."

The second story of The Hornet was almost like an old theater house. It took up the front half of the building and overlooked the stage below. I walked along to the back lounge where only a handful of people were sitting, drinking and smoking, and talking amongst themselves.

Behind the lounge was a large completely stocked bar. The counter was white and shined in contrast to the dark wood around the rest of the bar. The stools were all black wood with white vinyl tops. I could see the bartender behind the counter serving a few younger guys.

I walked up and leaned against the counter. "I'm dying of thirst. Got anything to drink?"

The bartender looked up at me and the fake smile plastered on his face vanished.

The bartender sent the two men on their way with their beers and then walked over to me.

"What's up, Gary?" I asked.

Gary was in his late forties with a head full of graying curly hair and a receding hairline that seemed to recede more every time I saw him. He might've been big once in his life, but now he was a mix of muscle and fat. He was wearing a black striped dress shirt with the sleeves rolled up and black slacks on. The dark curly hair on his chest spiraled up out of his open shirt.

Gary was human, but liberal. Jack didn't just help Weres and other supernatural types; he helped anyone he could with financial support. The Hornet was more or less owned by Jack who invested a lot of his own money in helping Gary get the place open nearly twenty years ago. Gary needed a loan and help, and Jack was offering it. I didn't like Gary, but I didn't dislike him either. The fact that he helped us out and didn't hate Vampires or Weres, so long as they didn't do badly by him, made him better in my eyes than most.

For some reason though, he looked more upset than pleased to see me.

"What took you so long, Kris?" He tossed the white cloth he used to wipe the counter into a bin at his feet.

"Nice to see you too, Gary."

"I called Jack about an hour ago." Gary licked his lips when he was nervous. A big grown boy from Chicago and he still licked his lips like a schoolboy when he got scared. Oh how precious.

I leaned over the bar and wasn't in the mood to bicker or argue or do anything other than take care of business and go hunting.

"What's wrong, Gary? You called and said someone was asking about Vamps?"

Gary looked around nervously, making sure no one could hear. He leaned in close. "Yeah. Two of them came around here. One of them asked me if I knew the area well. I told him I've lived here for over twenty-five years, I know it as well as anyone."

"So modest."

"Yeah, well he asked me if we have any problems that I know of."

"Problems?" I asked. "Problems being what? Vampires?"

Gary gave a nervous chuckle. "I asked him what he meant and he asked me if there were any Vamps or Weres running around. I told him that we haven't had any problems with no one in years around here. He was a big guy, Kris. I didn't get a good vibe. I know trouble when I see it."

I turned and glanced around the lounge. "They still here?"

Gary shook his head. "I think they left a few minutes ago. You took too long."

Of course I did.

"Well, there's not much I can do if they left already. If they come back again call Jack and have him send someone over." I sighed. The whole trip had been a waste of time.

"Should I even let them back in the club?" Gary asked.

I thought about it. "We don't know who they are. You kick them out and they have a reason to think that you lied to them. We don't want trouble, remember."

"Alright." Gary turned and saw a newcomer at the bar waiting to be served. "You staying here then?"

I couldn't hide how absurd that sounded to me. "No, I'm good."

Gary shrugged. "I know you, Kris. You go ahead and feed if you have to. You're always welcome here."

"Thanks, Gary."

The big man nodded, proud of himself and headed to the young punk in a collared shirt standing at the other end of the bar.

It looked like my work at The Hornet was done. I headed off towards the stairs.

"Finished already?" Mark asked.

"Yep."

"Heading out?"

"Yeah. Nice seeing you, Mark."

Mark grinned and slapped me on the shoulder. "Take it easy, Kris."

As far as humans went, Mark was a decent guy. I didn't know much about his profession as a bodyguard, but maybe I could have Jack set him up with a higher paying job. I doubted he liked standing around watching the stairs at a place like The Hornet.

I was halfway down the stairs when the heavy thrum of the music died down. The lights stopped flashing and shifted to a steadier rhythm. The music that came on was a slower, less-crazed song that changed the mood of the entire club drastically.

I watched the people on the dance floor stop their crazed grinding and flailing. Couples of all kinds started moving in a sensual, passionate sway that seemed more fluid and appealing than before.

And that's when I saw her.

She was wearing a red strapless top. Her skin was pale and her hair tied up so that I could see every inch of that smooth wonderful neck. Her eyes were closed as she danced to the music alone. She caressed her thin body, her hips moving. It was as if she was the only person that existed right then.

Something inside me was throbbing, pulsating. I thought it was my heart, but that wasn't possible. Once the night comes my good old heart quits beating. My hunger was like a living breathing thing inside of me that wanted nothing more than the woman on the dance floor.

I couldn't explain it. I'd never been drawn to anyone like that before. I knew in that instant that I had to have her.

I'd just found dinner and I was starving.

3

I couldn't think clearly. I was halfway across the dance floor when I realized what I was doing. I stopped dead in my tracks amidst the sea of writhing humans dancing around me.

I could see her through the crowd, still alone, still moving to the music of the night. She danced differently than the others. It was as if every move she made was slower, more intimate, more...everything.

I watched her hands play along her body, grazing her chest, caressing her hips and slender stomach. Her hands touched her the way a lover would, the way I wanted to. I wanted to be those hands. I wanted to feel every curve, every rise and fall of her tight body. I wanted to taste her on my lips and listen to her heart pounding beneath her breasts.

I needed to have her.

My legs were moving by themselves. My body felt separate from my mind.

I was right in front of her when she opened her eyes. I saw her dark irises reflecting the beams of light flashing overhead. It made her eyes glow. She looked me in the eye and wasn't afraid, she wasn't embarrassed or self-conscious. In fact, she knew exactly what she was doing. She kept dancing with her eyes locked on mine.

I was mesmerized plain and simple.

I watched her sway and crouch, her body in sync with the music. She went down and came back up, running her hands down her front. She never took her eyes off me. She liked that I was watching her. So did I.

The slow rhythmic music faded and a louder, faster one replaced it. A lot of couples were heading off to get more to drink, but most just started dancing like lunatics again as if the immediate change didn't faze them.

My unknown lady walked right past me and headed for the nearest lounge.

I followed her, admiring the way her ass looked in her tight black leggings. It looked firm, tight.

She turned around and smiled at me, finally looking embarrassed.

We made our way to the bar. She leaned over the counter, waiting for one of the three bartenders to come to her.

I leaned on the counter beside her, staring out at the racks of bottles and glasses. It took everything I had not to look at her. I breathed in her scent and I got chills. She smelled like winter mornings and fresh flowers dipped in sweet candy. It was perfect.

"You're an incredible dancer," I said loud enough to be heard over the music.

I think she smiled at that. "Excuse me?"

I looked at her then and I watched the vein in her throat pulsate. I focused on her eyes; they were the palest brown I'd ever seen.

"You're an incredible dancer."

She seemed to blush, but that perfect smile never left.

The bartender came over, a blond with a whole lot of makeup on and a push-up bra that made it seem like she was going to spill out of her black blouse. A beast compared to my beauty.

"Tequila Sunrise, please," she told the bartender.

"Sure thing," the blond said.

I reached over the counter and handed the bartender a twenty. She took it and asked, "Anything for you, sweetie?"

"No, I'm fine." I lied.

She took the answer and went off to make the drink.

"Thanks, I guess."

I looked to my left and into those pale brown eyes again.

"You don't want anything to drink?" she asked me.

"Not just yet."

She smiled and I felt the connection between us that I'd felt hundreds of times with so many other women. Sometimes all it takes is a look or a glance for someone to be attracted to you, to want you. This girl, she was attracted to me, and I was all kinds of fuzzy over her. She was mine.

I wanted her even more. I had to know who she was.

"What's your na—"

Someone bumped into me and I had to hold onto the counter to make sure I didn't bump into my future meal. I gripped the edge of the counter too hard. It cracked beneath my grip and I almost broke a chunk of it off.

I took a deep breath. I had to stay calm.

I turned to my right and some drunken weight lifter in a bright blue polo shirt was wiping beer off his arm. His face was bright red and his greasy black hair was spiked with enough gel to be considered a lethal weapon. Good old South Floridian preppy boys who could afford personal trainers.

"What's your deal, asshole?" he spat at me.

Great. I really didn't need that right then.

I ignored the human and turned back my next meal. I had to know her name; I didn't care about anything else.

She stepped away from the bar, confused.

Someone grabbed hold of my right arm and tried squeezing as hard as they could. I barely felt it.

I looked over my shoulder and saw the idiot who'd bumped into me.

"I was talking to you," he said, his words slurring a little. His eyes were glazed over.

I watched two other tools in their late twenties standing at the bar behind the guy holding me. They were just as drunk and just as stupid looking.

I didn't need a confrontation with anyone right then. I needed to just work my magic on the woman from the dance floor and feed off her. I don't know how, but I knew she'd taste incredible. I could feel it in my bones.

I tried being diplomatic as opposed to murderous. "Hey, my fault. You want me to buy you a drink?"

The man let go of my arm and shoved me in the shoulder. "What do you think I am, your *boyfriend*? Gonna buy me a drink? Fuck you."

"Boyfriend?" Well, there goes diplomacy.

I turned for just a moment and the woman from the dance floor was gone.

With the music and the idiots, I hadn't even heard her leave.

25

The guy in the polo shoved me and I grabbed onto the bar and stopped myself from stumbling. Oh, I was starting to get pissed.

"Hey, get the hell out of here," the blond bartender shouted from behind the counter.

I glanced at the bartender who was watching us all with hesitation. She was holding the Tequila Sunrise my would-be dinner had ordered. She must've left to avoid any trouble. Smart girl.

I turned completely around to the three punks. I sighed and looked them over.

The music was rising and rising, the speed of the beat going faster and faster. I thought about my prey getting away from me and knew I had to find her. I had to have *her*. No one else would do.

"You sure you want to do this?" I asked the drunk.

I don't think the kid even heard me.

I moved slowly so that I wouldn't draw too much attention, but faster than the kid was expecting. I grabbed him by the side of the head and smashed his thick skull upside the bar counter just to daze him a bit. I got around him and put my arm around his throat to choke him out.

His two friends stayed back, everyone around the bar frozen and watching us.

I could've literally crushed the kid's throat and it would've been as easy as snapping a stalk of celery. I didn't need people knowing what I was or suspecting it. I just remained calm enough to knock the kid out without permanently hurting or killing him.

I let his body slide down to the floor and he toppled over at my feet. Everyone in the lounge just stared at us. The loud music kept going, and the rest of the club wasn't even aware of the little scrap.

I looked at the two punks in front of me.

I looked down at their unconscious friend on the ground.

I turned and walked away from the bar. No one followed me. Smart punks.

Mark came running down the stairs, heading for me. "What did you do now?"

I held up my hands innocently.

Mark shook his head, but I saw him grin as he went to do his job. He told the bartenders not to call the police, that everything was fine.

I let Mark take care of the clean up. I had other things to worry about.

My brain wasn't working right. I couldn't concentrate on anything because of the music, because of my hunger…because of that girl. I wanted her. I needed her. If she got away, I was going to go back to those three punks and break their necks.

I followed the unmistakable scent of my prey and walked out of the lounge. I caught a glimpse of her leaving the club and my body tensed.

I could track her. I could follow her.

I'd find her.

Then the fun could start.

"Please don't kill me," she begged, tugging at the cloths binding her to the bedpost. Tears streamed down her face. I could taste her terror on the tip of my tongue as I watched her. The moon shone in through the window behind me. Her black robe and black panties didn't expose all of her perfect figure, but what did show of her pale flesh shimmered in the moonlight.

"I'm not going to kill you."

Well, probably not.

"Then untie me!"

I shook my head slowly, putting my finger to my lips and shushing her. I couldn't let her get too loud.

She was a smart girl. She continued to cry, but did her best to whisper, "Please."

People confuse me. They're never happy. You try to make things as comfortable as possible for them and they're still never satisfied. She's tied to her bed for God's sake. It's familiar, warm, and soft. I used silk to tie her hands. Freaking silk. Silk doesn't even hurt much. Honest. I do it because I care. Okay, I use silk because it doesn't bruise like handcuffs or leave burn marks like ropes. It keeps them comfortable and doesn't leave evidence, but that doesn't mean I'm not considerate.

I care. Promise.

Now, I go through all this effort when I could've just taken her in the parking lot of The Hornet and this is how she acts. Can we say ungrateful? She was the most delicious smelling person I'd ever met. I was trying to treat her good, like a lady deserves to be treated.

"Relax," I walked over to her bed and sat down beside her. The bed was soft, softer than gravel. Maybe I shouldn't be so nice. She didn't even appreciate me bringing her into her bedroom.

I looked her over. Now that we were alone, I could take my time and get a good look-see. She was slender, thin, but not too thin. Healthy was the best word for her. I liked how pale her skin was, a clean pale, not freckled or blemished. Her hair was a dark tangled mess behind her frightened face.

I followed her home from the club. It was a cheap apartment a few miles west of The Hornet. I don't usually go that far into Pompano, but for a taste of what was inside that woman, I would've gone anywhere. My legs were shaking. I wanted her. I had waited for her to shower, to get comfortable. I was outside the whole time. Her scent hung in the air like a trail of perfection.

I couldn't take it anymore and I finally had to make my move.

"Who are you?" she asked.

Like everyone else, she tried to make sense of something she couldn't understand.

"Nobody," I whispered.

Slowly, tenderly I caressed her cheek with the back of my hand. That simple touch made me crave her even more. As if the physical connection amplified how badly I wanted to feed off her.

I forced myself to calm down. I had to relax. I couldn't afford to be greedy or careless. With that one simple touch, I urged her to relax. I whispered to her soul to be free of all of that fear.

I can always tell by the eyes when they fall under my spell. This woman, this young, beautiful, *healthy* woman was mine. She looked at me and I knew she could feel my lust and hunger for her.

"Who are *you*?" I asked. I believe in a good bedside manner.

She didn't answer right away. She should've.

I leaned in closer. I whispered to her, as close as a lover.

"What's your name?"

I watched those dark eyes flutter. "Lauren," she told me. "Lauren Millar."

It was a nice name, but she didn't look like a Lauren to me. But she couldn't lie. Once I have them, once I've made the connection, it's impossible to tell me a lie. I smiled and it made her feel more than just relaxed. I felt what she felt like a whisper in my ear. I kept caressing her cheek, careful to keep touching her.

I have to keep physical contact so that I can stay in control. Once you've started reeling a fish in you don't let go of the rod do you?

I noticed something dark marring that perfect, pale skin. It was hidden just under the top of her dark silk panties. I ran my hand down her abdomen, over her stomach and just to the top of her underwear. I pulled the tip of the cloth down enough to make out the black tattoo on her hip. It was a plain, simple crucifix.

I ran my finger over the tattoo, the only imperfection I could see on her. I ran my hand back up her body. Crosses don't bother me.

People amuse me with their religion. Religion's just a word. It doesn't matter to Vampires. We're not afraid of it. Now I'm sure maybe some Vampires won't feed on a Buddhist because they're afraid of karma or something, but me, well, I'll take me anything from an Atheist to a devout Catholic, and everything in between. I'm not picky or superstitious. I've gone to church, tasted the Holy Water, stood before the Holy Cross, and was left feeling a lot of the Holy Nothing. Vampires and religion don't really mix since, as far as I know, Vampires predate any religion man's come up with. Christianity included.

"You don't have to be afraid, Lauren," I promised.

"I'm not." She meant it. I could see it in her eyes. She meant it as much as I wanted her to.

"Good." I reached into my coat with my free hand and pulled out my syringe. The needle caught Lauren's attention.

Her fear jolted up my arm and I had to focus on her again to bury that fear. It only took a second. When I held the needle up in front of her, she looked at it with a lustful gleam in her eye. I love it when the ladies look at my needle like that.

I watched the vein in her throat start to dance beneath her skin. I was drawn to it. For a second I thought about tossing the needle and just going for her throat with my fangs. All of that blood calling to me...I could do it.

No. Damn. I shook my head, trying to clear it. I had to stay focused. Whoever this Lauren was, she was affecting me differently than anyone else ever had.

I looked for a vein, that nice blue stream winding under her pale arm. It's called the median cubital vein, where all the big doctors take blood from their patients.

Carefully I pressed the needle to her arm, not breaking the skin. I looked up at Lauren's face. She was biting her lip, expectations, hesitations, and excitement flooding her mind. She wanted me to do it.

The needle punctured her skin.

Lauren's eyes rolled back and her body tensed. Her legs squirmed and she made small sounds from deep inside her throat. I kept touching her, rubbing my hand down her neck and between her breasts. She loved it. She loved it because I wanted her to love it.

I watched the blood fill the tube of my syringe.

Syringe, it's the civilized way of getting some good old-fashioned blood. Despite what you think, not too many people get off on having two one-inch long fangs pierce their neck. Finding a willing customer who likes being bitten is tough. Well, there were those twins in Vegas, but that was one crazy night. Besides, what bleeds in Vegas, stays in Vegas.

Even though it's not every Vampire's lifestyle, my way of getting blood suits me. There's no bite marks for people to identify. It's simple, keeps my life uncomplicated. Okay, biting someone and feeling all of that blood spray down your throat *is* invigorating, I'll admit, but a little archaic these days. I'm practical and practicality goes into surviving.

Getting my blood from people with a syringe is a nice idea I came up with. You take just enough to get by and you don't leave any evidence behind. It's great. I personally love making a nice cocktail. I make a mean virgin with a redhead chaser.

I only filled up three vials that night. No reason to get greedy.

I pocketed the vials and slowly pulled the needle out of Lauren's arm. She moaned a little as I did it. I looked down at her and she was practically radiating warmth. She was beautiful, even more attractive than before. I couldn't explain it.

I could smell her blood in the air. It sparked something inside me. I stared down at the spot of blood welling up out of her forearm. I wanted to lick it. I ran my hand down her abdomen, keeping the connection. There was so much more blood inside her. So much just waiting for me.

I took my hand off that pale skin and got to my feet, putting my syringe away. I didn't like how fuzzy she was making my head.

"Please, please don't hurt me." The panic returned to Lauren's voice as if it never left.

I didn't pay her any attention. I smiled as I held one of the little glass tubes of blood up to the window. It looked black in the moonlight.

I opened the tube and tossed my head back. I like my shots of blood straight.

The second I swallowed the blood I gasped.

It was so sudden, so intense. I felt Lauren inside of me, fueling me, making me just as strong and healthy, and alive as she was. That spark inside of me started to grow. It started to rise and burn deep within my chest and I wanted more. I wanted that spark to grow and burn brighter.

I turned back to the half-naked woman tied to her bed. I had to have more. I had to have all of it.

I went to the bed and nearly lost my balance. I felt dizzy. I'd never tasted anything so sweet, so…indescribably perfect. I turned around towards the window and put my hands onto the wall for support.

My mind was swimming. I wanted more blood. I wanted to feed. I wanted to consume all of her.

There was a picture hanging in a frame on the wall in front of me. I saw four friends standing in front of lockers smiling at the camera. I recognized the teenage girl in the center as the young woman lying behind me. The others didn't matter. The boy on her right didn't matter. He was just some punk with his arm wrapped around the most beautiful thing I'd ever tasted.

I could've torn her open and fed as much as I could. But I didn't. I wouldn't kill her. The thought of coming back, of keeping her alive so that I could return as often as I wanted was the only reason I didn't kill Lauren that night. That thought helped me get my senses back.

With her life still hot in my mouth, I turned and reached out for her arm. She started to scream. I made the connection again to calm her. Lauren wouldn't remember any of it. She'd go back to being scared of the dark. She would close her eyes and drift into her sleep. I'd be nothing but a nightmare she wouldn't even remember in the morning.

Me? I don't ever forget a good meal.

4

I was still feeling a little funny after feeding off Ms. Lauren. I don't even remember thinking about anything else but her the entire walk home. I took the two remaining vials of blood and got out of there as fast and silent as I could. I'd never had anyone taste so incredible. I couldn't get her out of my mind, and for the first three blocks, I had this intense urge to just run back up there and ravage the girl in more ways than one.

I don't ever lose control. I take pride in that. Something about that woman drew me to her, but I couldn't risk everything. I buried my desires and headed home. The night wasn't as fun as I wanted it to be, but I did get the best meal I'd ever had in my life.

I knew I'd have to go back there tomorrow for another taste.

What was it about her that made her taste so...unbelievable? I kept rolling over the thought of swimming in a pool of her blood as I strolled up to my house. It was only a little before four in the morning and I was already home. Lame.

I live right on the beach, literally. Right off A1A. I didn't need heightened senses to hear the waves crashing from the sidewalk or taste the salt in the air. It was a nice oceanfront home on a private beach.

It was everything a Vampire could ever ask for. Aren't I lucky?

I had gotten it cheap through Jack. One of his numerous business associates dabbled in real estate and got me a deal. I paid Jack the money for my rent each month, and he in turn gave it to the man who legally owned the house on paper. I didn't know the specifics, but I didn't ask questions. To be honest, I don't care about the minor details. I had somewhere to live and I liked it a lot. Why ask questions?

I spent last summer working on the house a bit. The home was built in the seventies and designed to weather the weather of South Florida. I painted the outside an off-white to be as simple as possible. It was better than my neighbor's bright pink house.

I walked up the driveway and headed inside.

The inside is pretty big. The front door opens right into the large living area that occupies almost half the house. The living space leads straight back into the kitchen. There's a large space cut out of the wall so that anyone in the kitchen could see into the living room and so I could see the television while I cooked. I even had a few stools on the little bar counter on the other side so that people could sit and talk to whoever was busy at the kitchen sink. In the daytime, a small window over the back counter and between the pantries lets in enough sun to light the entire kitchen naturally.

Straight back on the far wall is a sliding glass door that leads out to the wooden deck. The vertical blinds were closed tight and I couldn't see the moon reflecting off the ocean.

The lights and television were on when I got inside. I heard footsteps on the tile in the kitchen and I smelled cologne and sweat.

"Where were you all night?" a voice asked the second I locked the front door.

I looked at Kyle standing by the kitchen in a pair of jeans and a blue hoodie.

"Hey, Dad." I tossed my house keys on the small glass table beside the door.

"It's four in the morning, Kris."

I headed for my brown leather sofa, cherishing the nagging. "Thought I left my boyfriend at the bar."

I plopped down on the sofa and stared at my television. It was my pride and joy. My fifty-inch LED flat-screen powerhouse that's potential was being wasted by playing the local news in high-definition with surround sound. I hate the news.

"Did you feed?" Kyle asked.

"You know it."

"Great." I noticed the sarcasm.

"I thought you worked tonight." I realized Kyle wasn't in his scrubs. I could've sworn he had to work that night at the hospital.

"I, I got off early."

"You, you got off early?" I teased from the sofa.

Kyle Brody isn't just my roommate; he's also my human servant. He was an accident, and I didn't mean to make him my slave either. You see, Vampires have this lovely talent of being able to bind people into their service. It's like this magical little link you form with someone you trust and someone who would willingly devote their life to keeping you safe and care for you.

Sure, I'd prefer a tall slender blond to the short scrawny college student standing in front of me, but what can you do? Kyle was barely five-nine and weighed maybe a little over one hundred and thirty pounds. He had a head full of shaggy black hair and he needed to shave. It was as if I had the shorthaired brunette reincarnation of Kurt Cobain for a slave.

I admit I'm not what you would call the most experienced Vampire in the world. I'm still pretty young as far as the immortal go. I've only been a Vampire for the last twenty-three years. Turning someone into your human servant is something I don't particularly know how to do. I met Kyle randomly and fed from him the old-fashioned way…with my fangs. It was a spur of the moment kind of thing. I took a little too much blood and the next thing I know, my body makes some kind of bond with his. Wham, I've got a human servant.

Kyle didn't take the news that he would have to serve me for the rest of his life too well. I proved to him that I was a Vampire by lifting the back of a truck up with one hand and moving faster than he could see. He had something of a little nervous break down. He cursed, begged, and prayed for me to leave him alone, but it didn't work. I really didn't know how I made the link let alone how to sever it. He was mine for the last year and a half and would be for the rest of his life. Not bad having your own personal slave, right?

Unfortunately, Kyle is the worst human servant imaginable. He hates me. Listening isn't his strong suit and I haven't quite figured out enough of the magical tricks to get him to be silent and obedient. The truth is, I feel kind of bad. Kyle was a medical student and three months from finishing his internship at the nearby hospital. He would probably have had a decent life if I hadn't come along.

Oh well.

I personally think I'm the best master a human servant could have. The kid's loaded with money from his parents dying when he was starting his first year of med school. I gave him even more of the money I'd "collected" from a few of the more high-class meal—I mean donors—I've had over the last eight years. Kyle had a nice allowance and he could blow his money on all of the women and liquor he could handle for the rest of his life, but he didn't. For some reason he was intent on being a Debbie Downer. Lucky me.

"Who was it this time, Kris?" Kyle asked, still standing between the kitchen and the wooden table on the wall in front of the back patio doors like some weirdo. "I'm not going to hear about anything on the news am I?"

I mock-gasped and put a hand to my chest. "You know it hurts me that you would even ask such a thing."

Kyle stood hovering over me, scowling. "Where did you go? I don't like it when you feed so close to the house."

"I killed the neighbors. You better go pack your things before someone realizes they're dead."

"Funny."

Kyle came over to join me on the couch. "Kris, all joking aside, I need a favor."

Oh, déjà vu.

"How much money do you need for her to sleep with you?" I asked.

Kyle came around, popping his beer open and sipping the Corona. "You're an asshole."

"Hey, watch your mouth." I didn't even look away from the TV. "You keep it up and I'll make you go streaking down South Beach."

Kyle's lips tightened.

I couldn't help but smirk. The funny thing about Kyle is that he doesn't really know a whole lot about anything. He doesn't even know how old I am. He thinks I'm over three hundred years old. I do a decent French accent, bought a cheap painting to hang on the TV wall, and he thinks I'm from the Renaissance. Kyle bought it. Gullible, my little slave is.

The truth is I don't have much power over him. Sometimes we can sense what the other is feeling if we're close enough or if he's being emotional like most teenage girls. I know if the bond we had grew stronger we would develop more mystical tricks, but Kyle won't let me and I'm not that capable. One important thing I know about our connection is that if I die, he dies. The day I told him *that* fun bit of information, Kyle started listening a bit more. Too bad it's the truth. I wouldn't want to drag anyone down with me if I go, let alone some kid who just got caught up in a world he couldn't understand.

I patted Kyle on the back and he flinched a little. "Relax, I'm just screwing with you."

Kyle took a nervous sip of his beer.

"I'm in a good mood. What's the favor?" I asked.

"I've got a date tomorrow night."

That caught my attention. I sat up and chuckled. "A date? I don't believe it."

"Kris…"

I started imagining all the possibilities. "Does she have friends? Can she bring a bunch of friends over? We could double date. We never double date."

"Kris, please." Kyle hated when I talked fast. "I need the house to myself tomorrow."

I think my heart stopped beating…more.

"What?" I couldn't believe it.

Kyle put his beer down on the coffee table, making sure it was on the coaster. He was a bit of a neat freak. "Don't over exaggerate this, please."

"Over exaggerate?" I asked, offended. "Kyle, I'm cool. I'm one of the coolest guys you're ever going to meet. Wait a sec. Are you embarrassed by me?"

"Yes."

Oh.

"But that's not the point." Kyle rubbed his tired eyes with his fingers. "I just want to have one night by myself to have dinner with this girl."

I crossed my arms and sank back into the sofa, putting my sand-covered shoes on the coffee table. I was having such a good night too.

"Don't pout. What kind of Vampire pouts?" Kyle grabbed his beer and sank back into the couch too.

"I'm not pouting," I said under my breath.

We sat there watching the news on mute for a few moments.

"Who is this chick?" I asked.

"An old friend."

"How come you never told me about her?"

"I don't tell you anything."

"Touché."

"We had a thing in high school." Kyle sipped at his Corona. "We ran into each other a couple of days ago. She's in town on business. I invited her over for dinner."

"That's great…" I nudged him with my elbow. "Get laid tomorrow. That's your main priority."

Kyle sighed and got up from the sofa. "I'm going to bed."

"No. Kyle listen to me…get laid." Maybe some sex would make him relax.

Kyle finished his beer in the kitchen and headed off to his room. "Kris, do I have your word you're going to let me have the house tomorrow?"

I thought about it for a second. I planned to feed off Lauren tomorrow anyway, not stick around the house. I raised my hand. "Sure."

"Kris?"

"Scout's honor."

I heard Kyle shuffle off down the hall and his bedroom door shut.

"Get laid tomorrow! That's a command!" I shouted from the couch. "I command you to get laid!"

He didn't respond so I grabbed the remote and started skimming for something to watch. I settled on Alfred Hitchcock's *The Birds* and it helped kill time for the rest of the night. I sat there thinking about Lauren and couldn't wait to get back and feed from her again.

I could wait patiently for a whole day. Piece of cake.

5

It was a little after six-thirty in the morning. I watched the sunrise from my back deck.

All these years and I never got used to the feeling of the sun replacing the moon. I can feel my body changing before the very first light even spreads out over the ocean. That power stored away in every one of my cells starts to fade. It never disappears completely, but I feel different, less energized, less…everything. It's funny, I feel more alive at night when I'm dead than during the day when I have a pulse. Ironic.

The ocean breeze washed over me as I watched the sun come up. The heart in my chest started beating again and I listened to it find its rhythm like a ticking in my ear. Slow at first, then fast, as if it's catching up for all the beats it missed, then finally normal.

You see, those rumors you hear about Vampires are all wrong. I'm not allergic to sunlight, I don't burst into flames in the middle of the day, and I sure as shit don't sparkle. Vampires don't become corpses while the sun's up, and we don't have to hibernate in a coffin. Hell, teenagers sleep more during the day than I do.

We do change though. There's no denying that. Most people just don't know about it.

At night Vampires have all of the great tricks of the trade. I can lift an SUV like a tinker toy. I can move faster than the human eye can see if I try hard enough. My senses are heightened so that every smell and sound has a depth and meaning that can't be put into words. The night's alive in ways humans just can't understand and Vamps can see and hear it all. I am a predator, a monster who hunts silently and swiftly. I'm also immortal. That's the important part.

When the sun goes down and the moon takes over, Vampires gain their immortality. You see, when a human becomes a Vampire, their bodies become immune to disease, but time still ticks on. Most Vampires don't have the ability to stop their aging.

During the day, the clock keeps ticking and some Vamps get older and older every year. I'm strong enough, metaphysically speaking, to stop my aging completely. It took me twelve years, but I did it. I'll always look thirty-one. It's complicated, but there are a lot of little things people don't know.

During the day, all Vampires are mortal.

Sure, you become a Vampire. Maybe you even stop your aging if you become strong enough. You play it safe and you've managed to spend hundreds of years hunting as an immortal at night. Except one day you go outside and a bus hits you down the road. Bye-bye immortality.

I've heard stories of Vampires who spend their days locked away like recluses. They don't leave the house, like germophobes. I don't know how they do it. It's sad really. I'd kill myself if I couldn't leave the house. Why live forever if you're too afraid to live?

I headed back inside and put on a pot of coffee before going to take a shower.

The second half of the house is three rooms and two baths. The master bedroom with a private bathroom belongs to me and it's the far right room down the short hallway. Kyle's room is across from mine and the second bathroom is the door just before his. The third room is just before mine. It's our office where Kyle set up the computer and all that other lovely nerdy stuff that he's into. I love the Internet just as much as the rest of the world, but I don't see the purpose of looking at porn when you can just go out and get the real thing. Kyle says it's because I grew up in a different time.

Yeah, a time when people had sex in person instead of over webcams.

I closed the bedroom door behind me and started undressing. My room's large enough for a king-sized bed. The dark blue silk sheets under the matching comforter were crying for me, but I wasn't tired. All of the furniture in my room is a dark oak. I'm no interior decorator, but I'm not color-blind. A small LCD television hung on the wall across the room over my long dresser. The carpet was the same from the previous owner; white shag from the seventies that brought back good memories. The walls were originally white when we moved in, but Kyle and I painted them a deep burgundy red.

I know, it's cliché, but I like the color red.

I took off my coat and pulled out the syringe and vials of blood. I tossed the coat and the blue button-down shirt underneath it onto the bed. I sat down and looked at my two vials from last night.

Lauren Millar. I remembered how sweet she tasted.

I held the two vials of blood in my hand. Sunlight was already starting to shine in through the window behind me over my bed. I watched the light make the blood inside brighter, as if I was looking at Lauren's spark burning inside the glass.

I realized early on that the thirst or hunger that you read about Vampires having isn't necessarily true. Not in my case anyways. I kicked the habit pretty fast. Sure, I was biting people and taking loads of their blood for years, but eventually I learned that it was safer to take less and to save it.

No, I don't have a big walk-in cooler of blood in my closet, but the anticoagulant in my syringes keeps the blood from getting too thick to enjoy. I always take three vials from my victims if they taste good. I take one right away and save two for snacks later on. I popped open one of the vials.

Vampires do eat food. As far as blood is concerned, I take one in the morning before breakfast and another in the afternoon to hold me over. It keeps everything running inside. I was told that drinking blood regularly, even during the day has power for Vamps, hence the shots.

I looked down at the blood. I was excited that I was going to have another taste of such amazing life. I drank the vial, my tongue wet with anticipation. It tasted…normal?

I couldn't explain it. Every person I'd ever taken blood from tasted the same even after it had been in my coat for a while. Lauren's blood, it tasted different than it had last night. Less…perfect. But that couldn't be right. I guess the only thing to do was make sure I went and drank from the source. The idea of doing that again cheered me up, made the idea of it even sweeter.

I tossed the vial I emptied and put the other one on the dresser for safekeeping. If nothing else, blood was blood, and it would have to do in the afternoon. I put my syringe in the small wooden cigar box beside the vial.

I headed into the bathroom and flicked the lights on.

My bathroom's small compared to the rest of my room. The floor and walls were white tiles. The two sinks and the toilet were white as well, but the counter and towels decorating the bathroom were a matching dark blue. I leaned onto the counter and stared into the mirror at the mortal looking back at me.

I knew an attractive Vampire who looked like shit during the day. Me, I don't have any problem luring women back to my house whether the sun's out or not.

I stared into those light green eyes looking back at me, at that tan face, and that head of short brown hair. Everyone has blemishes, moles, dimples, wrinkles, lines along their eyes, and signs of gray hair near their temples, all of these tiny imperfections that go unnoticed even when they're hardly there. I notice though. It's hard not to when every night every imperfection melts away under cool pale skin and you look into a mirror and see what you would look like as a God. It does a number on anyone's self-image. A lot of Vamps can't handle it.

I rubbed my hand across the mirror as if to wipe that mortal face away. I rubbed my hands on my pants and felt them snag on the material. My hands were rough from the years. At night, they glided over flesh like silk. I bit back my frustration.

I'm not a fan of the flaws that come with my mortality. Maybe I'm vain.

I splashed water on my face and brushed my teeth to get the blood out of my mouth. Nothing stains teeth like coffee, tea, and blood. I had a long day ahead of me. I don't usually sleep during the day. Not much of a reason to. My body never felt the need to sleep unless I used up a lot of energy the night before. It's sort of like a mystical backlash. Vampirism is just one big balancing act, give and take. If I had to heal a lot of damage or didn't feed enough, then maybe I'd need some shut-eye. Other than that, I had a routine I generally followed every morning.

I'm in better shape than most men are these days. When I grew up, people ran outside and stayed active all day. People loved life and the outdoors and never even fathomed the idea of microwave dinners and McDonald's diets.

I'm lean muscle, not too defined or impossibly buff, just healthy. I've been lifting weights, running, and swimming just about every day for the last eight years. Since I moved into this territory two years ago, I've gotten into a nice routine. I run for a few miles during the day, swim in the ocean, and lift weights at the small neighborhood gym close to home.

I examined myself in the mirror. I ran my finger along the scar running down from the top of my ribs down to my lower abs. Like I said, during the day Vamps are mortal. You get cut, you heal slowly and if you make it until night, the wound disappears. Then the next day you're left with the scar. I had gotten careless once when I was first on my own. My cover was blown and humans don't tend to like Vampires as much as you'd think. I looked down at my right shoulder, at the nasty scar staring up at me from a knife. It was a gift a friend gave me years ago, my reminder that my life before I was on my own wasn't worth remembering.

Jack was afraid of people coming here and hunting us down like animals. I've run into hunters before. I know how a knife feels when they swing it and it cuts into you. I know what it's like to run, to hide.

I was careful. I adapted and learned. I hadn't been hunted by anyone for going on eight years now. I didn't think I had to worry about anyone finding out I was a Vampire while hiding out with my med-school roommate turned human slave.

Yep, what did I have to worry about?

6

Kyle asked me once why I don't just sleep the day away if it was safer to wait until night when I was immortal. Aside from not being tired, I just don't have the attention span to sit around at home all day. I was active when I was human, and that didn't change once I was turned. I had a rough first half of my immortal life; I was going to spend the rest of it on my own terms. The way I looked at it, I was on permanent retirement.

That morning I jogged five miles north along the beach to Deerfield Beach. If you've never tried jogging on sand, do it. There's a reason I'm in good shape.

After the run, I took my time and walked inland over the Intracoastal to a shopping strip. I stopped inside of a small bagel joint to refuel. I grabbed an asiago cheese bagel with cream cheese, a bag of sliced apples, and a cup of black coffee; breakfast of champions.

It was a little after nine by the time I got done eating so I walked over to the large Barnes and Noble on the corner of the plaza. I spent the morning scanning through the shelves for something to read. I read everything I can find that's good. From classical to modern literature, to even some decent fantasy, I'm willing to pick it up and lose myself in a good story. I even read a few of the more famous Vampire novels out there for a good laugh. The only books I stay away from are non-fiction and crime dramas. I'm not a fan of the real world. I've seen enough of it in my day and it doesn't entertain me. I'd rather get lost in someone's imagination.

I had just finished Albert Camus' *The Fall* and I wanted something a little easier on my mind. I settled on Stephen King's *Salem's Lot*. I had a copy at home, but it had been years since I'd read it. I sat in the café with a green tea and read for an hour until it was time to get on with my morning.

I usually get weight training in every other day. I go to a small local gym near US-1. It's a small place, but since I came to South

Florida, I've invested enough money to get newer equipment inside. There's a boxing ring in the corner, and punching bags and sparring mats on the second floor. The ground level is free weights and the machines with a few treadmills and bikes. I get free membership because of my under the table donations since I don't have the legal status to get a membership at a fancier establishment. I've also had the pleasure of spending an evening with the woman who works the front counter in the mornings. She's more than happy to let me go through and get an hour-long workout in.

After the gym, I jogged back to the house. My blood was pumping and I felt pretty damn good. It was time to start the more relaxing part of my mid-morning, so I changed out of my gym clothes and into a gray shirt, black swim shorts, and sandals. The weather was cool during the day; it was the time of year to start swimming again. The water would be cold at first, but a little cold never killed anybody. I walked along the beach looking for a seaside hotel. I planned on lounging and doing some laps in the pool instead of the ocean. In a perfect world, I'd own a private pool.

I eventually found a hotel with a pool and bar you could access from the beach. It was a Marriot and I'd been there before. Nobody in the hotel seemed to care if you came in off the beach if you weren't a guest as long as you tipped and spent some money at the bar. I did both in excess.

"How's it going?" The bartender in his white collared shirt and khakis handed me a bottle of water.

I downed as much of it as I could. "Good. But it's still early."

It was a little before noon.

"It's beautiful out today."

I looked around at the pool. It was already crowded with kids, teenagers, and their relatives splashing in the water or lounging on the chairs.

"Better enjoy it while it lasts. Soon it'll be hotter than all hell out. Give it another month," the man said.

"He's right," a woman added.

I turned to my right and saw the older woman sitting a few stools down wearing a black bikini top and a towel around her waist. Her short hair had streaks of blond highlights that her tan leather skin accented. I would've guessed late thirties, early forties. Not a bad figure, silicon C-cup. Yep, good old-fashioned South Florida's a big supporter of plastic surgery.

The woman didn't hide the fact that she was looking at more than just my eyes. Made me feel all warm and tingly inside.

I leaned against the bar and drank more of my water.

"How're you doing today?" she asked.

The bartender pretended to be busy serving another guest and walked away.

I grinned at my new friend. "So far so good."

As she laughed and sipped at her Mimosa, I noticed the ring on the woman's left hand and how little it stopped her from running her tongue along the tip of her straw. Some people just try too hard.

I held up my water bottle and flashed her a smile. "Have a good one."

It was too early for that kind of trouble.

"Have a good swim," she said, watching me walk away.

"I will." I headed for a lounge chair as far away from the potential adulteress as I could find.

I took off my shirt and put it on the ground beside my chair with my keys and cell phone. I pushed my sunglasses up higher on my nose and leaned back on the warm plastic chair. Lying there with my hands behind my head, I felt the warm sun on my skin. I listened to the people by the pool and the sound of the water splashing. It was one of the times when being me wasn't so bad.

Of course, my tranquility lasted about ten minutes.

I don't really know how to explain it. You ever get that strange feeling that you're being watched; like something is about to touch you on the back of your neck and send chills down your spine? That's how I felt and the second I did, I knew something that wasn't human was nearby.

The first rule of how to act when you're surprised is making sure you don't look surprised. I sat up carefully, leaning over to pick up my keys and phone. I scanned the pool as I moved though. Something was close. Something...different.

I can sense people who are less human than most. It comes in handy when trying to avoid trouble during the day. Hell, it helps when I go looking for it too.

I don't really know why I even noticed it, but I did right away. There were two or three people stopped at the fence leading to the beach by two kids. One was a young boy, maybe just over ten years old and the other was a little skinny girl a few years younger. They were wearing large jackets and jeans, and both had backpacks strapped to their backs. The older boy held onto the tiny girl's hand as they talked to the adults.

Both of them looked dirty, hungry, and tired. You didn't see too many homeless children on the beach these days. I watched them ask a man and wife if they could spare some money. The man shook his head and led his wife away, ignoring the beggars.

That was when the boy jerked the younger girl's arm and she closed her eyes as tight as she could. Her tiny face squinted in concentration.

The couple walking away turned around and the man pulled out his wallet. I don't know what bills he gave them, but it looked like he took every bit of cash on him and handed it to the boy.

The couple turned and walked out onto the beach, forgetting about the hotel entirely. The boy held his young accomplice by the hand and the two hurried over to the bar. I followed their every step. Did I really just see that?

The kids gave the bartender a few dollars and he looked unsure as he gave them both a bottle of water.

I leaned forward on my chair, forgetting about being discrete and just stared at the two little kids. The boy opened the bottle for the girl and she was about to drink when the trouble started.

"Hey, you two!"

One of the hotel managers was walking towards them.

The kids made a run for it. They went by my side of the pool and rushed past me. I sat there, frozen, as the girl broke free of the older boy's hand and stopped dead in her tracks. She was thin; almost sickly looking. The curly blond hair on her head was a thick, tangled mess. Her eyes had heavy bags, but they were full and bright with intelligence. They were the deepest green I'd ever seen.

The little girl was staring right at me.

I don't know how, but something brushed over my skin. It pressed against me in a gentle swipe of supernatural power.

Whatever that girl was, she wasn't human.

"Lila!" The boy snatched her by the scrawny arm and tried pulling her away.

The manager reached the girl, Lila, at the same time and grabbed her by the other frail arm.

They pulled at the girl like a wishbone.

"Let go of her!" The boy roared.

"I told you two no soliciting." The manager was dressed in black slacks and a white polo that fit snugly around his bulging stomach. "I called the police."

The boy reached into his jacket and grabbed a wad of crinkled bills. He threw it on the ground as hard as he could, "There! Now let her go!"

"No. You're waiting here for the police." The manager held onto the little girl. She wasn't even putting up a fight. I realized then that she just kept staring at me. She hadn't stopped staring.

Help us.

The voice entered my mind. It was soft. It was young.

Please.

It was *her* voice. The girl named Lila.

I heard her speaking to me and I stared at that poor girl.

My mouth was dry. She'd gotten my attention alright.

I got to my feet and pocketed my phone and keys. I put on my sandals and pulled my shirt on over my head as I walked towards trouble.

"What's going on?" I asked.

The manager turned to me. He was in his thirties, putting on weight, and hopefully smart enough to get through this easily. He turned back to the little girl and tugged harder on her arm.

"You're hurting her!" The boy snarled. He was a little over five feet with a head full of curly brown hair. He looked just as hungry and dirty as the girl.

"I'm not hurting her," the manager said.

I wasn't sure; the girl hadn't said a word yet, but it looked like he was holding her tighter than he had to.

"These two have been out here all morning harassing our guests. The bartender warned them three times."

"Hey, come on. They're just kids. Give them a break."

The boy stopped carrying on like a beast and looked up at me about as confused as the manager was.

I looked down at the little girl and she smiled up at me. I was flooded with warm happy feelings that weren't mine. At least I hoped they weren't mine.

The manager looked at me, his brows raised. "Sir, are you a guest at the hotel?"

"No, but—"

"Then I'm going to have to ask you to leave this to me, buddy."

Buddy?

"I've already called the police," he continued. "I'm taking care of it."

I got a bad taste in my mouth as I took it all in. I should've just hit the asshole in the nose and called it a day, but I didn't.

I took my sunglasses off and stared right into the man's eyes. I let him see the part inside of me that would be visiting him once the sun went down if he didn't back off. "Listen, you should let them get out of here."

The manager didn't like what he saw in my eyes. He took a nervous step back, but licked his lips and held his ground. Good for him. It was stupid, but brave.

"I already called the police. They'll take care of these two. Please go back—"

"Let go of her," I said in a voice that shut the manager up fast. "You're hurting her arm."

The manager let go of the girl and her brother grabbed her by the wrist and pulled her close.

I could feel everyone's eyes on me at the pool as I stepped closer to the manager. I could smell the fear oozing out of his pores.

"Go back in the air-conditioning. Everything's taken care of. You got it?"

He nodded.

I nodded. "Good."

Lila looked up at the manager who shot her a dirty look. She reached out and poked him in the arm with a thin finger. The moment she touched him she quickly pulled away and the boy she was with grabbed her hand to hold her back.

I watched the manager turn around and start walking away. Without saying a word, the grown man walked into the pool and fell in with a huge splash.

"What the hell?" I looked down at the little girl, shocked. Had she done that?

People started talking and everyone was staring at the kids and me while the manager was screaming and flailing around in the water as if he had no idea how he got there. Perfect.

I looked down at the kids and signaled them to start walking. It was time to go.

I followed behind them and all three of us left the hotel pool and walked out onto the beach.

The voice entered my head again the second we touched the sand.

Thank you.

I could still hear the manager cursing and shouting by the pool.

"Don't mention it."

7

I have never in my entire existence been a babysitter.

I mean, sure I've fed off a few kids here and there. I know it's not the most acceptable meal in society, but if you ever get desperate enough, you start going for the weakest of the herd. Haven't you ever watched Animal Planet? It's survival of the fittest.

I stood there on the beach and looked over the kids with the ocean at my back. I wasn't going to take any of their blood, but the way the little girl kept watching me made me nervous. When I get nervous I get hungry.

"What do you think you two are doing?" I wasn't sure how to talk to kids so I was blunt.

The boy looked at me like he was about to take off running any second.

Lila just kept staring at me.

I crouched down to her level. I tried reaching out with my senses and see if I could tell what she was. All Vampires have certain unique talents or abilities. One of mine, which is my own little secret, is that I can sense other Vampires. During the day, while we're mortal, Vampires don't give off the same otherworldly energy that helps other supernatural types sense one another. It's how most Vamps stay hidden during the day. Luckily, my little gift was how I managed to take my territory from the last Vampire.

There's nothing like walking up to someone in the middle of the day with a gun and two choices. He made his choice and I pulled the trigger. That Vampire was a big shot. Killing him put me on a pedestal of respect and power that I never had before.

The daylight hours are all Vampires' Achilles' heel. It doesn't matter how powerful you are at night because during the day, we all die just as easy.

I felt out with that part of me that could spot a Were from ten yards away. I felt a prickle of energy hovering around the girl. Lila definitely wasn't a Vampire, but maybe a Witch?

"What are you?" I reached out with my finger and poked her on the forehead to see if I felt any kind of reaction to that power.

Nothing happened. Lila just blinked and then reached out and poked me on the forehead back.

The boy pulled her away from me and stood between the two of us. "Don't touch her, pervert."

I got up and stared down at the kid. He had some spunk. "What are you, her bodyguard?"

"Yeah, now go away," he said.

"You know what she is?" I glanced to the girl.

The boy blinked as if he'd been smacked. I watched him glance back at her and say, "No way."

"'No way' what?" I asked.

The boy shook his head at her and then scowled back at me.

She must have been talking to him inside his head like she'd done to me at the pool.

"You need to leave us alone. Now." The boy led the girl away from me. "Thanks."

I watched them start to go, the girl struggling to keep eye contact with me.

Kids are so creepy. I should've let them walk away, but that little girl had entered my mind. I had to know what she was and what she was doing in my territory. I decided to play it safe.

"My name's Kristopher," I said as I casually strolled up alongside them.

The boy kept walking on, doing his best to ignore me.

"Kris, for short," I added. "What were your names again?"

They both kept walking.

"A little warm for jackets don't you think? Those backpacks look heavy. Need help?" I talked as if we were all just friends out for a nice stroll on the beach.

"Please." The boy stopped in his tracks, turning red in the face. Both of the kids were pale. They didn't look like Floridians. "I'm going to scream rape if you don't leave us alone."

I raised my hands up, surrendering. "Hey, relax little guy. I just helped you out back there. What's the problem?"

"The problem," a woman's voice whispered in my ear, "is that I've got a gun aimed at your spine."

I hadn't heard her coming. Even during the day my senses are sharper than any human's. The waves; I blamed the waves for my ego's sake.

I didn't turn around because I felt the barrel of a gun press against my lower back. How did I know it was a gun and not something less dangerous? Who cares? The fact that I could even tell was what bothered me. This was happening more frequently than I would've liked.

I put my hands down slowly. "I don't have any money on me."

"I don't want your money," the woman hissed in my ear. She sounded young. "I want you to keep walking and just leave."

I nodded. I could do that. Probably should have. I could go home and wait to track the kids' scents. Then I could find them and ask them questions when bullets would do less permanent damage. But that would take too long.

"What are you their mother?" I asked.

The gun pushed harder into my back. She must've been hiding it well because people on the beach weren't shouting and running for their lives. Not yet anyway.

"I'm whatever I have to be for you to leave us alone."

She pushed me and sent me on my way. I took a few steps before taking a gamble with my life and glancing back at the woman who had a gun pointed at me.

She wasn't a woman at all. She was a teenager. Her jacket was draped over her arm that was casually holding a small handgun. She did a good job concealing the weapon.

I smirked and turned completely around to get a good look at her.

The kids were behind her as if she were their protector.

My smirk pissed her off because she took a step toward me.

"You're going to shoot me on a public beach? Come on." I winked at the girl with the gun and she started to get flustered.

I looked at the little girl and she was concentrating on me.

Help us.

Lila's voice screeched through my mind. A sharp sting of pressure behind my eyes made me wince. There was panic, desperation in the girl's voice that time.

I turned to the oldest girl with the gun. "Why does the kid keep asking me for help?"

The girl holding the gun seemed shocked and looked at the younger girl in disbelief. "Lila, stop it."

I looked from Lila to the girl with the gun. They looked like sisters.

"No, we don't need—"

The older girl started to say, but then stopped. She looked at me as if any moment her eyes were going to pop out of her skull. She dissected me with that gaze and I watched her do it. She looked older right then, smarter. I guessed a senior in high school, maybe a freshman in college.

She lowered the gun a little.

"What do you mean he's a Vampire?"

My face went slack. Uh oh.

I think my little heart actually skipped a beat. I looked from the girl with the gun, to the tinier girl inside my head, to the little boy in the middle who looked furious that they were even still there.

How the hell did she know I was a Vampire?

A part of me saw the problem standing in front of me and told me to kill it. I didn't have my speed or strength during the day, but I could grab that gun and make sure they never said a word to anyone else about what I was.

It was the quickest solution.

People generally won't tolerate a Vampire in their cities and near their homes. If these kids sold me out to humans, I'd have to move out of town before some idiots tried killing me. That wasn't the real problem. If some of the other predators in the city, some of the Weres or other monsters, found out about my daytime life, then I'd be shit out of luck. I've got a couple of people I'd call enemies and my enemies tend to want to kill me.

Killing those three in cold blood right then, that looked like my best bet, but could I do it? I looked down at the little girl. She looked up at me, completely calm and trusting. I didn't like the thought of killing innocent kids. It left a bad taste in my mouth. If it came down to my life over theirs, I'd pick mine. I've been faced with that dilemma before and, well, I'm still here.

The teen lowered her gun finally.

The boy looked up at her like she was crazy. "What are you doing?"

"Lila says to trust him," the young woman answered. Her eyes didn't move off me.

I stared into her dark eyes and then looked her over. Her hair was naturally straight and light brown. It was pulled back in a ponytail and I caught the sweat glistening off her slender neck. She wore a red tank top and jeans that hugged her slender physique.

I was betting she was a cheerleader because of how much tanner she was than the other two. I may have even thought she was pretty if I didn't see the anger behind those eyes. She'd seen blood. I knew it right then and there. I wondered how far she'd have to be pushed to shoot me there on a public beach in front of witnesses.

"Lila!" The boy turned to the youngest of the trio. "Lila, how can we trust a Vampire?"

"Hey." I glanced around at the couple of people sunbathing and walking along the beach. "Let's keep our voices down."

"My sister says that we can trust you," the oldest said. "My name's Tara."

"Tara!" The boy squealed. "Come off it."

"This is Ben and the little girl talking inside your head is Lila."

I looked at Tara and Ben, and finally down at Lila.

"Lila says your name's Kristopher?"

I smirked, still ready to crush any of their windpipes if they said the V word too loud. "Call me Kris. A pleasure to meet you."

Tara nodded, but not in a friendly way. "Listen, do you live around here?"

I looked the three over again. "Yeah. I don't know if it's child-proof though."

"I'm eighteen, Ben's twelve, and Lila's eight. I have a gun and I'll shoot your dick off if you try anything. Lila says you can help us. Can you?"

I turned to Lila. I could see her mind working behind those green eyes. She was smart. Real smart. The thing that worried me was why she thought I could help her.

"Sure. Why not?" I finally decided.

The kids were better off with me. If that girl could sense I was a Vampire then I couldn't have her running around shouting it into everyone's skull. If I had to kill them, it would be better to do it back at the house.

If I didn't have to kill them, well that'd be good too.

Who says I'm not reasonable?

8

I walked onto the back deck with three bottles of water.

Tara was waiting to intercept me as soon as I stepped out of the house. She didn't trust me to give anything to the kids. I passed the bottles to her. "Here. You guys thirsty?"

"Thanks." Tara didn't sound very thankful. She walked over to the others. Ben was sitting with Lila on the deck, staring out at the ocean. They were still bundled in jackets, looking like miniature bums. Tara knelt down beside them and handed out the waters.

"Drink it," she whispered to them, rubbing Lila's back.

Tara stood up and caught me watching her. She straightened her posture and glanced at the gun lying on the table nearby. Can we say trust issues?

I walked over to the table to grab a seat. I had a round wooden outdoor table that I stained and refurbished to match the deck. It had a hole in the center for the umbrella, but that was in the garage. It wasn't hot enough to need it for shade yet. The four chairs around the table had black metal frames with cushioned seats, more modern than the table itself.

I sat down with the house to my back while Tara sat down across from me. She rested a hand on the table near her gun. She sat turned enough to keep her eyes on the kids. She earned a few points for being smart, I'd give her that much.

I examined the gun, grinning to myself. It was a small revolver, old and dirty. Call it a hunch, but I don't think that Ms. Tara was the original owner of the piece. I glanced at the three backpacks that were resting by the kids near the steps. Each of them had been wearing one. It looked like they'd been travelling for a while.

"So I have to ask. What brings you three to South Florida? Besides the beautiful weather." I looked at Tara and raised my brow, expecting answers. "It's a little early for spring break isn't it?"

Ben glanced back at Tara.

I noticed it. I didn't like it. The kid was worried. Worried about me finding out whatever Tara might tell me.

"How much trouble are you guys in?" I looked Tara dead in the eye.

Tara leaned forward in her seat. "I don't know what the hell is happening. Three weeks ago my life was fine, but now...I don't even have a life."

"You're alive."

Tara scoffed.

"That means you've got a life," I told her.

She just looked at me. Tara was young and she knew everything and the look in her eyes said that I didn't. "Yeah. Well my life's shit."

"Where do guys live?" I asked.

Tara's narrow jaw clenched. I could see the muscles working in her cheeks. She was so thin.

"What's it matter?" She looked at the two kids. "It won't help."

I shrugged. "Whatever."

That seemed to surprise Tara.

"Maybe it's best you kids get going then."

"What?" Tara was trying to read me, but couldn't. "I thought—"

"Listen, I'm not sure why the kid thinks I can help you, but I'm not bringing you into my life if I don't know what's after you. I've got a talent for spotting trouble and you kids are covered in it."

Lila got to her feet and walked over to me.

She ignored Ben and Tara's surprised stares and urging. Lila stopped right in front of my chair, staring into my eyes.

It was kind of creepy.

"Can I help you?" I asked.

Lila nodded. I watched her little brow crease as she tried concentrating.

I'm hungry.

Lila's voice was as smooth and perfect in my head as if it were my own thought. I looked into those deep green eyes. In the sunlight those eyes looked even greener, as if somehow they'd been painted a dark emerald that only shined in the daylight. They were pretty eyes. When she was older, they'd be beautiful.

It was then that Lila reminded me of someone. The only girl I'd ever loved. She reminded me of my baby sister. Their hair was similar, the eyes so hauntingly close that I started to get chills up my arms.

I looked away from those green eyes, from the reminder. I couldn't afford to be reminded of my sister when I looked at Lila. I couldn't afford to get attached. Not if I was going to have to kill her.

Tara was watching me. Ben came to stand at her side.

I looked at the two of them and then back to Lila. I had to focus on the present. I didn't have time to take a stroll down memory lane.

"Does she talk to you like that too?" I put a finger to my temple. "In here?"

Ben nodded. Tara looked down at the table.

Interesting. I leaned forward in my chair and examined Lila. She was so small, so innocent looking. She was someone's small, innocent little baby girl who'd gone missing. Yeah right. She could enter my mind. That made her dangerous.

I don't like people being in my head. There's barely enough room in there for me, let alone someone else.

"Lila can't talk," Tara answered.

I sat up at that. "You mean she's a mute?"

"Yeah. She was born that way."

I looked at Lila and imagined not ever being able to talk. I know a lot of people who fantasize about that scenario.

"Lila's hungry." I stood up quickly. I had some questions, but I didn't want to talk in front of the kids.

"I think I have a few frozen pizzas in the freezer."

"Don't. We can't take your food," Tara said.

"Well the little one says she's hungry. And you all look like you could use a bite to eat. This is me attempting to help. You want it or not?"

"Lila doesn't understand what's happening."

That made Lila turn to Tara with a scowl on her small, round face.

Tara raised her brows at her. "You don't."

"How did Lila know what I am?" I asked.

Lila looked up at me.

"How did you know?" I asked her.

I don't know.

"You don't know?" I asked.

I looked at the three runaways on my back patio. I was starting to get a headache. This is why I don't get involved in other people's business.

"What *do* you guys know?"

"Not much," Tara said. She looked older then, exhausted from running.

I glanced at Lila and Ben. Tara was looking out for them, protecting them. If I wanted answers, I didn't think I could get them with the squirts standing around listening.

"You said you're hungry?" I asked the little girl.

Lila nodded.

"How about you?"

Ben took a moment, but finally nodded.

"Good. Come on."

I got up and headed inside. The two kids grabbed their backpacks and water bottles and followed me inside. Tara watched from the doorway.

Kyle kept a few frozen dinners that he sometimes made when he didn't have time to cook and I was being lazy. I grabbed two of the flatbread pizzas and nuked them in the microwave for the kids. I set the sizzling plates down on my wooden dining table in front of the sliding glass doors. With their water bottles in tow, the two sat down and started picking at their meal.

"You two good?" I asked.

Lila blew softly on her pizza, trying to cool it off. Ben looked up at me from the head of the table and looked unsure.

"Good." I turned and Tara followed me back outside. She never put her back to me. Impressive.

I walked to the edge of the back deck and leaned on the wooden railing. I stared out at the waves bombarding the shore. The water was shimmering in the sunlight. I should've been swimming on a day like this rather than playing detective.

Tara came up beside me, her gun tucked in the waist of her jeans.

"What is Lila? A Witch?"

Tara laughed, "No...God, I don't know."

I searched her face to see if she was lying.

"Listen, if you want my help you need to tell me what's going on. I need to know what Lila is so I know if she's dangerous."

"Dangerous? She's only eight for God's sake." Her voice wavered. I could tell she didn't believe what she was saying.

Tara wouldn't look at me. She kept watching the ocean.

I looked out at the beach with her. A trio of sea gulls glided over the beach before landing in the sand. Tara and I watched them comb the private beach for food.

"What else can Lila do?"

"I don't know. She speaks inside your head. Sometimes she knows what people are thinking. I've seen her tell people what to do and they do it."

I thought back to the hotel. I'd seen her stare at that couple and they just gave her all the money they had. She also touched the manager's skin and he decided it was time to go for a morning dip in the pool with all his clothes on.

Tara turned to me. "I don't know what she is. But she's my sister."

"Where are you from?"

It took Tara a long time to answer. Her dark brown eyes looked auburn in the sunlight. Eyes always changed so drastically in the daytime. At night most people's eyes became darker, more cryptic. I knew Tara was young, but with her tan skin, those eyes, and the lighter streaks of brown in her hair, I was attracted to her. If she didn't wind up dead, Tara would make a beautiful woman one day.

"I'm tired of running." Tara spoke softly. "I can't do it anymore."

I just watched her. I watched the way she rubbed her tired eyes. I watched the way she pushed down the fear and exhaustion, and raised up whatever anger and determination she used to keep going. I watched her auburn eyes fill with something dark, something that only people who have to fight for survival get.

61

What had she been through that could make someone so beautiful get eyes like that?

I shouldn't have let it happen, but Tara intrigued me.

"Harrisburg. We're from Harrisburg."

"Harrisburg, Pennsylvania?" I couldn't believe it. "That's a long way."

Tara scoffed. "It's even longer when you're being hunted."

Hunted? Now that really peaked my interest.

"What's hunting you?" I had to be careful. The kid seemed volatile and I didn't want to push her so much that she clamped up on me.

Tara turned to me and I saw the fear seep through the courage in those eyes. "They're murderers. Goddamned psychopaths."

Tara gripped the railing tight enough to turn her knuckles white. The veins in her neck were standing out. I watched them thump with every bitter heartbeat. "They killed my father. Right in the middle of the day."

"Why?"

Tara glanced back to make sure that Lila and Ben were still eating. They were.

I looked at the two kids through the glass of the sliding door. Lila was laughing at something that Ben had told her. She had a smile that was so innocent and so pure. I wondered how long until Lila's smile vanished and her beautiful green eyes looked more like Tara's, more like mine.

"Lila?" I asked. "They're after Lila aren't they?"

Tara nodded slowly, like it hurt.

"Where's your mother?"

"She died five years ago. Cancer."

"Where's the rest of your family?"

"My mother and father were only children. I only have one grandmother left and she's here in Florida." Tara looked up at me, unsure.

"Where in Florida?"

"Boca Raton."

"You passed it already. Boca's just north of here."

"I know." Tara ran her hands down her skinny arms as if she were cold. "We tried looking for her, but I couldn't find her in the phone book. I don't know where the hell she even lives."

I took it all in. "Why come all this way to see your grandmother? Why didn't you go to the police in Harrisburg?"

Tara stared at me. "My sister can talk to you inside your mind. The police would've helped lynch her if they could."

It was the twenty-first century and that still didn't stop a good old-fashioned hate crime if you happened to be different from everyone else. Isn't evolution great?

"Is that who killed your father? A mob?"

"No. There was six of them and they didn't look like they were from town."

Tara stopped talking. Her walls were back up. Great.

"What?" I asked.

Tara bit at her bottom lip a little. "Lila's never wrong. If she says to trust you, I believe her, but..."

"But what?"

Tara seemed ashamed. "I've never met a Vampire before. How do I know we can trust you?"

I tried being honest. "You can't."

It took her by surprise. Her posture became more rigid and her hands were loose, ready to go for the gun if she had to.

I sighed and turned to lean my back against the railing. I crossed my arms and didn't know how to explain that I wasn't going to eat her.

"Tara, the truth is I brought you here because it's not safe for me personally if you know what I am and you're out wandering the beach. I can't afford to have your sister let it slip that I'm a Vampire."

I didn't like the coldness in Tara's eyes. "She can't talk."

"But she could accidentally put it in someone's mind, right? How's her control?"

Tara looked like any second she was going to draw her gun and flip out. That was exactly what I didn't need. See where honesty gets you?

I put my hands up. "I'm not going to kill you."

Probably.

Tara didn't seem to believe it either. "You hear on the news about Vampires killing people. I mean everyone's heard stories about them...you. I've seen a video on *YouTube* where these guys torched a Vampire with flamethrowers and shot him with machine guns. It showed the Vampire ripping one of their heads off." Tara didn't seem fond of the memory. It made me think better of her.

"Yeah, I caught that one too. There's a lot of videos like that out there these days," I said. It was true. I was on the Internet enough to see all kinds of videos and pictures of the "monsters" being taken down. People who were so full of hate and fear they slaughtered innocent creatures whose only crime was being something different.

Some of us monsters do deserve to die for the things we've done, but I could say the same for a lot of humans.

"My father always said Vampires are dangerous. He said they're dying out so they wouldn't be a problem in the future." Tara sounded uncomfortable. "He said that Weres are the real problem."

I didn't like politics, human or otherwise.

"If you don't trust me, why are you letting your brother and sister eat my food?"

Tara's hands went down to her sides. "I already told you. Lila's never been wrong."

I glanced at the gun in her pants. Up close I recognized it as an old Ruger Speed-Six. I knew a little bit about guns because of my line of work and because Jack and I went shooting at least once a month as a sort of bonding experience. It's good to know your way around guns, especially when you're getting shot at a lot or doing a lot of the shooting. In my case, it was usually the latter.

Tara's gun was a short barrel revolver with a six-round cylinder. The Ruger was a good sturdy gun that you could rely on. I think I've been shot by one of those before.

"Where'd you get that gun?"

"My dad. He gave it to me and told me to run."

"So he knew you were in trouble?"

"I don't know how my dad knew, but he said men were coming to hurt Lila. He said they'd take her and we'd never see her again." Tara glanced back at the house, as if making sure her little sister was really still there. "He made me promise to keep her safe."

"What about Ben? He's your brother?"

"Ben? Yeah, why?"

I shrugged. "Just wondering. Was your dad concerned about you or Ben? His other two children?"

"They're not after us." Tara started to get louder. "My dad was losing it. I've never seen him so scared before."

"Alright, relax."

Tara had to visibly calm down. Her eyes darted back to her siblings again.

"So what about your grandmother? How long ago did she move away?"

"Three years ago."

"What could your grandmother do for you that your father couldn't?"

Tara sighed. "I don't know. Gram's always been a little off. I mean, I remember her always talking about all kinds of stuff. Spirits and magic and energy. My dad didn't like her doing it around us. I think he was glad when she left."

"So, is it possible your grandmother's a Witch?" I didn't let any of the worry come through my voice. I didn't trust many Witches. Depending on what they practiced meant whether or not I wanted to be around them.

"I'm not sure. I mean, she could be, right? My dad just told me to find her. He said that she was the only one who could keep us safe."

I didn't like where this was going, but I had to know more.

"If he sent you guys away, how do you know your dad's dead?"

Tara didn't answer right away. She must've dug deep down to bring it out and she did, like a real soldier. I was impressed. A lot of people can't handle traumatic experiences. Others are survivors, they keep going no matter how screwed up they become along the way.

"He gave me all of his cash and the gun with some ammo and food in our backpacks. We couldn't take our cell phones. I tried not to go. I tried making him tell me what was happening, but..."

I watched the kid struggle. She looked at me as if begging me to tell her it was okay to stop, that she didn't have to talk about it, but I didn't. I needed answers.

The fear made her voice crack. Tara swallowed the pain of the memories. "He slapped me…he never hit me before. He told me that I had to go to Gram and keep Lila and Ben safe. He told me I had to be strong.

"I had to carry Lila in my arms and drag Ben out of the house. Lila wouldn't stop crying. Ben was terrified. There was an old Charger down near the shed away from the house. My dad built the little tarp and shed himself. The car was old; he'd been fixing it up for years. He gave me the keys. I had to hide in that car with my brother and sister while the trucks pulled up to the house.

"They didn't look like locals. These were huge brand new black SUVs and one Mercedes. The men got out in suits and ties. Two of them had machineguns. I watched my father walk down from the porch with his shotgun loaded and ready. He didn't look scared."

Tara's eyes were red and shimmering. I watched a tear slide down her cheek and she wiped it away, ashamed.

"He didn't even try to kill any of the bastards." She sounded bitter. "He shot at their tires. I screamed at Lila and Ben to keep their heads down so they didn't see. I had to look though. I had to see it. They shot at him. He fell, but he kept aiming for the cars. They kept putting bullets in him until he finally stopped shooting and stopped…just stopped…"

The tears ran down her face and her cheeks were red. I watched her and I didn't know what to do. Was I supposed to be there for her? I reached out to just put my hand on her shoulder, to do something, but she swatted me away.

"Don't touch me," she snapped, looking as if she couldn't stand to be in her own skin. "Just, just don't."

I pulled my hand back and watched her wipe the tears off her face and fight the pain.

"What happened next?" I asked.

Tara laughed and it was a dry, bitter laugh.

"I wanted to shoot at them. I wanted to kill them. All of them." Her voice trembled from rage. "I just drove. I couldn't think, couldn't stop crying, I couldn't do anything except drive. The bastards just watched us go. They couldn't drive after us."

I had to admire her father. He couldn't have taken them all on. If he'd tried, they would've just killed him and then drove after the kids anyways. Smart man. Tara didn't understand that he'd given his life to make sure they had a chance to get away. Maybe she did and she just didn't care because she was alone and he'd gotten out.

"Where's the car now?"

"South Carolina," Tara said. "The engine died on I-95 right in the middle of nowhere. I had to drag those two ten miles to the next exit. We'd been sleeping in the car the night before that. I bought us a hotel with the money I had, to give the kids a bed to sleep in while I tried finding us a better car. I only had three hundred bucks, I couldn't get a car with that so I...I had to find one."

I didn't like the sound of that. "What do you mean?"

There was a memory playing in Tara's mind that she tried ignoring.

"I found us a car and drove us to Georgia. We hitchhiked the rest of the way, only with people Lila said we could trust and then got onto buses." Tara turned her back to me for the first time since we met.

"You okay?" I didn't try touching her that time.

"I'm tired. I didn't ask for this."

I nodded. That made two of us.

I stood there staring at the young woman and then at the two kids in my kitchen watching us from the table. There was that part of my brain that I usually listened to that shouted, "Do not get involved, I repeat, do *not* get involved". Then there was that part that wondered what Lila was and what these three kids had dragged into my territory.

Sometimes I rush into things. I speak before I think. I'd like to say that was one of those times.

"I'll see what I can do to help you," I told her. "You're safe. No one will find you here."

Tara wasn't sold. "You sure?"

I nodded, even though I didn't like what I was offering. "Yeah, I'm sure. As long as you don't mind hanging around a big bad Vampire."

Tara looked me up and down. "You're not really scary."

It made me laugh.

Tara smirked and it was infinitely better than her crying and scowling. "I think I could take you."

"Don't push your luck." I nodded back to the house. "Let's go get you something to eat too. You hungry?"

Tara nodded. She didn't say thank you. I was glad she didn't. I didn't want anyone thanking me just yet.

If there were a group of men willing to kill in cold blood to get that little girl, it meant she was worth something. I just had to find out what that was and how I could profit from it. That meant I had something to occupy my time with for the time being.

I love having hobbies.

9

Lila and Ben sat on my sofa, mesmerized by my television. Lila kept flipping through the channels over and over again. Every time Ben saw something he liked he'd make a sound and then watch it go as Lila continued her endless search. It cost an arm and a leg to have over five hundred channels and I think she was on her third lap.

I watched them from the kitchen table. I was trying hard to think of a game plan. It wasn't working out too well. I glanced at the microwave on the kitchen counter to check the time. It was a little after two in the afternoon.

The kids were cleaned up and in fresh clothes. Lila's hair was combed and still a little wet, but the tangles were out. The kids' backpacks had a few clothes in them, some with tags on them so I assumed they were stolen. At least they were out of their oversized, ripe smelling jackets. Ben was in jeans and a navy blue hoodie with a white shirt underneath. Lila was in jeans as well and a purple long-sleeved shirt that looked a little too big for her. I was just happy they didn't smell.

I told the kids that they could go rinse off. They had a bit of an odor going on and I wasn't going to let them stink up the house. Call me fussy, but I've got a superhuman sense of smell. There's nothing worse than the stench of someone's body odor on your couch for months. Trust me.

Tara didn't like the thought of leaving me alone with the kids while she showered. I didn't disagree with her and in the end Lila and Ben convinced her it was okay.

I really wished I knew how Lila was so sure I wasn't going to kill them. Kids were usually pretty creepy to me, but one who could get inside my head was downright terrifying.

My house was built in the seventies and the plumbing was proof of that. Even without the acute hearing it would be tough to miss the squeaking and groaning of the pipes in the walls as Tara took a shower in the spare bathroom. The water had been running for twenty minutes straight; I don't know what she was doing in there. I'm not cheap, but my water bill was going to be through the roof.

I had my cell phone on the table in front of me. I had to come up with a plan for what to do with the kids. I didn't know what was after them, but I knew that there was a chance Jack would. He knew everything. As I said, Jack was the best business partner a Vamp could have. I trusted him.

I called Jack's cell phone first, but it went straight to voicemail. Good thing I wasn't dying in a ditch somewhere.

I called Mikey's next and a female voice I didn't recognize picked up on the second ring. "Mikey's Bar, Charlene speaking. How may I help you?"

"Is Jack there?" I asked. Charlene was overly happy on the phone. I hate when people are so loud and cheerful on the phone.

"He's not taking any phone calls at the moment. May I ask who's calling and I'll take a message for Mr. Weaver?"

"Just tell him that Kris called, alright? I'm a former lover of his."

Charlene sounded at a loss for words. "Umm...okay?"

"Thanks." I hung up my cell and tossed it onto the table. I really wanted to talk with Jack about what was going on. I liked to keep him informed about what was happening in the territory. He generally did the same. It was just common courtesy.

"What's *Jailhouse Momma's*?" Ben glanced back at me from the couch.

I looked at the TV and saw that they were looking at the shows Kyle and I had on our DVR. *Jailhouse Momma's* was right there on the screen with the picture of a female guard seducing a nervous inmate.

I wasn't good with kids. Do you lie to them or treat them different than you would anyone else? Ben was what, twelve? These days there were twelve-year-olds with babies.

I shrugged. "It's porn."

Ben just stared at me.

Lila turned around, kneeling on the couch with her mouth open a little in surprise.

I just watched them both. "What?"

The two kids looked at one another and Lila gagged before resuming their endless search of channels.

I grinned. That was easy. I could totally be a parent.

The house phone started ringing in the kitchen and I got up to answer it.

"Put something on already," I shouted to Lila.

Lila stopped changing the channel instantly. *Nosferatu* played in black and white on my beautiful television. Oh the sweet irony. I hate that movie.

I turned my back on the living room and looked to see who was calling my private line. It was Mikey's Bar. Thank God.

I picked it up. "Jack?"

"Yeah. Kris, I got your phone call. What's wrong?"

"Are you going to be in the bar tonight?"

There was silence on the other end. I could hear really old/bad country music in the background. Jack was in his office. "Always am, Kris."

"Good."

"What's this about? You scared Charlene. She's new. Doesn't understand why you didn't leave a number for me to call back. Oh, and I'm gonna ask you to stop referring to yourself as 'my former lover'. It's not as funny as you think it is."

I smirked. It was pretty funny.

"Quit your grinning. I'm serious. Next time you come down here I'm gonna have them tie you up and chain you to the ceiling. Maybe even torture you."

I sat back down at the kitchen table. "Kinky."

Jack sometimes felt the need to prove his dominance to others. I blamed it on his animal.

"What did you want from me now?" I could hear him smiling.

"I need some information." I glanced back to check on the kids. They were watching that terrible old film, mesmerized by the fake Vampire's grotesque figure. Ugh.

"Information? I thought you were calling about last night."

Last night? "What do you mean?"

I heard the gruff sigh from the old man. "About what happened at The Hornet last night."

71

Holy shit. I sat straight up in my kitchen chair and felt a little overwhelmed. I completely forgot. That wasn't a good sign. I didn't forget about anything. I slipped up because of that delicious girl, Lauren. Shit.

"Dammit, sorry Jack."

"It's alright. I called Gary this morning. He said you showed up too late to see the guys who were asking around. Good thing they didn't start any trouble."

"Yeah." I still couldn't believe that I'd forgotten. No girl ever affected me like that before.

"He told me you knocked some kid out at one of the bars then ran off." Jack sounded irritated. "That what you call laying low?"

"Yeah. You know me."

"So what's this about needing information?"

I looked at Ben and Lila on the sofa. "I can't really get into it right this second."

"You in trouble again?"

"No." I thought about the men after the kids. "It's too early to tell."

"Uh huh." Jack sighed. "I've got a business meeting early in the evening. I'll be able to talk with you around eight thirty. Come over then. That's bright and early for you isn't it?"

It made me laugh. "I appreciate it, old man. What's the business meeting about?"

I let Jack handle the paperwork and the logistics of running the territory. I was the muscle and the overseer who played cleaner sometimes. Just the way I like it.

"I'll tell you when you get here. Hopefully it goes smoothly."

I didn't like the sound of that.

"Don't worry about a thing, kid. I'll get you up to date when you come over tonight. See you when I see you."

Jack hung up and I put the phone back on the receiver.

If I could tell Jack what I'd stumbled on, he'd know the best thing to do. But eight thirty was a long time away. That was a long time to sit around and do nothing. That wasn't my style. I had a lot of sunlight left to go visit another old friend who may be able to help.

I only trusted one other supernatural acquaintance well enough to call them my friend. She'd know more about what Lila was than I did and the more I knew before talking to Jack, the better.

I was about to head into the living room to get *Nosferatu* off my television when I heard the screaming through the walls.

Then there came the gunshot.

I ran to the back of the house and down the hall.

The spare bathroom door flung open and Kyle came rushing out, smacking into the other wall. He was in just his boxers and I could feel his pulse pounding in his chest like a drum as if it were my own. I could feel his terror.

"KRIS!" He screamed.

I didn't smell any blood in the air. Thank God. The last thing I needed was a dead body.

The shower water was still running. Tara came out holding a towel around her as best she could. She had her gun in one hand, raised at Kyle.

I watched the beads of water on the nape of her neck. Her hair was soaking wet and clung to her back. She looked incredible. She also looked pissed.

"Everybody relax." I looked at that stupid gun. "Put that thing away."

Tara ignored me.

Kyle had his hands raised, his face bright red. "Who the hell is she?"

"The new maid."

Tara glanced at me and her hand steadied.

"She shot at me!" Kyle screamed.

Tara was perfectly calm and rational. She turned to me. "I thought he was you."

That was comforting.

"I was going to take a piss." Kyle lowered his arms, walking towards me so that I was between him and the girl with the gun. "I didn't know who was in my shower. I thought it was you, Kris."

"Why would I use your shower?"

"I don't know," Kyle whined. He got whiney when he was frantic and scared to death. It was irritating. "I just woke up. Jesus Christ, it's *my* bathroom."

Tara lowered her gun finally and held the green towel around her better. I liked the color against her tan skin.

"I'm sorry I shot at you."

"You're sorry?" Kyle was brave without the gun pointed at him.

"I thought I locked the door."

Kyle turned on me like a rabid dog. "The lock sticks. Kris was supposed to fix it a month ago."

I'd been busy. "I'm working on it."

Tara looked at me and then went back into the bathroom, gently closing the door behind her. I think she kicked the door to make sure it was shut.

Kyle was breathing heavily.

I looked him over and wondered if he'd start hyperventilating soon. He told me he had had asthma as a kid. If he did start to hyperventilate, he was on his own.

"You okay?"

Kyle's face turned scarlet.

"Am I okay?" He was whispering in that furious forced whisper that wasn't really a whisper. "Am I freakin' okay? She tried to kill me."

"You're fine. You aren't even bleeding."

"Who the hell is she?"

I turned to head back into the living room, Kyle following me.

"She's a guest. One of three," I told him.

We walked into the living room and Ben and Lila were both standing in front of the coffee table with their backs to the television. The two were holding each other's hands as tight as they could. Lila looked like she had forgotten to breathe and Ben looked ready to run.

"It's alright," I told them.

Kyle grabbed me and squeezed my arm as tight as he could. I turned back to him and raised my eyebrow at him. It wasn't often that Kyle got mad or bold enough to get rough with me. He really was upset.

"What the hell are you doing?" he asked.

I smirked. "I've got a question for you first."

"What?"

"In the shower…you see anything?"

Kyle started to blush and he took a step closer to me. "I'm getting dressed. I'm coming right back, Kris. You better not hurt those kids."

I pretended to be shocked. "That hurts. What do you think I am, a monster?"

Kyle headed back into his bedroom. He slammed the door shut behind him and the walls rattled.

I couldn't believe it. I was borderline jealous. Kyle hadn't even done anything and he got to see Tara naked already.

I was the one who brought her and her siblings back to my house, fed them, let them take a shower and Kyle was the one who'd gotten a sneak peek. Why is it that the innocent ones have all the luck?

10

Being a Vampire and living on the beach in South Florida means that you have to take certain precautions. I have neighbors, human neighbors. Mr. and Mrs. Schwartz on my left are the nosiest little old couple I think I've ever met. Now if every time a gun went off in my house or someone started screaming and I had those two old crazies breathing down my neck and calling the police then I wouldn't ever have any fun. Luckily for me, I've got pretty useful friends.

One of which is a Witch. Just about the best Witch at forging spells that I've ever seen. She set me up with a nice protective spell plan that surrounds my home.

It's a basic package. There's a spell around my property that makes the inside of my house soundproof. It was because of that nifty little piece of magic that I wasn't worried about anyone overhearing Tara's failed assassination attempt.

The other part of the spell is that no one can enter my home by force. If someone were dumb enough to try, they'd get a nasty shock that would send them flying back onto the lawn. I still remembered the first trial. Kyle was my guinea pig. I had to rub Neosporin on his back from where he slid along the driveway. The sound he made when he went flying was kind of worth it though.

"Sorry about your wall," Tara said, tying her hair into a ponytail.

I looked straight at the small bullet hole marring the white tile on my wall. I put my finger in it. The little sucker went straight through. Lovely.

I glanced back at her. "Lucky you're a bad shot. I'd be mad if you killed Kyle."

"Yeah…sorry." Tara was wearing dark jeans and a gray hoodie. The zipper was down enough to show the white tank she had underneath. It made her perky breasts even perkier. I wanted to say natural B's. Not too shabby.

I noticed the tag hanging from the sleeve of the hoodie.

"You guys rob a Gap on your trip?"

Tara noticed the tag and pulled it off. She tossed into the garbage can near the toilet.

"No. An Old Navy."

"Oh, silly me."

"So, who is he?"

"Who?"

"That Kyle guy. Another Vampire?"

I laughed at that. "No."

I walked out of the bathroom and into the hallway. Tara stood in the doorway of the bathroom. I followed the trajectory of the bullet and saw a similar hole in the wall of the hallway right by the spare room.

"Who is he then? Your roommate?"

I glanced at the hole and saw that the bullet hadn't gotten through the drywall. I knew that I'd have to patch up the walls later. The tile in the bathroom would be a pain in the ass to fix.

"He's my servant." I turned back to Tara, wondering if she knew just how much it cost to replace a tile wall in a bathroom.

"Your what?"

"My servant. My slave. He's kind of like, what do the kids say these days? He's like my bitch."

I walked past her and she followed me out into the living room.

"You think he's mad?" Tara asked.

I thought about it. "Probably. Kyle gets mad about everything."

Kyle sat on the sofa beside the two kids. He had thrown on a pair of old faded jeans and black sneakers. He had his black long-sleeved Motley Crue shirt on. Kyle loved music and he had decent taste. If there was one thing that Kyle liked about me it was the fact that some of the "old" bands that he loved were bands I actually saw perform live when I was a kid, back before I was turned. Oh, the eighties.

Kyle had the remote and CNN was on the television.

Ben and Lila looked absolutely bored and I couldn't blame them.

Tara walked up behind the sofa and ran her hands through Ben's hair. He looked up at her, worried. I was starting to think that Ben worried too much.

"You okay?" he asked.

Lila just looked up at her big sister.

"Everything's fine." Tara smiled to reassure them.

I could hear it in her voice. Tara didn't believe what she was saying. I don't think the kids bought it either.

Kyle put up his hands when he saw Tara. "Please, don't shoot. I'm just watching TV."

Tara glared at him from over the kids' heads. "I said I was sorry."

Kyle wasn't satisfied. He turned to me and asked, "Could I talk to you outside for a second?"

Lovely.

I turned to Tara and the kids. "You want anything, you know where the fridge is."

Ben turned around on the sofa at that. I remembered being just as hungry at that age.

I turned and headed through the kitchen and onto the back patio. Kyle followed me out.

"What's going on, Kris?" Kyle whispered frantically as he slid the glass door shut. "You've never brought kids back before."

"It's not like that."

"What about her? She's got a fuckin' gun, man."

I explained to Kyle how I found them on the beach. I left out the part about Tara catching me off guard with the gun. That just didn't seem too important.

Kyle glanced back at the young trio in our living room. Tara was sitting on the couch with Lila and Ben. She was trying to make them smile, trying to relax them. I remembered what she said about her mother dying. It was just her dad and her raising those two. I knew that feeling; the feeling of having to take care of your siblings like they were your kids. You stop being an older brother and you act more like a father. Tara was more of a mother to Lila and Ben than a sister. I pitied her for it. That was a lot of pressure for a kid.

"The small one knew what you are?" Kyle couldn't believe it. "She's not a Witch is she?"

I shrugged. I didn't know for sure what she was.

"I've never met a Witch before." Kyle didn't like magic, Vampires, or anything that didn't fit into the picture-perfect mess of a normal life he once had. It was sad really. He should've been exposed to more as a child. It would've made him more liberal and open-minded.

"Witches can be dangerous. The older they are the more years of practice they have. She's just a kid so I don't know if she's technically dangerous, yet." I rolled that around in my mind. "Their grandmother might be a Witch though."

Kyle didn't like that. "Which means she's potentially very dangerous?"

"I think that's a possibility."

"Why are you helping them then?" Kyle whispered. "What do you get out of this?"

"I'm doing this out of the kindness of my heart."

"Bullshit."

The truth was that if Lila's grandmother was a Witch and I helped reunite that family then the Witch would be in my debt. It was never a bad idea to have powerful friends. Most people who trusted me enough to call me a "friend", owed me a debt that they had to pay off eventually.

I'm practical. Sometimes friends are like stocks. You invest time and money into them and eventually they pay off when times get rough. It's a curse you know, the being practical and all.

"Kris? Why are you really doing this?"

I looked at Kyle and I didn't know or feel like explaining anything to him. He wouldn't like my answers anyway.

"I don't have to explain this to you."

"Screw you," Kyle snapped. "Seriously, tell me."

I stepped up close to Kyle and he took a step back. I was six feet tall and he was a few inches shorter. I looked down at him and I could almost smell the fear rising out of his pores. I spoke softly, no bullshit.

"No, *seriously* Kyle, I don't have to tell you anything." I held him with my eyes and made sure he knew it was one of those moments when all joking was over. "I'm the master. You're the servant. You remember that?"

Kyle was trying desperately not to blink or look away from me. It was a brave thing to do. He was getting bolder. It made me kind of proud of him. Unfortunately, we were close enough that I could feel his fear. Even after everything I did for him, everything I gave him, he was just a scared college kid who still got spooked by the monsters.

I smiled a big smile and patted him on the back, which scared him even more.

"Relax, buddy. I know what I'm doing. This is gonna be fun."

Kyle was a little paler than before. "Fun for you is psychotic."

"It's still fun though." I glanced back at the three strangers in my house. "They asked me for help. So I'm going to help them out."

"I bet."

I smirked at the kid. "I may need you to watch them tonight for me. I've got business."

"Really?" Kyle wasn't whispering anymore. "I have that date tonight, remember?"

Shit. I was pretty sure that Vampires couldn't get Alzheimer's. I'd have to Google it later. Na, it was easier just to blame it on the stress of finding three runaways, one of whom may be a Witch.

"You may have to call that one off, Kyle."

"Nope." Kyle smiled a cocky little smile and walked over to the patio doors. "Sorry, Master. I've got plans tonight. I've also got the house to myself. You want to play babysitter? Go right ahead. But you told me that you'd leave the house to me tonight. You're in charge, remember?"

I'm told that in a true Vampire and human servant relationship there's a bond that literally forces the servant to do whatever the master says. I think somewhere along the way I screwed up with Kyle. I don't think I'm cut out to be anyone's master. The kid stands up for himself and I admire him for it instead of punishing him. Eh, what can you do? I grew up in the seventies when people in America were still fighting for equality. Slavery isn't my forte.

I couldn't even hide my grin from him. I couldn't force Kyle to do anything anyway and that argument wasn't worth the breath.

I'd intended to go to Jack's and try finding their grandmother alone. I guess I could just bring them with me. Why not? They were safer with me than Kyle anyway. He's just a human and he's not even good at that.

I followed Kyle inside and shoved him with my elbow.

"You're an ass," I told him.

"I'm learning," Kyle replied.

"Kris…" Tara called from the couch.

I looked from her to the television and didn't have to ask what was wrong. It was right there on the bottom of a CNN news report in all its high-definition glory.

"WEREWOLF BURNING IN GAINESVILLE, FL"

My throat started to get dry.

"Turn it up."

Tara grabbed the remote beside her and cranked up the volume.

"…remains of two Werewolves were found this morning outside of a small trailer lot near Gainesville, FL.," the male newscaster said. "The two monsters were suspected of being involved in three prior attacks on human beings. We are now being told that the victims' corpses are nearly a week old. That is the extent of the information we have at the moment. Police are speculating that these killings may have some connection with the other recent Were-killings on the East Coast."

I watched the images of police sealing off a crime scene. I caught a glimpse of the two human bodies sealed up in dark plastic. Weres always turn back to human when they die, no matter what the breed. Everyone at that crime scene was wearing gloves, boots and masks to prevent catching lycanthropy. I couldn't blame them. If catching lycanthropy meant you could end up like those two on the television, then you didn't want to take the chance.

The TV cut back to the CNN reporter standing in the studio set. "We will have more information as the story develops. In the meantime, look us up on Twitter and take our online poll: Do you think that whoever is behind these Were-killings should be prosecuted? At the moment, seventy-two percent say no. Another—"

"Turn it off."

Tara glanced back at me and turned off the TV before I could hear another pathetic word.

I hate the news. Almost as much as I hate the humans who report the news.

"Kris?" I heard Kyle's voice.

I turned to him but didn't say anything. What the hell was there to say?

Gainesville. That was only five hours away from here. The thought of a group of people out there hunting down whatever they could find didn't sit well with me. I hoped real hard they didn't make their way into my territory...for their sake.

I didn't need any more trouble.

I didn't say another word. I headed to my bedroom to clean up and get dressed.

"Where are you going?" Kyle called after me.

I turned to face him and the others. They were all looking at me, waiting for me to say something. I decided right then and there I wanted the little problem with the kids straightened out fast.

"We're going to run some errands."

Kyle could tell something was bothering me.

"You're coming too." I didn't ask.

I wasn't going to waste time arguing with Kyle if he decided to put up a fight. I headed down the hall to my room. I couldn't shake this feeling that Jack had been right to be worried before. But Jack and I were two different people.

If something worries me, I kill it the first chance I get.

11

The garage door roared open and the sunlight pierced my eyes.

I put my sunglasses on and turned to Kyle. He was acting chauffeur.

My Honda CR-V came to life. I nicknamed her Sandy. She's got a sexy black exterior with matching leather interior and loaded with more features than I could ever really need. I kept her immaculate. Sandy was my present to Kyle for being such a team player and for being my slave. I hardly ever drove her because Kyle had her at night to go to work.

I sat in the passenger seat and buckled up. You don't risk immortality just because you forgot to put your seatbelt on. You can't afford to trust other drivers on the road, especially in South Florida.

Sandy seats five. The kids sat in the back with Lila in the middle.

"Buckle up, kids," I said glancing back at them.

Lila and Ben already had their seatbelts on. Tara just looked at me.

"You serious?" she asked.

"Dead serious."

Tara reluctantly clicked hers on and raised her eyebrows stubbornly. "Happy?"

"I could burst."

I looked at Kyle. "Let's get it going."

Kyle rolled his eyes at my sincere enthusiasm as we pulled out of the driveway. I clicked the garage door shut with the remote control as we drove down the street.

"Where are we going?" Kyle asked.

I grabbed hold of the GPS and plugged in our destination. Kyle, like so many kids these days, relied completely on electronics. I accepted this and rolled with the times. If the kid could get us to where we were going faster with a computer shouting at him than me, so be it.

"Just follow the map." I reclined my seat a bit and put the window down enough to feel the fresh air on my face.

"I'd like to know where you're taking us." Tara's voice was close to my ear. She was leaning forward in her seat. I instantly wondered where her gun was and realized I didn't like her behind me with a loaded weapon. Call me paranoid.

"Visiting an old friend."

"Dressed like that?"

I turned around in my seat to look at Tara and the two kids. "What's wrong with my outfit?"

I had taken a quick shower—it only took twenty minutes, a new record—and threw on a pair of black jeans and a button-down gray shirt as dark as smoke. The top few buttons were open so that you could see the wifebeater underneath. I even had gel in my hair to give it a bit of a spiky look.

Tara seemed at a loss for words. "You look like you're going on a date."

"He always dresses like this..." Kyle glanced at me. "When he's trying to get laid."

"Trying?" I laughed at that. "I wouldn't even call it trying. Sort of just happens."

"What's that smell?" Ben asked.

"Hey." I breathed in my cologne. It was some crap out of Kyle's bathroom. I usually never wore cologne, but I figured I'd give it a shot. I turned in my seat to get a look at Tara. "You think I smell bad?"

Tara didn't answer. She shrugged and looked out the window at the passing buildings as we got onto A1A. The flirt that was my very essence was intrigued.

"Do I look alright?" I asked her directly.

Tara kept staring out of her window. "I guess."

I turned back around in my seat and settled. Smirking, I caught Kyle watching me and I smiled even wider. I'm told I have a natural charm with women. What can I say? Maybe in a past life I was a whore.

I think you look pretty.

I got shivers from the voice inside my head. It had just seeped into my thoughts. I looked over my shoulder at Lila and she was smiling at me. I had to smile back at her. She was a cute kid, a nice kid. It was bittersweet seeing her smile. She looked like my sister did when she was that age, except for the smile. My sis had a prettier smile I think.

Thank you for helping us.

I nodded at the kid. "Anytime."

"We're visiting a friend of yours?" Kyle asked.

"Yep."

"Which friend is this?"

It was going to be a much less hectic and irritating car ride if I didn't tell them the truth. So, instead of saying a word I turned on the radio and started looking for something to listen to.

"Kris…" Kyle spoke so I turned the volume up louder.

I stopped on Aerosmith's hit, "Love in an Elevator".

I turned the volume up even more. The mirrors rattled and the wind rushed by my face from the window. There was nothing like a car ride listening to music. I'm not picky about what I listen to. I've been around to see so many changes in music that I could give you my top fifty songs from the last four decades. I like rock n' roll, classic rock, all the way to grunge, and even indie bands. I've spent nights listening to blues and jazz, and whole days relaxing to David Bowie like I did when I was younger and human.

I've never met Steven Tyler, but I knew I'd rather be partying with him and the band than carpooling a bunch of runaways and an ungrateful human servant around on a beautiful afternoon. In a perfect world, I'd be famous and going wild with movie stars and musicians. Instead, look where I was.

My immortal life sucks sometimes.

12

It was almost four in the afternoon when the GPS said we'd arrived.

"Is this the place?" Kyle asked me.

I stayed in my seat, staring out the window. I could already feel her on my skin even inside the car.

"Oh, this is definitely the place."

We had driven all the way down to Dania Beach to the Townhomes of Aruba. It was too small for my taste, but the location was decent. It was a five-minute walk to the beach. Thick pine trees and a small forest surrounded the buildings, making it pretty secluded. Each building was divided into three separate two-story townhouses. A tall slash pine hung in front of building C and that was how I remembered which of the units belonged to my friend. I knew the townhouse number, but the tree helped since every unit was painted the same dull blue with white trim.

"Park there," I told Kyle. He pulled the SUV into a guest parking spot in front of the complex.

"Now can you tell us who your friend is?" Tara asked.

I sighed. No point in keeping it from them any longer. We were already there. "She's a Witch."

Kyle was the first. "Hold on a sec—"

I got out of the car casually to avoid the whining. I didn't want to hear it.

I stretched my legs in the parking lot. I don't enjoy being cooped up in cars for too long. My left knee locked up on me sometimes. Oh, the woes of being mortal during the day.

The three car doors opened and slammed almost all together. The kids and my slave spilled out into the parking lot.

"A Witch?" Kyle's voice was squeaking a little. "What do you mean a Witch?"

"You're joking right?" Tara couldn't believe it.

I knew they were going to react like that. "Relax. She's a sweetheart."

I headed up to the townhouse in the center of the unit. I hadn't come to visit her for at least two months. I wondered if she'd be mad.

The small forest surrounding the homes was lush, but not large enough to block out the sound of traffic from the nearest major street. Still, the place had a sort of seclusion to it that I admired.

As I approached with the ducklings trailing behind me, the front door opened up and there she was.

Her hair was cut and cropped short, black spiky shadows clinging to her tan scalp. An oversized red t-shirt that she cut and wore loosely over her shoulders like it was still the eighties, made her tan skin look even darker. You could tell she wasn't wearing a bra and I took the time to skim over her busty bust. She was wearing tight blue jeans with holes scattered about. At five-seven, Abigail Silva resembled a Brazilian supermodel. I wanted her in more ways than one the second I saw her.

Too bad Abby didn't like men as often as she liked women.

"Abby," I held out my arms as if to hug her from twenty feet away. "I've missed you so much."

"Go away." Abby raised an eyebrow and I felt that rush of supernatural power crawl along my face and give me chills.

I hated when she did that. It aroused and terrified me all at once. Aroused me because she was so attractive, terrified me because it meant she was pissed. You never wanted to piss off a Witch, especially a skilled one.

Abby might be a Witch, but she's also one of the only people alive who I did business with during the day. That's because we trusted each other with our lives.

Most Vampires don't trust Witches. Hell, most Witches don't trust other Witches unless they're in a coven together. Abby was different though. She used to be the second-ranked Witch in her old coven in South Carolina. Being second was a big deal. It meant that she wasn't only knowledgeable, but powerful. Some Witches know more magical spells and tricks than others, but lack the power to be really great. Others have the potential, but no wisdom to learn and grow from.

Abby was a double-threat and it was her job to protect the head of the coven.

I don't know the exact details, but Abby had more or less failed her number one priority. She hadn't been able to keep the head of the coven safe. That was six years ago and since then, she exiled herself to Florida alone. She set up a small underground business to make money and keep to herself. Abby made money by helping clients with defensive spells and protective charms. She was the Witch responsible for the magical guards protecting my house.

Like I said, I trust her.

Unfortunately, she was obviously still pissed off at me.

"Abby, come off it." I couldn't stop grinning as I walked up to her. "You're not still mad at me are you?"

Abby had her arms crossed and leaned against the frame of the door. "You fed off my ex."

"Now Abby, that's not fair and you know it. It wasn't my idea," I said.

"You did it on my sofa."

"Not true." Abby looked curious. "It was my sofa."

Abby headed back inside and slammed the door shut behind her.

"Smooth," Tara said.

I glanced back. "Don't worry, she'll come around."

"What are we even doing here?" Tara asked.

"Research," I tried figuring out how I was going to win Abby over.

"I don't like this," Tara said. "How can we trust a Witch?"

I understood the fear. Witches weren't angels. Some covens were devoted entirely to getting in touch with nature or finding a deep center of one's self or some crap like that. Others just wanted power and to own more territory and make more money. Witches were human after all; they couldn't help what was in their nature.

"Abby's a friend. She wouldn't hurt any of you."

Couldn't was more like it. Abby was a hardcore pacifist, a reformed fighter who literally refused to kill anyone. I guess failing her coven had left her scarred in more ways than one. No matter what happened, Abby swore that she would never physically harm another living soul. She meant it more than I had the capacity to understand.

I met Abby the first few months I moved down to Florida. She used to live closer to Miami in a nice apartment complex. Unfortunately, a group of radicals had been giving her a hard time. You know the type, Church loving, honest members of society who were good Christian murderers that would lynch a Witch or skin a Were so long as it was God's will.

A group of them went to her apartment and set the entire building on fire. What no one thought to worry about was the other people living there. Three were injured, but everyone got out alive. Abby said she was lucky that she got her neighbors out in time. It was an old woman and her granddaughter who wouldn't have made it out before the floor collapsed if not for the Witch living next door.

I was driving through the neighborhood looking for food when I spotted the flames. I was feeling nosey so I checked it out. I got there in time to see Abby in her pajamas, kneeling on the ground outside her burning home. She was crying while a bunch of men spat and kicked dirt on her. They were humiliating her and preaching to everyone around as if it was some big show. Abby refused to move, to do anything to provoke them. She refused to fight back.

It didn't make sense to me then and it never will. Abby could've worked her magic to stop the men from spitting at her. She could've fought to stop their cursing and screaming. It would've been easy to punish them all and she would've been justified in my book. But Abby wouldn't make a move.

It didn't take long for one of the men to get brave enough to walk up to her and hit her. He kicked her in the chest while she kneeled there in front of them. Abby fell on her back coughing and clutching at her chest. I expected her to react like a normal person would. Instead, she just got back on her knees and looked straight ahead. Tears were running down her face and her eyes looked like she'd gone somewhere very far away.

The guy was about to kick her again, laughing the whole time. I stopped him.

Everyone sort of started panicking and forgot about the Witch the second they saw a man go flying forty feet into a parked mini-van. If it were up to me, I'd have snapped the man's neck like a twig. But I was new in town and I had to keep a low profile. I settled for breaking his back. I don't know why she let me, but Abby didn't stop me from picking her up and carrying her away in my arms.

No one was dumb enough to say a word or try to stop me as I carried her off.

I saved Abby's life because she wouldn't do it herself. Abby told me later that her neighbors said the fire department didn't even try to put the fire out. They said it was a lost cause. "Lost cause" meant that there was nothing they could do because a Witch lived there and that was that.

"Abby!" I called through the front door. I didn't dare pound on the door or knock. I knew what spells she had up and I was wearing too nice an outfit to go flying across the parking lot.

"Abby, I need your help."

No response.

"You really fed off her boyfriend?" Kyle asked.

"Abby, come on." I started to shout. "I'll make a scene if I have to. Please don't make me make a scene."

She still wouldn't open up. Abby was getting even more stubborn. Great.

"What was his name?" Kyle asked.

I stepped away from the door, trying to figure out what I'd do if she wouldn't let me in.

"Amanda," I said absent-mindedly.

Kyle's eyes widened. "Oh."

The door opened up and Abby's anger spilled out.

"Megan! Her name was Megan."

"Then who was Amanda?"

I looked into Abby's burning brown eyes and felt her wicked powers swirl around her like a living flame. It was nothing you could see so much as sense.

I heard a gasp from Lila and Abby heard it too.

She looked down at the girl and then at the others behind me as if she just saw that they existed.

"Who're they?" Abby asked.

I noticed that Abby was looking at Lila. The two were staring at each other without blinking.

I wondered if Abby could feel what I felt around Lila. The two kept staring at one another and I was getting the impression that little Lila was having her own private conversation with Abby.

"Kris." Abby turned away from Lila and looked right at me. "Get inside. Now."

13

We all sat on the trio of black leather sofas in Abby's living room.

Abby's home always felt small but cozy to me. The townhouse had all wooden floors, polished and shining with no trace of dirt or dust. Some of the walls dark blue while others were a pine green. Sunlight spilled in through the double sliding glass door windows that led out to a back screened-in patio. The blinds were spread wide open and you could see all of the herbs and plants thriving in Abby's backyard. They hung from the ceiling in pots and vases and lined the entire patio. There were exotic flowers and plants and vines I didn't care enough about to ever be able to name. The backyard was lush with wild grasses and flowers that looked too bright and vibrant to be real.

Abby was a botanist. Her thumb was greener than all of my fingers combined. Every time I came over, I admired how beautiful her private garden was. With a tall wooden fence keeping the outside world from spying on her small backyard, Abby had enough room to keep practicing witchcraft even though she wasn't in a coven anymore.

"Can I get you kids anything to drink?" Abby asked from the kitchen.

The kitchen overlooked the living room with a small counter covered with a variety of scented candles. A few bowls were filled with unlit incense. Abby's place always had a scent that relaxed you right when you walked in.

"Can I have a Pepsi?" Ben asked.

Tara nudged him. "Ben."

"What?" Ben looked at his older sister as if she were crazy. "I'm thirsty."

"I don't have Pepsi. How about an iced tea?" Abby was leaning over the sink looking at us all.

I watched Ben think about the offer for a moment before he finally nodded.

Abby looked happy. "Anyone else want some tea?"

I watched Tara's face when Lila's hand shot up. Tara didn't trust Abby. I could understand her thinking. It was perfectly rational not to want to drink something a Witch was offering you. But Abby wasn't a threat and I didn't need Tara being rude to my friend.

I made eye contact with Tara and nodded. She trusted me enough to let it go, but she didn't like it. She crossed her arms and didn't say another word. Good girl.

"Alright. Two teas it is."

While Abby clanked ice in a glass and poured her homemade tea for the two kids, I turned to Kyle on my left. We were sitting on the sofa against the wall, facing the rest of the apartment. The three sofas in the room were arranged to make a U-pattern in the back corner of the townhouse. Tara, Lila, and Ben were on the three-seat sofa to my right.

Kyle's leg kept shaking up and down nervously. He hadn't said a word since we walked through the door.

"What's wrong with you?" I asked him.

He looked paler than usual and kept shifting his gaze to Abby. He watched her move in the kitchen. He hadn't stopped watching her every move.

"Nothing."

Kyle licked his lips, worried. He leaned closer to me and whispered, "Is she really a Witch?"

Oh, precious. "Yes."

"Okay..." Kyle sat straight up as Abby came into the living room with two cold, sweaty glasses of iced tea. She handed Ben and Lila their glasses, met Kyle's eyes, and smiled at him pleasantly.

I leaned over as close as I could to him and whispered, "I think she likes you."

Kyle's eyes widened and he glared at me.

Abby crossed in front of Kyle and I, and sat down on the sofa beside us.

"How's the tea?" Abby asked the kids.

I wasn't a big fan of tea. Abby had made one or two for me before, but they were either too bitter or too sweet. I was expecting the kids not to like them, but they took their sips and looked genuinely surprised. Ben was especially blown away, looking at the tea in shock.

"It's pretty good," he marveled.

Lila was all smiles, holding the large glass with two hands, careful not to spill a drop. She nodded enthusiastically and took another sip.

"Good." Abby turned to Tara. "You sure you don't want anything?"

Tara looked a little uncomfortable around the older woman. "I'm fine."

Abby's eyes stayed on Tara a second too long before she turned to Kyle.

"So you're Kyle?"

I turned to my slave and he was turning a slight shade of pink.

"Yeah, not much is he?" I asked.

Kyle waved at Abby and was all smiles. He wasn't a bad-looking kid. He just acted too serious and thought too much to use his looks to ever get laid. He said it was because he didn't view women as items to have, and was looking for someone that he would enjoy spending time with…give me a break.

I'm all for finding the love of your life—I've had two or three—but come off it. That mentality wasn't getting him anywhere. He was young; he should've started exploring and having fun a long time ago.

"How is it living with Kris?" Abby asked.

I rolled my eyes. This wasn't going to go anywhere good.

"You know him, it's…kind of like babysitting."

That hurt.

Abby smirked and looked at me. "I sympathize."

"You help me out Abby, and you and Kyle can switch places for a few nights. Could be fun." I smiled at her, spreading my legs and getting comfortable on the sofa.

"Please." Abby crossed her long legs. She looked me in the eyes for a few moments, I watched her face relax, and her eyes darken. "Why'd you come here?"

I sat forward on the edge of the couch. I looked at Lila and then Tara. She met my eyes and was trying to figure out what was going on in my head. Too bad she wasn't her little sister.

I looked back at Abby and I didn't know how I was going to tell her what I had to. "Let's go outside."

Abby knew me well enough to trust my call. "Okay."

She got up and we both headed for the sliding glass door.

"Kris," Tara and Kyle said together.

I glanced back at them.

"We'll be right back. It's business. Just drink your tea," I told them.

Kyle ignored me and watched the muscles in Abby's shoulder blades work as she slid the door open. Ben and Lila sat silently sipping their teas. Only Tara had her eyes on me, and she was thinking hard about something. I could see it in those brown eyes, a real intelligence. She didn't trust me completely and her instincts were making her nervous. Those were good instincts to have if you wanted to survive. I was starting to admire the kid's natural intuition. She was a survivor, no doubt about it.

I turned and followed Abby out onto the patio. I closed the door behind us and headed out into the backyard. The air smelled so sweet and fresh. I could practically taste every incredible scent. It always overwhelmed my senses when I stepped into Abby's garden. Luckily, my nose isn't as sharp during the day.

We both walked out through the screened-in patio and out into the backyard. I noticed several plants and ferns climbing up the wooden fence that I'd never seen before. They looked like something from the Amazon.

"Maybe you should sell some of these flowers," I suggested.

Abby turned to me and smacked me upside the head.

"What the hell was that for?"

"That's for Megan."

"Oh, get over it. She was a slut. You can do better. I told you that."

Abby punched me in the shoulder.

"Quit it."

"She left me because of you. Why'd you have to sleep with her?"

My ego wouldn't allow me to hide my grin. "Because you turned me down."

I could feel Abby's anger like a living darkness creeping up my spine. See, people don't tend to like my smirk.

Abby swatted at my face again, but that time I caught her by the wrist. "Hey, okay enough. I'm sorry, alright?"

Abby didn't seem too thrilled, but she backed off and I let go of her wrist.

"I shouldn't have slept with her. I'm sorry."

Abby raised her eyebrow like she always did when she was pissed. I wondered if she'd curse me if I upset her enough.

I put my arms out as if to hug her. "Come on. Was she really worth it?"

Abby just kept staring at me. "Turns out you weren't the first man she slept with while she was with me."

Not really a surprise to me. "No way."

"Yeah," Abby sounded cold. "I never told her that she couldn't be with men. Hell, I would've done it with her if she wanted."

I swear I did my best not to smirk or make any joke. But my best wasn't good enough.

"I think I just came."

I got Abby to laugh at that.

"Are we okay?" I asked.

Abby nodded thoughtfully. "Your human servant's pretty cute."

"Not as cute as me."

Abby gently caressed the side of my face. Her hand was warm and smooth. I didn't say anything to her, but that touch felt nice. It felt right.

Abby's angelic touch became painful as she pinched my cheek as hard as she could. "Oh, you're right, you're so cute."

She stopped pinching my cheek and laughed. I liked hearing Abby laugh. It was nice.

"What do you want Kris?"

"Help. A lot of it," I told her. Something in my voice made her realize I wasn't joking around.

"What's wrong?"

"Have you been watching the news lately?" I asked. "Oh wait, you don't own a TV."

"I don't need one." Abby didn't believe in televisions. She said that the media was brainwashing society.

I told Abby what I saw on the CNN report. I mentioned Jack being worried about the killings up north and warning me to lay low. As I spoke, I could already see the wheels turning in Abby's mind. She was a smart girl. You have to have a gifted mind to be a gifted Witch. Fun fact.

"That's why I came to you. I need help."

"What can I do?"

"I found those kids on the beach this morning."

"Found them?"

"Yeah. Do you sense anything different about the tiny one?"

Abby nodded, not surprised. "Of course. She's a Psychic."

"A Psychic?" Well, that made sense.

A Psychic was a human with an above-average level of psychic power flowing through them. Most Psychics weren't strong enough to do more than just sense some spirits or see glimpses of ghosts. Some just got a few lucky guesses that didn't have much to do with luck. But every once in a while, you had a human with enough mental power to start living in the realm of weird that separates us monsters from the rest of the world. There were those who could use telekinesis, telepathy, some who could even force their wills onto others. I'd read a news article about a man in Dallas who flipped a car with his mind and killed the driver. He was tried for murder and got the death sentence. Texas isn't the most tolerant state of the supernatural.

Dangerous Psychics are hard to come by.

I was a Vampire, and as far as I knew, all Vampires had some psychic ability. It helped make feeding easier. I personally had to keep physical contact with my donors to make sure they stayed under my influence. It made things go a bit more professional than them screaming for their lives and all that. I just didn't know how to make a connection from across a room. I could push feelings into them, get them to feel sedated, and even enjoy me, but I couldn't make them hurt themselves. I practiced it a few times, just to see if I could.

The Vampire who owned this territory before me could influence people from a distance. I heard he used to make people torture themselves in front of him. He was strong; psychically more powerful than I thought possible. Too bad he had to die when I took his territory. Maybe he could've taught me a few things.

"You couldn't tell she was a Psychic?" Abby sounded surprised. She had taken it upon herself to educate me with as much supernatural knowledge as she could. Every time I didn't know something and she did, she rubbed it in my face. What are friends for?

I looked at her and wasn't in the mood for the condescending look on her face. "To be honest, I thought she was a Witch."

"No." Abby rolled her eyes. "You've never met a Psychic before have you?"

I shook my head.

"Witches draw their energy from the world and life around them. We have to summon the energy and then manipulate it by reciting spells and chanting. Psychics, on the other hand, are only limited by their willpower and the strength of their mind."

"Did she talk to you outside?"

Abby nodded. "She's young. Telepathy is hard for most Psychics to learn. It looks like she has to concentrate, but Kris, the fact that she even can is impressive. You said you found them on the beach?"

I caught Abby up to date with my run-in with the runaways. I didn't leave anything out about what Tara had told me.

Abby glanced back at the house. I did as well, but couldn't see through the reflection of the yard in the glass doors. I wondered what Kyle and the kids were doing on the other side.

"You trust them?" Abby was talking low.

I looked into her beautiful face. "The truth?"

"Always."

"No."

"Why not?"

"Their story…I don't like it. I also don't like that the girl can get inside my head."

"You said she's a mute. It's her only way to communicate, Kris."

"Not that, though that's creepy as hell too."

"What then?"

"She knew what I was, Abby. Right there on the spot. Somehow, she knew. She had to have gotten inside my head and read my mind."

"I don't think she's doing it on purpose. She may not have control over her abilities." Abby sighed. "She's so young."

"I still don't like it." The thought of some stranger in my mind rubbed me the wrong way. I didn't even like some of the memories stored away in there. Good luck to whoever stumbled inside my head and saw the nightmares I had for flashbacks.

"What do the kids have to do with the killings up north?"

I shrugged. "Tara says she doesn't know who's after them. I don't know who's been killing Weres and Vamps and I don't know who killed their father. That's two groups of killers too many that I don't know anything about. Pennsylvania, Abby. That's north, right on the East Coast."

"Really? Are you sure?"

"...I'm not a big believer in coincidence."

"What's your plan then?" Abby asked.

"Plan?" I had to laugh at that. "Abby, I'm winging this."

"Kristopher,"

Uh oh. I knew I was in trouble when Abby used my full name.

"What are you going to do with that girl if she's being tracked?"

"Tracked?" I didn't like the way that Abby said that word. Like it was a word I should know, but didn't.

"Tracked. Really? Psychics can find other Psychics, Kris. They can feel their mental auras. It's just like ghosts being able to find other ghosts."

"Oh, of course." That was news to me.

Abby smacked me on the arm. "Some Psychics have such an acute sense of detection that they actually get paid to search for other Psychics all over the world."

I didn't like that part.

"Kris, if there are people after Lila and they know what she is then they're going to try tracking her. It's the easiest way."

Shit. My mind started racing. I didn't know who was after these kids and I had been dragging them around with me all day. Lila had a huge rope tethered to her and there were people on the other end reeling it in that I had a feeling I didn't want to meet. Why the hell did I have to go and bring that kid back to my house? Why the hell did I even help them in the first place?

Then it donned on me. I knew why I helped them. Because she asked me to. Because a little girl entered my mind and asked me for help and I was dumb enough to go with it. I messed up. I risked everything because I was curious. Screw the cat. Curiosity killed the Vampire.

Abby put her hand under my chin and forced me to look up. I saw something too close to fear in her eyes and it made my stomach tighten.

"Kris, I don't know about any killings, but I do know one thing. Unless you want their trouble to be your trouble too, you need to do something about those kids. Fast."

"I know. Shit." I stepped back out of Abby's reach. For once, I didn't feel like being touched.

"Have you tried finding their grandmother?"

Their grandmother. That was a dead end. "I thought that maybe their grandmother was a Witch, like Lila. That's why I came here. I figured if the kid was a Witch you might know their grandmother or a coven she might be a part of."

"I'm sorry. Even if she was a Witch, I don't know of a coven or anyone who practices in Boca who hasn't been down here for less than ten years."

I had to take a deep breath. "Do you know any powerful Psychics? Tara made it seem like her grandmother was different like Lila."

"Kris, I'm sorry. I just—"

Abby's eyes widened and she wasn't focused on me anymore.

"Abby?"

"Kris," Abby whispered. "I felt Lila for a moment."

Shit.

"I think she read my mind." Abby's voice was shaky.

Double shit.

I turned to look back at the house. I still couldn't see anything beyond the reflection of the yard.

Tires screeched and an engine roared nearby. I listened to the familiar sound of a car driving away. It sounded like a certain SUV I knew.

Triple shit.

I rushed to the patio and went for the sliding glass door when it slid open.

Kyle stood there looking at me with a bright red welt on his forehead. "We've got a problem."

14

"Why the hell didn't you try to stop them?" I shouted at Kyle. I was pacing in the middle of the living room. I pace when I can't hit anything.

Abby was standing in the center of the room, watching me. Kyle was sitting on the couch holding a bag of frozen edamame on his forehead. Abby was a vegetarian.

"She had a gun," Kyle whined.

"Good excuse."

"Why didn't you take it from her after she shot at me the first time?"

I stopped pacing and stared at Kyle. The kid had a point. But I was pissed so that meant he was wrong.

"At least if you put up a fight she'd have shot you and we would've heard them leave," I said.

"Oh, funny. You're an asshole." Kyle pulled the bag away from his face and got to his feet. "You're the one who got caught up with those kids. So screw you."

I had no good way of venting. An eighteen year-old maniac with a gun and her two pre-pubescent partners stole my SUV. I couldn't call the police because that would just open a door to trouble I couldn't handle. I had no way of tracking the damned kids by scent because the sun was still shining. If it were night, I could've followed them all over the state and caught up to them by now. But sunset wouldn't be for another couple of hours and their trail would be impossible to find by then.

The worst part was that I didn't know Tara, but I knew she was reckless. She left a crime scene and drove all the way down the East Coast from Pennsylvania. For all I knew, the police were already looking for her and her siblings. If she crashed my car or got pulled over for speeding, they'd trace my car back to Kyle and then to my house and my money.

I really wished it were dark out. I really wanted to punch a hole through something.

"Kris, you need to calm down," Abby said.

I turned to the Witch and scoffed. "Calm down? Sure. You know what, on second thought, I'll just kill Tara." I thought about it for a second. "Yeah. I like that plan."

Abby wasn't amused. "They only ran away because Lila read our thoughts and heard our conversation."

"I bet."

"Kris, it must've terrified her."

"Yeah," Kyle said. "The kid looked like she was going to freak. Next thing I know Tara's got her gun in my face. She said that if they were being tracked then they had to keep moving."

Great. Leave it to a bunch of kids to do something stupid.

"Kris?"

I was starting to get a headache.

"What's tracking them?" Kyle asked.

I wished I knew.

Kyle stared at me and scoffed. "You don't even know do you?"

"Abby?" I kept my eyes on Kyle. "You know a spell to shut Kyle up?"

Kyle looked at Abby and she looked at him without blinking.

"I could make his flesh grow over his lips. He wouldn't be able to talk," Abby said matter-of-factly. "He wouldn't be able to eat though either."

I watched the color drain from Kyle's cheeks. "You can't do that."

Abby raised one of her eyebrows.

"Can she do that?" Kyle looked at me, borderline panicking. He didn't know shit about witchcraft. Seeing the uncertainty and fear in his eyes cheered me up a bit.

Abby took a step forward and Kyle took one back, nearly falling onto the couch behind him.

"I know a way you can find them," Abby said as she sat down on the sofa and crossed her legs.

She stared up at me with her soft lips spread in a wide smirk.

I was intrigued. "How?"

"I can locate them. All I need is something from their body for the spell to work."

"What, like hair?" Kyle asked.

I glanced at him. "Kyle, stop talking. You're embarrassing me in front of my Witch."

Abby ignored us both. "Actually hair would do. But..."

She leaned forward and reached out for one of the glasses resting on the coffee table in front of her. She held up the glass of half-drank iced tea into the sunlight coming in from the back of the house. I could see the tiny smudge marks from Lila's lips at the top.

"Saliva works just as well."

I loved having a Witch on my team.

"I'll need blood though for the spell." Abby turned to me. "Care to share?"

"Does it have to be mine?" I asked. I knew that some spells required blood to work. I even knew that if the blood came from something supernatural, like a Vampire, then it had more of a kick to it. My body generated blood during the day like everyone else, but it still had mystical properties. I wasn't eager to donate. Blood was something I took and didn't like giving up. Not unless I absolutely had to.

Abby shook her head. "Any blood will work."

We both turned to Kyle.

"No," he said vigorously. "Hell, no."

I crossed my arms. "You want to get the car back? Quit being a baby."

"No, Kris. Seriously, no."

"Just a drop," I said. I turned back to Abby, not really sure. "Just a drop, right?"

"Just a drop."

Kyle started to leave the living room, never turning his back to me. "Please, Kris. You know I can't stand the sight of blood. You remember what happened the first time you tried to take my blood?"

I remembered.

"I threw up everywhere, Kris. I don't want to throw up everywhere."

"If you wanna be a doctor, you're gonna have to get over it," I told him, taking a step closer.

"Please don't make me do it." Kyle looked like he was going to be sick. "Please."

"You're being ridiculous."

"Screw you. I'm not doing it."

I shushed him and held out my hand. "It's just a little prick on the thumb. Be a good boy and maybe I'll get you a lollipop."

Kyle was almost nearing the kitchen when Abby got up from the couch and walked right up to him.

"Stop it," she said. "Leave him alone."

I stood there; hurt that she would take Kyle's side.

Kyle didn't even budge as Abby walked right up to him. I couldn't believe it.

"You undermine my authority like this and he won't ever respect me."

Abby gently took Kyle's hand and looked up into his eyes. Kyle looked down at her and looked instantly calmer.

"Just breathe," she whispered to him.

Kyle let out a slow, steady breath that he'd been holding in. He let Abby's smooth tender hands rub his fingers and explore his palm like a mind reader. I watched the way Kyle looked at her. Abby was staring only at his hands, but Kyle couldn't take his eyes off her.

I could feel how beautiful he thought she was. I could feel how she silenced that fear inside of him. She calmed his anxiety and excited him all at the same time.

"You won't feel a thing." She spoke softly to him, her words stroking his soul. "I promise. Just close your eyes."

Kyle glanced at me and then the bastard closed his eyes as if he trusted Abby with his life. It hurt a part of me that I didn't know was there. After all the time we shared together, he didn't trust me at all. He was more willing to trust a beautiful Witch he just met over me.

I couldn't blame him, but I didn't like it. What did that say about me as a master?

Abby reached into her pocket and pulled out a thin black sewing needle. She massaged Kyle's palm with one hand and pressed the needle into the top of his index finger. The kid's face didn't even flicker as a mound of fresh ruby life welled up to the surface.

She rubbed the needle in it until Kyle's blood covered the tip.

Abby let go of Kyle and his hand fell to his side.

"All done."

Kyle opened his eyes and stared at his fingertip. It was already healed and there was no blood in sight. Oh, the wonders of magic.

Abby reached into the front pocket of her jeans and pulled out her iPod Touch.

She began searching through it with the needle in her free hand.

"What are you doing?" I asked.

"Looking for a location spell strong enough to find them with just a little saliva."

"You keep your spells on your iPod?" I asked.

"I may not have a television, but I'm not ignorant. I've got a computer upstairs and an external hard-drive with all of my back-up recipes for potions and lists of spells." Abby glanced up at me. "Welcome to the twenty-first century, Mr. Grant."

I shrugged. "I remember when computers were as big as my dresser."

Kyle was staring at Abby, calmer than before now that his sacrifice was over and done with painlessly. "You see what I have to deal with?"

Abby ignored him and held the iPod closer to get a good look at it. "Alright, I found one. Just give me a few."

"How long's 'a few'?" I asked. Patience wasn't one of my strongest qualities.

Abby headed for the kitchen and began rummaging through cabinets. "If you stop talking to me, not long. I have most of the ingredients already prepared."

It was one of the many things I loved about Abby. She was always prepared.

Kyle walked up close to me, his arms crossed uncomfortably.

"What?" I asked.

He stood close enough to whisper to me. "Could she really sew my mouth shut?"

"I could break your jaw and then we could wire it shut. How about that?"

Kyle got upset and turned to watch Abby in the kitchen. She was grinding God knows what with a marble mortar and pestle.

We stood there side-by-side, watching the Witch work her magic.

"How's your head?" I asked.

For however much of a disrespectful pain in the ass Kyle was, he was still my responsibility. I'd have Abby try to heal him if he was hurt more than he looked. Being hit with the butt of a gun hurts, trust me.

"What do you care?" Kyle asked bitterly.

I didn't respond. We both just kept watching Abby as she poured the purple powder she had ground up onto Lila's glass where her lips touched. Then she touched the glass with the needle covered with Kyle's blood and started to whisper under her breath.

"I'm fine," Kyle replied. "She didn't hit me too hard. I don't think she wanted to hurt me."

I thought about that. He was probably right. Tara had taken the kids and the car and fled because she was terrified about being found by whatever was chasing them. You do what you have to if you want to survive. I understood that better than most.

Kyle took my silence to mean something bad. He knew I didn't have a problem killing. I guess he figured I'd kill the kids for stealing my car. I've killed for less.

"They're just kids," he told me as if I didn't already know. "They're scared."

He was really concerned. I stared back at him and wondered just what kind of monster he saw when he looked at me. I didn't get why he thought I was such a bad guy. Maybe I was. I made his life hell sometimes, but I made up for it with everything I gave him. Still, it bothered me a little that he felt the need to try and stand up for the kids to protect them.

Truth was, I wasn't going to hurt them. At least not Lila and Ben. Tara might have to be roughed up a bit though. She was playing the types of games I couldn't afford to play. If there's one thing you never do, it's mess with a man's immortality.

"I'm ready." Abby walked out of the kitchen holding a small glass. There was a mixture of purple liquid in it that looked like pale grape juice. It smelled like lavender.

"Kris, if you drink this it'll link you to Lila."

"Link us? How?" I reached for the glass.

"You'll feel yourself being pulled to her."

I guess I looked as confused as I felt.

"You'll know what I mean." Abby looked at me and I could see she was worried. "What do you plan on doing when you find them?"

"Get my car back."

I put the glass close to my nose and breathed it in. Yep, smelled like lavender. I hate lavender. I hated lavender even more when the thing I was supposed to drink smelled like it.

"This is gonna taste like shit isn't it?" I asked.

Abby nodded. "Probably."

Of course it would. Why couldn't a potion ever taste like lemonade or Vodka? Hell, I'd settle for a potion that tasted like plain water.

I downed the glass as fast as I could, trying not to taste anything. I failed. I gagged, but managed not to throw up. I held the glass out for Abby to take and she did, smiling from the look on my face.

"How do you feel?"

"Oh…that's gross." I winced and shivered from the taste. "I taste grass. I quite literally taste fresh grass in my mouth."

"Do you feel any different?" Abby ignored my whining.

I thought about it, closing my eyes to concentrate. I didn't feel anything. I was going to be pissed if I drank that crap for nothing.

"Kris?" Abby asked me again.

"No, I don't feel anything. You sure you did it ri—"

It was as if someone had lassoed a rope around my intestines and yanked with all their might. I stumbled forward, almost losing my balance. There was a rush of intense vertigo and all at once, it disappeared. I think I closed my eyes because everything went black for a moment.

I could smell the interior of my car. I could feel the air conditioner blowing on my skin. My heart was racing because I was afraid and worried. I knew I shouldn't have dragged anyone else into my mess. I missed my father...

I opened my eyes and there was Abby and Kyle kneeling on either side of me.

Apparently, I'd fallen back and nobody had bothered to catch me.

There was the tugging at my insides. Whatever I was tied to was getting farther away and the cord around us was being pulled tighter.

"I think it worked," I moaned.

I held out my hand for Kyle to help me up. He ignored me and just stood up.

"Thanks." I sat up by myself and took a deep breath.

Abby stayed knelt down next to me, a true friend. "You okay?"

I nodded, trying to get used to the sensation inside.

"You sure?"

"No." I took a few deep breaths. "How long is this gonna last?"

"Until you find her. You just have to touch her and the spell will break."

Great. "Thanks for the help, Abby. I think."

She smiled and had a hand on my arm as I dragged myself to my feet. "You're sure the spell went alright? I don't want to watch you burn from the inside out."

I glared at Abby. I didn't want to know if she was joking or not.

"Yeah." It felt better to be on my feet.

Abby took me at my word.

The spell connecting me with Lila was working. I could feel her presence getting farther away. I knew I had to get to her fast because the feeling of that spell inside my gut sucked. I also had to get to them before Tara made any more problems for me.

I turned to Abby. There was something else she could help with.

"I need one more favor from you."

Abby didn't like that.

"What?"

"I'm gonna need to borrow your car."

15

Abby's red Toyota Yaris raced along US-1.

I weaved in and out of traffic. The speed limit was forty-five, but I was pushing sixty. The engine of the small sedan roared in my ears. I don't think Abby ever opened up the little guy on the road before. Poor thing. Cars are made to be driven. If the law doesn't want me to drive so fast, don't put so much horsepower in the engines.

I stuck to the roads I knew, avoiding as much of the five o'clock traffic as possible.

Kyle was strapped in and gripping the side of his door. "Why couldn't I drive?"

"You drive too slow."

I was still following the constant pull on my insides. The more I drove in the right direction the more that mystical rope binding us slackened. I was getting closer to Lila every second.

"You're going to get pulled over. Slow down." Kyle was holding his breath as I sped by an old woman driving a little blue Lincoln.

I had to find those kids and get my car back. Once I did that, I really didn't have much of a game plan. It was a little past five. In just over an hour it'd be nearing dark. Then I could quit playing around.

I got a feeling to head closer towards the ocean so I got off US-1 and headed east down some back streets. As we drove, the spell told me I'd made the right call. It made sense. It seemed like Tara had been keeping the kids close to the ocean. A1A, US-1, and I-95 were all easier roads to navigate than the less familiar ones further inland.

We were getting closer and closer to the ocean when the spell shifted so suddenly that I gasped. It was as if the taught line I'd been reeling in went slack. I knew deep in my gut—literally—that they'd stopped somewhere. That meant I was catching up fast. Good. The sooner I found Lila and my car, the better.

"What's up?" Kyle asked.

I knew Kyle felt what I was feeling. Oh, the perks of me being his master. It was so rare for him to feel my emotions that it always startled me when it happened.

"I think they stopped driving."

The light up ahead turned red and I slowed down at the intersection to make a left onto the next road. I knew they were northwest of us.

There was traffic coming and I didn't see any cops nearby. I floored it and drove across the intersection before the other traffic could go.

"What are you doing?" Kyle shouted.

"What?"

"You can't make a left turn on a red light."

"Sure you can." Usually I didn't risk getting in a car accident, I swear, but I was in a rush. Besides, nobody got killed.

Kyle didn't say a word out of frustration as we drove. He stared out the window watching the hotels and condos pass by.

"How much longer is this going to take?" He finally asked. I had been waiting for the bitching to start. It looked like the wait was over.

"I don't know." I was annoyed. I was getting so close to the kids so fast that the spell was starting to make me nauseous. Abby's locator spell really sucked. I'd make sure to tell her later.

"Well it's already after five o'clock."

"Can you just quit whining for five minutes? Please? Could you do me that one little favor?"

"I'm not whining," Kyle whined. "I've got plans tonight."

"What plans?"

"My date. Remember? Oh, wait. Why would you remember? It's not about you."

I ignored the pressure in my abdomen as I drove and bickered. "Oh. I'm sorry. Somewhere between finding a Psychic kid on the beach and having my car stolen I forgot about your little dinner date."

"As soon as we get the car I'm driving back home." Kyle pointed a finger at me. "You dragged me around with you all day and I'm done with it."

I couldn't believe what I was hearing. "Where do you get off?"

"Excuse me?"

"The servant's not supposed to order the master around. It's in the rules."

"You're full of it." Kyle sat forward in his seat. "I've been shot at and hit over the head with the same gun from the *same* lunatic you brought into our house. You wanna run around all day and get yourself killed, go ahead. I'm all for it. But do it by yourself."

"If I die, you die, buddy old pal," I told him. "You forget that?"

"So when we find the car I'll drive it back and you drive Abby's car back to her. It'll be dark by then. You can find your own way home in the morning." Just like Kyle could feel my emotions, I could feel his at times. Right then I could tell he was feeling nervous and proud all at the same time. He'd stuck up for himself. To him, he wasn't doing anything wrong. To me, he was just being an idiot.

Feeling Kyle's emotions and having the spell warp my stomach drained me. I didn't feel like bickering any more. Thankfully, neither did Kyle.

We were driving along a shopping mall strip right on the beach. The end of the street became a large loop with a fountain in the middle. It was huge, with a large statue of a merman with a trident plunging out of the water. It was the first time I had ever been to that part of town.

"Look." Kyle pointed straight ahead. "Is that them?"

I didn't see them at first. It was a shopping plaza in the early evening so there were people everywhere. It took a second, but I spotted them.

The three kids were on the west side of the street, moving with the traffic of people on the sidewalk. Tara was in the middle holding both of the little kids' hands. They were walking faster than everyone else was, as if they had somewhere to be. They were on foot. They'd ditched my SUV, hopefully somewhere safe and close.

Since the road was going to end at the fountain and I'd have to loop around, it made more sense to get out and get the kids by foot. I didn't want them to see us coming. They would probably panic. Panicking was never good.

The traffic wasn't bad in the strip. I pulled up along the side of the curb and parked Abby's car.

"What are you doing?" Kyle asked.

"If they run we have to chase them." I turned the car off. "They won't run in the street and we can't chase them through parking lots and buildings in a car."

Kyle looked out his window. "Do you have money for the meter?"

I gave Kyle a harsh look.

He threw up his hands, "Fine, let's go."

We both got out of the car and into the cool evening air. I put on my sunglasses and surveyed the street. I spotted the kids still walking on the sidewalk. They looked like they were in a hurry. I had to get to them and talk with Tara without causing a scene.

I turned to Kyle. "You try to cut them off up ahead."

I pointed north on our side of the street. "I'll come up from behind."

"What if she shoots you?" Kyle looked at me from the other side of the car. It was a reasonable question.

"She won't." At least I hoped she wouldn't. Firing a gun, let alone shooting someone on a crowded public street was a surefire way to get the police after you. Tara wouldn't want that and neither did I.

I jogged across the street and slowed down once I was on the sidewalk. I could feel the knot in my stomach tightening. That metaphysical rope connecting Lila and me shrank with every step I took. I could see Tara's ponytail bobbing behind her. They were less than thirty feet away.

I wove in and out of people, brushing against some, while nearly pushing others who were in my way. There were a lot of people out shopping and strolling. There were way too many witnesses for Tara to just shoot Kyle or me. At least that's what I kept telling myself.

I could see Kyle jogging on the other side of the street, bumping into strangers and apologizing as he desperately tried getting ahead of our prey. If he wasn't a bit more inconspicuous, Tara was going to see him. I hoped she didn't.

I was a hunter. I kept my eyes on my target, just like I'd been taught. I kept up my steady pace, making progress. There was only a single couple between the kids and me.

I was moments away when it happened.

A musky scent overpowered the ocean air. I felt the presence in the back of my mind like a growling rumble that didn't belong to me. I felt the thrill of the hunt, the fear of losing control. I could sense him without even trying. There was a Were nearby, one who lacked the self-control that most of the Weres I knew had. The fact that I could sense him so strongly meant that he was new, new and fighting for control over the beast inside.

I didn't know exactly what, who, or where it was, but that didn't matter. What mattered was that I could feel him, and that was the problem. I didn't hang around many Weres during the day. It wasn't healthy. Unlike Vampires, a Were keeps all of its strength and other supernatural abilities during the day, including its regenerative abilities. They're not as strong as a Vamp at night, but they were close. I know, unfair right?

I acted on instinct. What choice did I have? I jogged around the last couple and shifted into a casual fast pace alongside my three runaways. I tried keeping the thought of the Were as far back in my mind as I could. I didn't need Lila picking up on it and freaking out.

They were holding hands. Ben was closest to the curb and he saw me first. He stopped for a fraction of a second before jerking Tara's arm.

The second Tara saw me I put my finger to my lips.

"Relax. Don't say anything."

I said a prayer that Tara wouldn't bolt or make a scene. I wished she were smart enough to just keep walking and listen to me.

Thankfully, my wish came true.

"Go away," Ben said harshly.

Tara yanked on his arm to quiet him.

"I'm not here to hurt you guys." I glanced around the busy shopping strip. I couldn't see anyone who looked like they were interested in us. I couldn't even see Kyle.

"Listen to me. Just follow my lead. There's something nearby that could be a real problem." I stared at Tara and hoped she could tell I wasn't kidding.

"What is it?" Tara swallowed hard, trying to keep the two kids walking regularly as if there was nothing wrong. Smart girl.

"I can sense something close. I need you to come with me. Alright?"

Tara looked down at Lila and then started glancing around the street.

"Don't," I urged.

Tara kept her eyes straight ahead.

"Just keep walking."

"What do we do?" Tara sounded nervous.

That was a good question. If there was a Were nearby and it just so happened to be following Lila then I was in trouble. I looked around. I didn't know the area that well, but I saw a sign on the other side of the street saying that the beach was privately owned. That meant no crowd. I worked with what I had.

"I'm going to stay behind you. Cross the street, keep looking ahead, and go towards the beach. There should be a pier nearby. Head for it."

"I'm sorry I took your car," Tara said. She didn't sound sorry.

"It doesn't matter. Just act normal and do what I say."

I didn't even wait for her to nod. I slowed down, glancing to my left at one of the nearby store windows.

Tara and the kids kept on going ahead of me and crossed the street looking like three normal kids.

I kept staring into the large front window of the small novelty store. It reflected the entire street and I could see Tara leading the kids to the other sidewalk. What I couldn't see was anyone going for them.

I reached out with that part of my mind that let me sense other Vampires. I instantly felt that innate thrill that ran through any excited Were who felt the hunger of the hunt. I couldn't pinpoint the damned thing like I could with Vampires. It felt more natural locating my own kind. Sensing a Were was more like feeling this sudden rush of adrenaline that gives you chills and makes your knees tremble. It's like feeling their beast's hunger and excitement when they spot their next meal.

I stepped away from the store to follow Tara and the others calmly when Tara made the dumbest decision of her life.

All three of the kids bolted.

"Shit."

Tara let go of her brother and sister's hands and all three of them were running as fast as they could to the beach behind the edge of the shopping strip. It wasn't subtle at all and it wasn't what I had told them to do.

I really hate when people don't listen to me.

I ran in front of a car and was halfway across the street when Kyle came running alongside me. He must've gotten ahead of them and crossed the street already when they ran.

"What did you do?" he asked.

I didn't have time to say a word because at that exact moment I saw someone else starting to run out of the corner of my eye. I looked up, and there he was on top of a connecting building across the street. A man was running along the roof, moving faster than any normal human could.

He was agile and graceful as he leapt up onto higher parts of the connecting buildings and then flipped down onto the lower parts. I lost sight of him as he headed towards the back of the roof near the beach. He was chasing after something and I had a good idea what.

Tara and the others rushed by people on the street. They ducked under the roped off barricade separating the shopping plaza from the private beach. Did Tara really think she could get away from me by running along an empty beach?

I *really* overestimated Tara's intelligence.

Too bad. I had to act fast.

"Don't lose them!" I shouted to Kyle.

"What?" he asked, but I was already gone.

I started running back down the street. I avoided the humans and the traffic and every glare and shout and gasp as I moved. I had to haul ass.

Aside from the blood pumping in my ears all I heard was Kyle screaming, "Where are you going?"

I sprinted as fast as I could right in the middle of the street. I skidded to a halt and fumbled for the keys as I flung open the Yaris door and got in as quick as I could. The engine roared and I sped away from the curb.

There are certain times when you have to do things that are anything but conventional. I was all about staying alive. That meant lying low and never showing up on the police's or anyone else's radar that could ruin my life.

I drove in the middle of the two-lane street going as fast as the car could go. I honked the horn and people ran and dove out of my way. The windows were up and I could still hear some of them screaming at me. None of it mattered.

I was mortal during the day. I had a Were chasing after a Psychic and I had no idea why. All I knew was that I had to stop him, but there's not much you can do to a man who could lift a pick-up truck without breaking a sweat.

Yeah, I was throwing conventional right out the window with this one.

16

I cut the wheel hard to the right. The tires screeched and the stench of burning rubber filled the car.

I drove straight through the shrubs and bushes blocking the end of the shopping strip from the private beach behind it. The rope barricade snapped as if it wasn't even there.

I had a split-second to decide whether to head north or south along the beach. I'd seen them go north. My gut was telling me to head that way too. The spell was still working; it was down there somewhere beneath all of the adrenaline. God, I love me some good old adrenaline.

I turned the wheel too hard. The Yaris drifted along the sand for a few yards before I got control of it again. I pushed down on the gas pedal until it wouldn't go any further. Abby's tiny car roared desperately to pick up speed. I gripped the wheel with one hand as hard as I could. I clicked my seatbelt on. Safety. Couldn't forget safety.

The entire car rocked from the uneven terrain of the beach. My stomach lurched as I drove over a small mound in the sand. I got a good foot of air before the car touched down again, the suspension hissing at me.

I was lucky that the private beach was empty. Usually there are people who don't really follow the rules. That day, a higher power was looking out for them. It was just the Atlantic Ocean on my right and palm trees and shrubs on my left for a mile or so down the beach.

Oh, and the five people I was speeding towards.

I saw the kids. Everyone was still alive. They hadn't gotten too far, but the Were had caught up to them.

Tara and the kids had the ocean to their backs. Tara had her gun pointed at a very large panther. It was crouched low, as if any second it would pounce. It was nothing but solid muscle beneath cream-colored fur. I saw Kyle to my left, far back from the rest of the party. He was getting to his feet, shouting something at me as I sped by. The Werepanther must've thrown him.

I kept my eyes trained on that big cat. There was enough room between it and the kids to do what I wanted.

I gripped the wheel with both hands as tightly as I could to keep it steady. I sped up, stomping the pedal to the floor.

You see, there's not much a human can do to stop a Were.

But you hit anything with a car going fifty miles per hour and it doesn't matter how strong you are. It doesn't even matter how fast you heal because guess what?

It's still gonna hurt like hell. That's physics.

The panther saw me coming, but it was too late. I knew he was a new Were. He didn't even notice a speeding car coming at him. The bastard couldn't focus on anything but his prey.

He tried leaping out of the way when the Yaris hit.

The sound of the impact rattled me. The body of brown fur flipped over the hood and smashed into the windshield. The glass cracked, but didn't shatter and I listened to the body roll along the roof a few times before the silence came.

I slammed on the brakes and lost control of the car.

Everything started spinning. I closed my eyes and braced myself for whatever was going to happen. After what felt like a lifetime of spinning and the sound of the tires grinding into the sand, everything finally stopped.

I opened my eyes to see a spider web-like crack in the windshield. Blood stained the center of the web. I cocked my head to the side to see the unusual sight. The Were's blood covered the hood and ran horizontally across the windshield from the car spinning.

I hadn't seen that happen before and I've hit a few people with cars on purpose.

The adrenaline was surging through my veins. Nothing else mattered but moving right then. I had just hit a Werepanther with a car going fifty. That didn't mean he was dead though. And if he wasn't, he was sure as hell going to be pissed.

I had to get out to make sure he didn't get up. I had to kill him before he killed me. I had been dumb enough to leave the house without a gun. Tara had her father's. I could use that. If nothing else, it would buy us some time.

I opened the door first and tried to get out, but couldn't. It took me a second to figure out why. I wasn't thinking clearly. My seatbelt was still on. I fumbled to get out of the car and spilled out onto the sand.

Lila was crying and screaming at the top of her lungs while Ben held her. They were kneeling in the sand, crying.

Tara still had her gun out. It was aimed at me.

I really wasn't in the mood for that.

I ignored the kid with the gun and looked for the body of the Werepanther. Priorities.

He was gone.

Shit.

I was still dizzy as I stepped away from the car. I was at least twenty feet from the ungrateful kid pointing a gun at me. I saw my tire marks up along the beach and the figure eights I'd made when I lost control of the car. The only thing that mattered was the spot of crimson soaking into the sand amidst my tire marks.

I stumbled over to it. I had to see. I put myself parallel from the kids. I could feel the barrel of the gun on me.

I looked down and saw the bloodstained paw prints of a panther in the sand. The tracks led off towards the small forest preserve along the coast. I followed the trail with my eyes and watched the panther tracks become human footprints.

If it was able to shift back to its human form, that Werepanther was very much alive. Great.

I looked over at Tara and the gun she had pointed at me. I think that was when I snapped a little.

"Stop pointing that goddamn gun at me," I growled.

She didn't waver. "Leave us alone."

"He saved us," Ben screamed over Lila's sobs.

"Shut up," Tara screamed even louder.

"No!" Tears were running down Ben's cheeks. "That thing was going to kill us."

Tara ignored her brother.

"I told you to stay calm." I straightened up and looked that stupid little teenager right in the eyes. My sunglasses were gone, hopefully somewhere in the car. Tara had no problem seeing the anger in my eyes. My neck and shoulders were already stiff from whiplash. I hate being mortal.

I walked towards them and Tara spread her feet wider apart. Someone had taught her to shoot. Good old dad probably.

"Why did you come after us?" Tara asked. "What do you want?"

"What do I want?" I couldn't control my anger. I trudged through the sand towards the barrel of that gun. "I want to know what's after you."

"I'll shoot you," Tara swore. "Stop!"

I stopped immediately. I didn't know anything about Tara, but I knew there was a chance she was crazy enough to shoot me.

Tara was fighting back something. I could see it in her eyes. Either she wanted to tell me something and couldn't, or she wanted to shoot me and wouldn't.

"Tara," Ben started again. "He—"

"Just shut up!" Tara screamed at the boy. "I'm in charge!"

Ben closed his mouth and stared right at me. He wanted my help. He knew they needed it. Hell, I knew they needed it. Everyone could see that but Tara. She refused to.

Lila had stopped crying and she looked at me through those red swollen eyes. Her blond hair was covering her face and her round cheeks were as red as I'd ever seen. I had a sudden image of my baby sister crying. I could still see her crying out for me because I wasn't going to be around anymore. Crying because I abandoned her, because I left her when I was turned.

A part of me that still held onto my past crumbled and gave way. I looked at Lila and I didn't want to see her cry. I was waiting to hear her voice in my head. I wanted to hear her. Hear her say that she wanted my help again.

She never said a word.

I stared at Tara and that gun. The pity, the concern I had for her went away for a second. I looked at her and I wanted her to see that she was the one making Lila cry. That running was going to get that little girl, hell, all of them, killed.

"Your car is back at the shopping strip. Behind the Starbucks." Tara kept her gun on me but reached out for Ben with one hand.

Ben just looked up at his sister as if he didn't know her.

"Benjamin!" Tara screamed.

I watched Ben reluctantly take Tara's hand. He dragged Lila to her feet.

Tara started backing up with the kids behind her, the gun still on me. "I put the key on the front left tire."

"I can help you," I told her.

She shook her head. "No. No, Lila was wrong. You can't help us."

Tara waved the gun up the beach. "Go. Please. You follow us and I swear to God I'll shoot you."

I looked Tara in the eyes as she ignored the help I offered her. It was her and two kids up against a Werepanther and who knows what else. Abby was right. They were in deep shit and it was all going to spill over on me if I got involved. Involved. I ran a Werepanther over with a car. I think that counted as me being involved.

I limped over to Abby's wrecked car. I got inside and listened to the engine idle. I had forgot to turn the car off. I sat there, biting back my anger. I kept telling myself there was nothing I could do. That I wasn't wanted and that was all there was to it. They wanted to go it alone? Fine. They weren't my responsibility.

I flicked the windshield wipers on and watched the spray mix with the blood. Some of the bloodstained water slipped through the cracks in the glass and leaked into the car. I just sat there watching the two blades try washing all that blood away. When I could finally see out the windshield I slammed my door shut and put the car in drive.

The kids watched me go as I drove back up the beach. I stared out the window and saw Lila's little face and Ben's heavy brow. I sped up and drove away. I watched Tara finally lower her gun in the rear view. She fell to her knees and Lila wrapped her arms around her.

I adjusted the rearview mirror so I couldn't see them anymore.

Kyle was walking towards me, limping a little and holding his left arm close to him as if it were hurt.

I stopped and he got in. I noticed sand sticking to a large scrape on his temple. He winced as he sat down on the seat.

Kyle looked at me and he didn't even have to ask.

"It was a Werepanther," I told him.

He took a deep breath. "You kill it?"

"No."

"What about them?"

"They're not coming." I swallowed all my rage and just focused on driving.

We drove back up the beach and back the way we came without saying another word.

17

My car was right where Tara had said it was. The keys were even on the front left tire. I didn't see any dents, scratches, or bodies under the car. Unfortunately, seeing Sandy in all of her big black Sports Utility Vehicle glory wasn't enough to cheer me up.

I was pissed.

That stupid location spell kept pulling at my insides the further I got from Lila. I didn't get to touch the kid so the spell hadn't broken yet. But that was okay with me. I'd use it later if I didn't start throwing up all over the place.

Kyle followed me back to Abby's in my car while I drove the Yaris. There was so much sand in the wheels and transmission that I had to listen to a constant grinding the whole drive. It didn't sound healthy. The Yaris' alignment was shot to shit and the front fender was drastically dented from hitting the Were. Every time I turned the wheel too hard to the right, the tire would catch on the bumper. Overall, I'd say Abby's car was just a little worse off than when I got it.

I parked in a parking spot as far back from Abby's building as I could. I really didn't want her to see the car while I was nearby. There was a pad of yellow notebook paper on the floor in the back. I tore out a page and used the pen clipped to it to jot down a quick note.

Kyle pulled up in the spot next to me and rolled down his window. "What are you doing?"

I didn't answer. I walked to the front of the Yaris and lifted one of the windshield wipers up. The blade snapped in my hand. "Shit."

I laid the broken blade back where it came from and carefully placed my note under the remaining wiper blade. I put her car keys next to it.

The note said, "THANKS AGAIN, I OWE YOU." with a small black heart doodled at the bottom.

I got into the passenger seat of my SUV so we could leave without being seen.

"Drive," I told Kyle.

He reversed out of the parking spot and we started the drive back home. "Why did you park so far away?"

"She's going to be pissed when she sees her car."

"You're afraid of her?"

I glanced at him. "No. It's just not healthy pissing off a Witch."

"You're totally scared of her." Kyle looked amused.

I wasn't scared of Abby. She could do all sorts of things to hurt me and she was strong enough to kill me if she wanted, especially since she knew where I lived during the day. But she wouldn't. Abby liked me and she wouldn't kill me because she was too much of a pacifist.

Okay, maybe I was a little scared of her.

I watched the sun slowly sink into the horizon. The moon was a pale crescent in the east, growing brighter every second. I could feel its latent energy growing in the air. Soon it'd be dark enough for me to gain my abilities back. The anticipation was killing me.

It's not precise when my Vampiric abilities will return. I hear that every Vampire is different. My body has a certain Vampiric circadian rhythm ticking inside. There's a time of day when my abilities return naturally with no problems. If I had to though, I could bring the change earlier. But that meant paying a price. Everything about Vampires has a cost, a way of balancing the scale.

Calling my abilities early was like yanking and dragging them up to the surface against their will. I had done it a few times before, but the sudden change is a little rougher. You bring out your immortality, but you get buried under a raging bloodlust. I'm all about being in control and civilized. But when I force the abilities to come, I need more than just shots of blood from a syringe to sate my hunger. That usually meant anyone around me was fresh meat.

When I was first turned, I was forced to call my abilities out. My record was an hour before sunset. A couple of men died that day. I ripped them to pieces. One of them was a friend. When you lose control, everyone's just meat waiting for you to sink your fangs into. There's no such thing as friends, or lovers, or family. There's just the killing, just the blood.

Changing early was for emergencies only. Even though things weren't looking up, I didn't classify this as an emergency just yet.

"Do you want me to drop you off somewhere?" Kyle broke my concentration.

I forgot about his little date, again. I didn't want to deal with another pointless argument. Kyle could have his night alone if he wanted. I had other things to take care of.

"I have to pick up a few things and change," I told him. "Then the house is all yours."

"It's just until morning," Kyle tried to assure me. I guess because I didn't give him a hard time he was grateful. Go figure.

"It's alright. I'm going to be out all night anyway." I watched the streetlights pass by in the window. They all started blinking to life for the coming night.

"That Werepanther..." Kyle's voice was deeper than usual.

"What about him?" I turned and got a good look at Kyle. His eyes were on the road, but he wasn't watching it. The gash on his forehead was fresh. I looked at the blood coagulating with the sweat and sand. A part of me wanted to run my finger across it and taste it. Another part of me regretted that I'd left the kid alone to chase after a Werepanther. It could've ended much worse for Kyle.

"He was strong." Kyle glanced at me and realized I was watching him. "The kids were in front and the Were was chasing after them. Tara spun around and once he saw the gun the thing stopped. I tried tackling him, but he knew I was coming. He turned around and threw me like I weighed nothing. I hit the ground and skidded on the sand. It hurt like hell. I'm lucky nothing's broken."

"You're lucky you're not dead."

Neither of us said anything for what felt like a lifetime. I hated awkward silences.

"I got up and watched you drive into him..." Kyle shook his head. "You're insane."

I thought I heard something that sounded like admiration in his voice.

The car turned and I realized we were already coming to A1A. We were only a couple of miles from the house. I watched the familiar street pass us by as he drove on. It's funny how coming back home always seems like it takes longer.

Kyle was talkative that night. "I wasn't very close, but that panther was huge, right? I mean, bigger than normal?"

The size of a Were's animal depended on the individual's strength. Usually an older, more powerful Were will be nearly twice as large as the animal was in the wild. The panther I ran over was big, but probably not much larger than an average wild panther. I knew he was a new Were from the excitement I felt from him. That just meant he was strong.

"It was a pretty big cat."

"Do you think it's alone?" Kyle glanced at me. He was more curious than afraid.

"I don't know."

Wasn't that the truth. I didn't know what was going on in my territory. That was a problem. Those kids had fallen into my lap and I should've just sent them on their way and ignored the whole damn thing. Now I ran over a Werepanther and I didn't even kill him.

I didn't know how strong that guy was, but most Weres can heal almost any wound. A new Were could get shot in the chest with a shotgun and still take off running. It would take time, but in a few hours they'd be good as new. An older, stronger Were could take the same shot and heal in minutes if they had enough willpower. The real kicker was, if any Were got seriously injured they could change and heal instantly. That left you with an upset supernaturally strong animal ready to tear you apart.

There's a reason humans hunted Weres down. There'd been one too many times in history when one rogue Were with a few screws loose or a twisted morality decided they'd go on a rampage and massacre as many people as they could. In Germany back in the thirties, they put Weres in camps. They'd gas them, burn them, or pump them full of silver and burn the bodies to ash.

They say that places like that don't exist anymore. The Were community doesn't tend to agree. Does the government run tests on Weres? Probably. Are places outside of the Land of the Free still eradicating as many Weres as they can find? Definitely. Even in the United States, once word gets out that you've got lycanthropy, you're a target in one way or another.

There's a video online of a teenage Wererat being beaten in broad daylight in New York back in the early nineties. Five grown men beat her with silver baseball bats. Eventually she fought back and kicked one of them hard enough to shatter his spine against a taxicab. Everyone backed off her and the video ended with her limping off down the street begging for someone to help her. Nobody would.

The next day, they ran the news report that a female with lycanthropy who had killed a man in New York was found dead in a subway tunnel. She'd been shot several times by police officers. The official statement was that she attacked the officers first.

Things like that happened all the time, and for the most part, people didn't seem to mind. We're just the monsters after all. Who cares how many of us die?

"Kris?"

I looked out the window and realized we were pulling into the garage.

"We're home."

So we were.

"You okay?"

The sun was almost down and I sat there in the seat feeling my powers rise up through my body like a growing storm. Finally.

I got out of the car and walked around to the back of the garage. I stood there staring out at the western horizon. The sky was an ocean of dark blues and purples consuming the dying sun. I closed my eyes and felt that part inside of me start to stir.

My hearing improved drastically. I heard the ocean waves and the birds gliding on the wind behind my house. Kyle's pulse whispered in my ear like a familiar friend. I could taste the salt in the air. I took a slow, deep breath and I was flooded with scents. The patch of grass out front, the ocean air, Kyle's body spray, and the stench of oil from the car. I could smell it all.

The energy in my body began to grow and grow, with no end in sight. There's only one way I can describe the change: it's like finally waking up. As if all day I was just sleepwalking through life until the sun went down. It felt good. Real good.

I focused and dialed my senses back down to just slightly above normal.

I turned to Kyle and he was rattled.

His eyes searched my face and he shook his head. "It freaks me out when that happens in front of me."

I examined my own hands. They were smooth and flawless. I knew my face and the rest of my body had changed as well. I looked at Kyle standing there in the garage. I should've fed from him, got him to donate some blood so that I wouldn't have to hunt. Unfortunately for me I didn't. I ignored the throbbing vein in his neck and the warm steady flow of sustenance that ran throughout his young body.

I never feed from Kyle. He hated it and I didn't have time to listen to him bitch.

There was still a shot from the night before. It would have to do.

I turned and headed inside the house from the garage. Kyle was right on my heels.

"So…" he sounded nervous, anxious, "When are you heading out?"

I glanced back at him. I'd been itching all day for the sun to set so that I could get to the bottom of all of this. I didn't have to be afraid of any Psychic kid and her gun-waving lunatic of a sister. Usually I'd be cautious of a Werepanther, but at night, I can manhandle any pussy. The fact that Kyle was still worrying about me being out of the house for his date was irritating, to say the least.

"I'll leave when I'm ready, Kyle."

Kyle stopped at the doorway as I went into my room.

A vial of blood was still on the dresser. Lauren. I couldn't believe I'd forgotten about her. Last night seemed so far away. As if it never even happened. I was supposed to hunt her down again. Have more of that incredible blood. I thought of Lila, Tara, and

Ben…damn. I wasn't going to be hunting anyone other than those three tonight.

I snatched the vial and downed the shot. The spectacular, incredible blood that made my mouth water tasted plain again. I couldn't explain it. It tasted even plainer than the second shot of blood I had drank that morning.

I cursed under my breath and headed into the bathroom. I threw the vial into the garbage bin near the toilet. The blood wasn't what I was hoping for, but it would do. It had to. I had business to take care of, whether I liked it or not.

I looked into the mirror and saw the God-like figure staring back at me. Every blemish, each random speck of imperfection on my face, was gone. The small crow's feet around my eyes, the lines on my brow and at the corner of my mouth, had vanished. I was flawless. I was immortal again and it felt amazing.

I ran my tongue along my mouth to make sure I got every drop of blood. I ran the sink water and rinsed my face off.

"You taking a shower?" Kyle called from the room.

A shower? I had planned on taking one, but I didn't feel much like wasting more time. I wanted to get away from Kyle before I broke his arm for trying to rush me out of *my* house. I grabbed the Listerine and rinsed all of the blood off my teeth.

I came out of the bathroom, unbuttoning my gray dress shirt.

Kyle was leaning against the frame of the door, watching me.

"What are you going to do?"

I tossed my shirt into the hamper bin by my dresser and looked for a new shirt to wear.

"You going after those kids?"

Going after the kids? Oh, I was going after the kids alright. I was getting answers. Nothing was going to stop me.

I grabbed a plain black long-sleeved shirt. I threw it on over my wifebeater and made sure my cell phone was still in my pocket.

"Kris?" Kyle's voice was getting on my nerves.

"I'm leaving. Relax."

"I just wanted to know what you planned on doing tonight. You going to hurt them?"

I really didn't know. *I* wasn't psychic.

"Kris?"

I turned to Kyle. "I'm going to take care of things."

Kyle scoffed at that. "I bet. You sure got a lot done today."

I moved with a burst of speed. To me it's just moving. I run to a place as fast as I can and the shorter the distance the harder it is for the human eye to see. I was already in Kyle's face with my hand gripping the side of the doorframe when he gasped and stumbled back into the hallway. His back hit the wall hard. His chest was rising and falling rapidly, his heart was like a clock ticking in my ear. Kyle didn't dare take his eyes off me.

I stayed in the doorway, scowling at the little shit.

"Kid, I'm not in the mood. I'm going out because *you're* the useless one. You let those kids drive off with my car. You stay here with your little friend. It keeps you from fucking things up more, you useless, whiney little shit."

I let go of the doorframe and stepped into the hall. I didn't have time to deal with Kyle and he didn't want me around. I had to find out what was going on in my territory. That was more important.

I walked down the hall, leaving my human servant behind.

I glanced back just once to see Kyle sliding down the hallway wall. He stayed slumped forward on his knees. He buried his face in his hands and I could smell his fear. I could taste it. His anger and hate was a warm breeze on my back.

I didn't have time to deal with Kyle's little problems with me being what I am. He was making us weak and I wasn't going to put up with it much longer. He had to get over it and make the best of it. He didn't have a choice. This was the way things were, for better or worse.

I was at the door to the garage when I stopped. For a second I thought about going back and saying something. Maybe even apologizing. The thought made me grind my teeth. I was pissed and frustrated about Tara's stupidity and not being able to go after Lauren's delicious blood again. It was like going through withdrawal.

I walked over to Kyle and it startled him. He looked up at me, terrified. I bent down and grabbed the car keys that he'd dropped on the floor next to him.

I turned and walked out of the house without saying a word.

I was the master and Kyle was my human servant. Even if I wanted to apologize, I couldn't. Kyle had to get over it on his own.

What else could I do?

18

I had an appointment with Jack at eight-thirty. I pulled up to Mikey's parking lot at half past seven.

I don't usually drive at night; I prefer walking. But Kyle didn't ask to borrow the car, just the house. I took Sandy because if I found the kids, I needed something to drive them in. Okay, I mostly did it out of spite. I'm immature sometimes. I'm Vampire enough to admit.

I have a few fake licenses and insurance cards just in case some cop pulls me over. Better safe than sorry. I didn't need any problems with the police that night. I already had enough to deal with.

The sun was nothing but a memory in the sky as real darkness started to take over. The darker shades of purples and blues on the western horizon were fading fast. The lot at Mikey's was already full and it wasn't even eight. I had to park near the back of the lot, close to A1A.

I got out of the car and headed to the bar. I put my hands in my pockets and walked up the cement walkway to the front entrance.

As soon as I stepped inside, I was overwhelmed with a typhoon of odors. Smoke, alcohol, perfumes and colognes, and sweat and grease. I listened to all of the conversations going on over the radio playing classic rock. I concentrated on tuning all the static noise out.

The bar at Mikey's was right in front of you when you first walked in. It was in the center of the building with black leather stools circling around it. There were wooden booths and tables on both sides of the bar for family dining. The back of the place had a few high tables and chairs to sit at while you played pool or darts. That night, the bar was loaded with people. For such a dingy hole in the wall, it definitely stayed busy.

I glanced to the far right corner of the establishment. There was a narrow hall that led to the kitchen, the restrooms, and last but not least, Jack's office.

"Kristopher!" a familiar voice shouted.

I headed over to the crowded bar to see the beauty shouting my name.

Julie was one of the prettiest bartenders I'd ever met. Her hair was a darker brown than mine with blond streaks running through it with the tail end falling down between her shoulder blades. It framed her slender neck like a dark portrait. Julie's skin was a permanent tan that never seemed to fade. It made her hair look even darker. Her eyes were a dark auburn that in the dim lighting of the bar appeared black. That night she had on dark jeans and a black tank top that seemed painted over her petite figure. Julie was in better shape than most men were.

I watched her finish pouring a beer on tap for an older gentleman at the bar before she turned her attention to me.

"Long time no see." Julie gave me that warm smile that she always seemed to have when I was around. "Where have you been hiding?"

I leaned against the bar. "I was here last night. Where were you?"

"Tuesday's my one night off from this place."

"I'll have to stop coming in on Tuesdays then."

"Jack told me you'd be stopping by tonight." Julie was only a little over five-five so she had to stand on her toes for me to see more of her body over the counter. She held her arms out to show off her unspectacular wardrobe. "I dressed up just for you."

Her smile made me laugh. Julie was one of the sweetest, prettiest women I'd met in Florida. Sadly, she was a Werefox and worked at Mikey's. Jack made it very clear that I wasn't allowed to sleep with the help, human or otherwise.

That usually wouldn't have stopped me. The fact I had never once fed off or slept with Julie is proof of my loyalty to Jack. The things we sacrifice to keep the peace.

"I've got an appointment with Papa Bear," I told her, surveying the bar. I looked at human faces that I didn't recognize and didn't care to know. "I'm just a little early."

"About an hour early." Julie tossed her white rag over her shoulder and leaned onto the wooden countertop towards me. It accented her breasts nicely.

"What's Jack doing? Hibernating?"

She laughed. "You never get tired of making bear jokes do you?"

"Nope."

"He's in a meeting right now."

"A meeting? What kind of meeting?"

"You don't know?"

"No."

"Then it looks like the kind of meeting you don't get to know about." Julie flashed me her perfect smile and swatted my hand with her rag playfully.

I was about to say something when one of the men at the bar pounded his fist onto the counter. "Quit your flirtin'. I need a beer!"

Julie's pleasant features turned sharp and cold. She turned to the customer and gave him the finger. "Quit your bein' a dick."

The second bartender, a young guy named Al turned around. He had short blond hair and dressed in all black just like his partner. He put a hand on Julie's shoulder to calm her down.

"I'll get you your beer, Earl."

Mikey's was busy enough and had a large enough bar that they usually had two bartenders working it at night. Al was human, but when he touched Julie I could see that he affected her in more ways than a friendly co-worker's touch should.

Julie glanced back at him and the smile she gave him was different from the one she gave me. It made her features look, I don't know, softer.

"Thanks," she told him.

I was getting the strange feeling something was going on between those two. Al was a good kid who worked days as a mechanic in some shop just south of Boca. Jack kept telling me to go to him if I had any car problems. He said he'd get me a good deal. Considering what I'd done to Abby's car, I might have to actually look into it.

Al was young, maybe twenty-eight. He lifted weights enough to make him bulkier than I was. Standing beside someone as small as Julie made him look even bigger. Still, even though he looked like a blond Clark Kent, my money was on Julie in a fight.

"You think your boss would cut his meeting early for me? I've got a problem."

Julie seemed genuinely worried for a moment as she looked at me. "You're serious. This is the first time I've seen you that you haven't said anything about my ass."

I frowned. "I need to see him. Now."

Julie nodded and turned to Al. "I'm takin' a break. You good?"

"I'm good," Al reassured her, pouring two beers from the tap at once.

"Good." Julie walked around to the side of the bar and lifted the wooden counter divider. She came around to me and got close enough to have a conversation without anyone else overhearing.

"Everything alright?"

I just looked down at her.

Julie understood. "Come on, let's go."

"Thanks."

Julie led me away from the bar and I walked right behind her, glancing at the smooth firm curves beneath those jeans. Once we got in the hall out of sight, I grabbed her by the wrist and she turned to look at me.

"What?"

I leaned in close and whispered, "Your ass does look great tonight."

She smirked and continued walking. "I know."

I got chills and a part of me wished that Jack wasn't as good a friend as he was.

Julie knocked on the door with a cliché sign on the front labeled, "EMPLOYEES ONLY".

No one answered the door and I couldn't hear anything on the other side even if I tried. That's magic for you. Jack had his own Witch who helped secure his business and home. There was a spell around the office that kept the sound trapped inside. I'd gotten the idea to have Abby do a similar spell around my house because of Jack.

Julie knocked a second time and before she could finish, the door opened. I saw Rick's familiar face. He looked upset already as he stared at Julie. When he saw me behind her he managed to get even angrier. Rick was six feet tall and bulky enough to look like a giant compared to Julie.

"We're in a meeting."

"It's an emergency," Julie said. "Get out of the way."

"I can't let you in," Rick replied. I wasn't sure if he was talking to Julie or me. Probably both.

"Jack!" Julie shouted in Rick's face.

Rick seemed so perplexed he didn't know what to do. Julie pushed the door open and forced her way through. I liked Julie's style.

"Jules? What's going on?" I heard Jack say.

I stepped into the office and saw Jack's eyes turn to me. I shut the door behind me and noticed a few things at once. The first was that Jack had his Desert Eagle sitting on his desk with his hand resting on it. The barrel was facing the man sitting in the chair in front of his desk; the same seat I sat in just last night.

The second thing I spotted was that the man sitting in front of Jack wasn't a man at all, at least not a human one.

He was dressed completely in black. A black jacket with a black cotton hood hid his face. Black jeans and large black leather boots with matching gloves made it so every inch of him was covered. I couldn't see any part of his flesh other than his left hand. His glove was in his lap while his hand rested on the arm of the wooden chair.

I stared at that hand and a part of me froze up for a second. Dark and pale green scales covered his skin. His fingernails were sharp, pointed orange claws with dark black tips. They looked dense, strong, and sharp enough to cause all kinds of hurt if they wanted to.

I didn't dare look away from the creature in front of me. He slowly turned his head towards me. The shadows clung under the hood of his jacket as if they were trying to hide his flesh as well. But it wasn't just shadows. He had black cloth wrapped around his head to hide his face.

I could only see his eyes. They gleamed in the soft light from the lamps on the walls. Those eyes weren't human. They were reptilian. Where normal people's eyes were white, his were black. His irises were narrow golden slits that shone bright amidst the sea of black surrounding them.

I couldn't sense anything from him. I couldn't tell if he was a Were, or something I'd never met before. There was nothing but my own hesitation, my own anxiety. I'd never admit it out loud, but I was nervous.

"It isn't eight-thirty yet." Jack's voice pulled me away from those serpent eyes.

I turned to him and I was having trouble thinking, more than usual.

"I told you to come at eight-thirty."

I glanced back at the lizard-man and watched him put the glove back on his hand calmly, as if no one else was in the room. It was a casual gesture, as if he were more sophisticated than terrifying.

"This is Kala," Jack signaled to the man/thing sitting across from him.

I looked back into those terrible eyes and the man nodded politely.

"Kala, this is Kristopher. He's the Territory Master here. My business partner."

Kala stood up and he was well over six foot four. He had broad shoulders and a wide chest, but a narrow waist. He had the build of an Olympic sprinter. Lean, powerful-looking muscles were masked by the black outfit. He stared at me and made sure his hood was in place before he turned back to Jack.

"I have said all that I have to say." Kala's voice was normal at least. It was deep and raspy, but he spoke clear. I don't know what I would've done if he hissed at the end of his words. Probably laughed.

"I'm sorry our meeting was cut short." Jack looked at me and it wasn't friendly.

"I hope that we can all do business in the future." Kala turned and walked past Julie and I to leave the office.

Nobody said anything after the Snake Man left for a few awkward seconds.

Rick was the first to speak. "Jack, I don't think—"

"Get out." Jack's eyes were fierce. He was rarely in a bad mood.

"But, Jack…" Rick looked like a puppy dog that just got kicked and couldn't understand what it had done.

"Go keep an eye on Kala. Make sure he gets out of the bar alright."

Rick looked concerned. I didn't blame him.

"Julie, get back to the bar."

Julie looked at Rick and swatted him on the chest. "Come on. Let's go."

The two left and Julie wished me a silent good-luck before she closed the door behind her.

"What the fuck do you think you're doing?" Jack was on his feet and walked over to a filing cabinet on the wall to his right.

I turned and saw that the Desert Eagle was still on the desk and not in his hand. Good. At least he wasn't pissed enough to shoot me. Yet.

"I'm sorry." I wasn't really. "What the hell did I just interrupt?"

Jack ran a hand through his salt and pepper hair, frustrated. "Business. Dangerous business that I don't think I'm up for."

"Anything I should worry about?" I sat down in the same seat Kala had been sitting in.

"No." Jack looked older, more tired than usual. He walked back to his desk and sat down to try and relax. I could hear his heart pounding like a ram inside his chest. He grabbed his gun and put the safety on before putting it back in his desk drawer. Jack's Desert Eagle was the Werebear's favorite handgun. If the fact that it was a huge Desert Eagle wasn't scary enough, it was also loaded with silver bullets.

I didn't know who Kala was, but if Jack felt the need to keep his gun out for his business proposal, then I don't think I really wanted to find out. Still, Kala's was one more face I didn't recognize. There were too many of those going around lately.

"Is Kala a Were?" I asked.

Jack nodded. "Yeah. I don't know what kind though. Can't even sense him. Could you?"

"No. Where's he from?" Sometimes location was a simple way of seeing what animals bit whom to make them what. Most Were-animals stayed relatively close to where they were found naturally. It made blending in easier when they hunted. You don't see many Werelions on South Beach for a reason.

"I don't know. I've heard about him though. He's bad news." Jack took a deep breath and just sat there looking at me for a while. Jack wasn't telling me everything. Usually I would've cared, but I already had enough problems to deal with.

"What's going on with you now, Kris?"

I forced the sight of Kala's hand and those eyes out of my head and tried to focus on business. I didn't have a real easy way of telling Jack what was going on, so I told him everything I could with as much detail as possible. I laid it all out there for him to see for himself. I was counting on him to be able to come up with something.

When I finished, Jack didn't say anything for the longest time. The two of us just looked at one another and let the seconds tick by. It wasn't awkward or uncomfortable; it was just me giving Jack the time he needed to absorb everything I'd told him.

"You think whatever's after the kids is involved with the killings on the news?" Jack didn't seem so sure.

"Seems like it. Hell, I don't know." I leaned forward in the chair, frustrated. "All I know for sure is that the little girl's a Psychic and there's a chance she's been tracked to our territory."

"You think the Werepanther's hunting this girl?"

"He was going right for the kids, Jack."

"You sure?"

"Positive."

Jack didn't seem convinced.

"I've never met a Werepanther before. This Were's animal looked like a mountain lion, a puma, or whatever you want to call it."

"I know what a panther is, Kris."

"I'm just saying. Are there other Werepanthers in my territory? I wasn't aware we had any."

"We don't. Not since Adam left a few years back."

"So this Werepanther's come here without speaking to us first. That's reason enough for me to find him and kill him."

Jack whistled. "Feeling feisty tonight, huh?"

I was getting confused. "You don't agree?"

"I didn't say that. I just don't know if he's involved with the killings."

"Why not?"

"Come on, Kris. One young Werepanther taking down a handful of other Weres, Vamps, and even a few Witches? It's hard to believe."

More like impossible. "There could be more than one."

"Maybe." The old bear sighed. "I heard about a few radicals from a friend in San Diego. Something about the movements their 'brothers' on the East Coast are starting."

"Great. That doesn't explain the over-sized cat I ran over though. Why would it be after the kids?"

"Money? He might be getting paid to bring them in." Jack laughed and it was bitter. "Hell, most people will do anything for money these days. Even us."

"Those kids could bring a lot of trouble here. This Werepanther, whatever else…they're in my territory without my approval."

"Or mine," Jack added. "But I have a question for you."

"Go for it."

"How much of what the girl told you is the truth?"

Good question. "I don't know. But as soon as I leave here I'm finding out."

"You gonna take it easy on them? Or just take what you want?" Jack was dead serious when he asked me.

"I don't want to hurt these kids."

"You just don't want to get played."

I leaned back in the chair and grinned at the old man. I loved when people psychoanalyzed me.

Jack smirked. "You don't want them to ruin the life you've got here. Right?"

"That wrong of me?"

Jack sat forward in his chair and leaned onto his desk. "Why'd you get involved then?"

I sighed. "Because I'm an idiot?"

Jack stared at me like he knew more about me than I did. I hated when he acted all wise and creepy.

"You said those kids were looking for their grandmother didn't you?"

"That's what I was told."

Jack opened his desk drawer and started rummaging through it. "I only know one Psychic in Boca with enough power behind her to be worth mentioning."

That was a start.

I watched Jack search. "Abby said that Lila's strong. According to her, the kid's gifted."

"Yep. Telepathy's a pain in the ass to get good at. If she's pulling it off, she's got a lot of potential to her." Jack pulled out a large brown leather journal. He opened it up and started skimming through the pages. "My Psychic friend likes to keep a low profile. That's probably why Abby doesn't know her. Her name's Portia."

"Is she legit?"

Jack chuckled as he scribbled something on a piece of paper. "Go see for yourself."

He handed me the note with Portia's address written on it. "No telephone number?"

"Doesn't use one," Jack said. "She doesn't like electronics."

"Old-fashioned huh?"

Jack chuckled again. "You won't need to call her to let her know you're coming. She tends to know when she's getting visitors."

"Bullshit." I laughed, not sure if Jack was joking.

Jack shrugged and leaned back in his comfortable leather chair.

Great. He wasn't kidding.

I got to my feet and stared down at Jack. "Thanks for the help."

"You going after the kids right now?"

I nodded. "I've still got Abby's spell twisting my insides up. I can find them."

Jack sighed. "You remember last night when I told you to lay low?"

"Yep."

"When are you going to start listening to me?"

I pocketed the address and smirked at the nervous bear.

"Probably never."

Jack gave me a big old smile that I didn't see him wear much. It made him look younger.

"Just be careful. I'll look into the Werepanther situation. If he's hunting in the area without seeing me first, well, that's a problem. I'll give you a call if I find anything."

"Thanks, Jack."

I turned and left his office for the second time in two nights. This time I left with an address in my pocket and a spell pulling me towards my next destination. It was more help than I usually had to go on.

All I had to do was find the kids before that Werepanther and whatever else was after them did. That wouldn't be too hard, right? I'd feel it if Lila's tiny little body was ripped apart by a Were, wouldn't I?

I imagined that scenario with my overactive imagination…

It was going to be a long night.

19

That mystical cord pulling me in Lila's direction had me driving north along US-1. I drove for thirty minutes heading towards Lila, wherever she was. I had the windows down and the cool night air swept through the car.

It was a beautiful evening, the kind of nights when most people went out in South Florida. It wasn't humid or muggy, and there was a constant breeze to keep you cool. You could walk around in jeans and a sweater comfortably without having to worry about drowning in your own sweat.

It was the kind of night that made hunting thrilling. Too bad I wasn't doing the kind of hunting I wanted to.

I should've just said, "the hell with it" to everything and went out to feed. I could practically taste all of the beautiful women in clubs and bars ripe and ready for me. I got chills just thinking about it. I'd feed first, guy or girl, whoever was easiest to stick my syringe into and then the real fun could start. With all of the stress I'd been under the last few hours, I could go for a nice redhead or maybe a blond. Maybe even both.

I was remembering the last redhead I'd slept with—I couldn't think of her name—when I felt that otherworldly pull in my stomach started to slack drastically again.

I was getting closer to Lila. I switched lanes to my left and I felt the spell tighten my insides. They weren't west of me. I switched lanes again, getting as close as possible to the right side of the road, and felt the magical cord slack a bit.

They'd kept to the ocean.

I followed my guts and headed to A1A. I kept heading north, closer and closer to my little psychic friend. As I drove, I noticed the scenery start to change. The buildings were getting nicer and bigger. The beach was covered in hotels and condominiums that grew more elegant and expensive with every passing mile. The architecture started to change and the beachfront shopping strips and parks had been replaced with million-dollar homes.

Welcome to Boca Raton.

Tara had dragged those kids farther than I thought. They must've taken a bus to travel so far so fast. It looked like they hadn't quite given up finding their long lost Grandma after all. I gave Tara an A for determination. But where else did she have to go? She had flipped her shit on the Vampire who had tried helping them. It didn't leave many options.

I was impressed that Abby's spell was still working. Don't get me wrong, I never underestimate her, I just wondered how long it would last before it just vanished. Maybe I could go out and party in Miami and just find the kids some other time. I actually considered it until I realized I'd have the spell upsetting my insides all night. That ruined the moment.

The spell was telling me that Lila was close. I parked my car in front of a small coffee house facing the ocean and set out on foot.

I searched for the kids as if I was on the hunt and they were my prey. I always hunted better on foot. I headed in the general direction the spell pulled me in and opened my senses up to scan the area.

I headed towards the beach. I walked along the shore with the ocean waves crashing a few feet away. The streetlamps and lights shining from the hotel windows didn't touch the beach. It was dark, the perfect time to hide if you were looking to hide. A few couples and some loners meandered up and down the beach with only the moon shining off the ocean to light their way.

My night vision is almost perfect. I could walk around my house at night without any lights on and see everything. It's like the world shifts to a darker tone of black and gray; I can see everything and make out every detail.

I could see the whole beach that night as if it were the middle of the day.

Unfortunately, my sight wasn't going to help me find the kids as much as my other senses would. I concentrated and heightened my hearing. I could hear a man and woman along the beach. They were holding each other and talking about how beautiful the moon looked on the ocean. I heard every word they spoke. I heard the sound of their breathing and the sand crunching beneath their feet as they shifted their weight. I heard it as if they were talking directly into my ear. They were dozens of yards away.

I stopped walking and broadened the area I was focusing on. The ocean waves were like thunder. I concentrated to block them out. Footsteps scuffling through the sand, people talking, laughing, coughing. I heard birds in the distance, and cars, and more people just talking, and talking, and talking. It was too much. I couldn't discern out the familiar voices of Ben and Tara. I closed the door on my hearing and the world sounded normal again.

I started walking and breathed in the cool night air.

I caught the stenches of the ocean, sunscreens, deodorants, perfumes, and colognes. I smelled fear like a wet musk seeping out of people's pores. I caught the dry, exciting scent of lust and love. I turned my head and focused on certain scents, detergents, and body odor.

I kept breathing in this world of scents as I strolled up the beach. The spell was telling me I was close. I was. It didn't take long before I caught Tara's familiar scent. It was the smell of her smooth tan skin I recognized. I smelled my own soap and shampoo that she had used when she took a shower back at my house. I was down wind of them.

I took a deep breath and focused entirely on that one scent. When I lock onto a scent, it's as if every other smell becomes less noticeable while the one I'm focused on amplifies. My brain just hones in on what my nose is remembering. I breathed in Tara's scent. It was all I needed to track them.

Abby's spell coincided with my nose and I followed it away from the ocean and further up the beach. The few people on the beach were farther and fewer between as I went. Good. I didn't like witnesses. They tended to be a pain.

I spotted the bright green fence and the construction signs and I knew I was in the right place. There was a three-story building being built on the beach and it stood right in front of me, unfinished and bare.

"Gotcha." It was about time.

I examined the corporation signs, and the construction machines, and equipment lying around. I walked behind a green outhouse casually. I couldn't hear or see anyone nearby on the beach.

Casually I jumped over the eight-foot-tall fence. On the other side, I crouched down in the sand and concentrated. I heard Ben and Tara talking. I could smell all of them and hear the two's voices as they whispered to one another.

I stalked towards the unfinished building. The cement walls were bare with rods sticking out and an unfinished elevator shaft in the center of the first floor. It was going to be some sort of small office building, but the construction company hadn't even gotten electricity running through it yet. Still, on the third floor of the building I saw a flicker of light and heard the whispers of the three strays.

I'd found them. All there was left to do was get my answers and offer the kids my help one last time. That was if I liked the answers I got. If Tara lied to me, I'd find out and then…well, I hoped the kid hadn't lied, for her sake.

I was wondering what the best way to get up there without scaring them all half to death was when I saw Tara. She walked up to the edge of the building, away from the flicker of light. She was looking for something. It only took a second for her to see me.

I didn't know much about Psychics, but I got a strange feeling that Lila had sensed that I was nearby.

Shit.

Tara turned and started to run back to the kids, shouting, "Move!"

I couldn't let that happen though. I wasn't going to let them get away. Tara and the others knew I was a Vampire, but they only saw me during the day. I was weak during the day. I was a little more than human. But it was night and I was going to show them what a Vampire was really capable of.

I rushed towards the building, heading for the parked forklift. I jumped onto the roof of the machine and leapt towards the building. I grabbed hold of the ledge of the third floor. I pulled myself up and ran towards Tara. In the time it took me to get there, she had only run a few feet.

I remembered the times she pointed her gun at me, the way she told me to leave me alone after I risked my life to save her from a Werepanther for God's sake. I let my frustration take control as I ran up from behind and wrapped my arms around her.

I held on tight and I lifted her off her feet as I kept running forward. She was weightless in my arms as I rushed by Ben and Lila; the two kids huddled together in front of a flashlight. They could barely see Tara or me as I ran straight through the other side of the unfinished building and leapt out into the open air.

Tara screamed as we soared through the air.

I cleared the construction site, over the fence, and landed just into the shrubs amidst the native palms. My feet hit the ground hard and sand erupted around me. I let go of Tara and she went flying to the ground, tumbling along the dry shrubs leading to the beach.

I watched her roll for a few feet before she finally stopped. The kid lay there grunting and gasping for air. I could taste her terror and I was glad that she was afraid of me. You should always be afraid of a Vampire, especially at night. It's the best advice I can give.

Tara scrambled to her feet and stumbled into a palm tree. She kept looking around, dazed. She looked at me and then at the building, unsure of what just happened.

I glanced back to see Ben and Lila near the edge of the third floor, watching us from their vantage. I turned back to Tara. She looked like she was going into shock.

"How…"

"I'm a Vampire." I walked towards her. "You forget already?"

For the first time since I met Tara, she finally backed down. She kept her eyes on me, too smart to put me at her back, but she was backing up quick.

"Where's your gun?" I asked.

Tara's eyes flickered past me to the kids. She didn't have the gun on her.

"Oh, that's too bad."

"How did you find us?" Tara's voice was strained. "How?"

I took another step forward and she went further back into the shrubs. Tara moved around one of the palm trees. She was trying to circle around me to get me from between her and the kids. Tara reminded me of an animal, a mother who wouldn't be forced away from her cubs, wouldn't abandon them. If she hadn't pissed me off so much earlier, I might have admired her for it.

"What do you want? I gave you your car back."

"I want answers."

"What did we do? Leave us alone!" Tara screamed it at the top of her lungs and I was on her before she finished her breath.

I cupped one hand over her mouth and pushed her into the trunk of the palm tree. I pinned her there and leaned in close, staring into those petrified eyes.

"Don't," I growled. That was the only warning she'd get.

Tara's eyes were wide, gleaming with tears about to break through the surface and spill down her cheek.

"I want the truth," I whispered.

I didn't have any more time to waste. There was only one way to get the answers I wanted without dealing with the bullshit. I took my free hand and grabbed the side of Tara's face. I felt the blood beneath her cheeks and her trembling lips. I'd be lying if I said it didn't excite me.

I made the connection I made with all of my prey. Only this time, I forced my way into her mind. I dove right in. I wasn't experienced in digging through someone's mind, but I gave it a shot.

Tara's memories crashed into me like a tidal wave.

I was in the kitchen with my father. He was telling me to run. He was telling me that I was in charge. He made me promise to take them to Grams', that she'd keep us safe.

I was so afraid. I couldn't do it. I couldn't do it by myself. He hit me; he slapped me and I hated him for it. I hated that he loved her more than he loved me. That keeping her safe was more important than my life.

"Take them and run," he said.

He handed me the gun he had with him. It was his favorite gun.

"You kill whatever you have to kill to stay alive. You understand?"

I took the gun. It was heavier than ever. He taught me to shoot with it. Taught me to hunt, to fight to protect myself. He said he spent his whole life trying to get me ready to protect my family like he did.

I hated him so much for it. But when I held the gun, I felt powerful. I wasn't afraid.

I packed what I could. I left so much behind. Ben was screaming at dad. Lila was crying. Her words were so loud in my head I couldn't understand her. Dad gave her a shot. He told her to relax. He said they would hear her.

I carried Lila, Ben carried our bags, and we left.

I left my father behind to die.

I got the kids in the back and hadn't started the car yet when they came. I could hear the tires on the gravel driveway.

I watched my father come onto the porch with his shotgun. The men got out and were talking to him. I couldn't hear them in the car. I was too far away.

I watched my father shoot at their cars, those big expensive cars. He called them hunters; killers who were trying to fix what didn't need fixing.

I watched blood spray from dad's stomach. I didn't see their guns. They all just stood there. My father fell to his knees, his head went back, and his neck was slashed open.

Ben cried and screamed. I couldn't stop shaking. I had to start the car. I had to get away. I almost lost control; I slammed on the gas so hard that I fishtailed.

I drove away. My father died in our front yard. I didn't stop driving.

I was sitting in someone's car. A stranger's. He was a big fat man with a red face and a beard that itched when he tried licking my neck. His hands were so rough. They felt like sandpaper on my thigh as he felt me up. His breath smelled like whiskey and his eyes were blue and glazed.

I was in the passenger seat. We were just up the road from the hotel. I told Ben and Lila I'd be right back. I had to just get us a ride.

Dad's gun was in my pack at my feet. It was right there. I was supposed to scare him into giving us his truck. I just didn't know when. I didn't know if I could. I'd never threatened to shoot someone before.

He pushed me back on the seat and my heart was racing. He started to undo my jeans and I smacked him upside the face. He liked it. Oh God, he liked it. He forced me to touch him. I felt him through his jeans. He laughed and licked my neck, telling me he'd pay me anything just for a taste.

What was I doing?

His hand went just inside my jeans. I felt his rough hand on me and I screamed.

I elbowed him in the ear. He cursed and screamed and I tried getting the door open. He grabbed at me, but he couldn't touch me. I snatched my bag up and fell out the door. I landed in the tall grass.

His door opened. He was yelling and coming for me.

I couldn't get the pack open.

I didn't even look up. He was coming. He was almost there.

I reached the gun, raised it, and pulled the trigger.

I looked down at his body. The headlights of the truck were on him. I've never seen so much blood.

I climbed into the truck and went back to the hotel. I took a long shower. I tried not letting Ben and Lila see me cry.

We had to leave. We drove away and left the car behind the next day. We took a train and a bus the rest of the way. I watched the news; I looked at papers along the way. I didn't see anything about my father, about the body, or us, or anything. It was as if it all never happened. As if I was lost in some crazy dream.

I could still feel his itchy beard on my neck.

I'm afraid.

I peeled my hand off Tara and just stared down at her. I couldn't believe what I'd seen.

My other hand was still cupped over her mouth and Tara was gasping for air. Tears streamed down her face and onto my fingers. The look in her eyes was sad enough to make a part of me wish I hadn't found her at all.

I didn't know what to say. There was nothing I could say. I just looked into those eyes and I froze.

The gunshot exploded. Sand erupted up from the ground a few feet away.

I stepped away from Tara and she collapsed at the base of the palm tree. I turned back and saw Ben holding his father's Ruger Speed-Six in his hands.

I didn't do anything at first. I was still reeling from being inside Tara's mind. I felt stunned, sluggish. I snapped out of it though once I remembered that gunfire always drew attention.

"Quit shooting, kid."

Ben fired again and the bullet hit the ground a few yards behind me.

I turned back to Tara, or the crumpled, broken remains of Tara, and said, "Tell him to stop—"

I felt the impact of the bullet go through my throat and come out the other side.

The shot knocked me off balance.

He fucking shot me. I couldn't believe it. The little shit actually shot me.

Tara was on her feet and running back to the construction site. "Run!" she screamed.

I watched Tara run as fast as she could. She couldn't get far.

I chased after Tara and picked her up again, a bit gentler this time. I leapt up over the fence back onto the other side of the site. I used her as a shield, keeping her held against me with one arm wrapped around her front as I walked closer to the building.

I looked up at Ben. He still had that damned gun aimed at me.

My throat was on fire. "Don't do that again."

Tara squirmed and was fighting to break free. She couldn't do it. I could literally crush her body in half with one arm if I wanted. There was no getting out of my grip unless I wanted you to.

I leaned in close to Tara's ear. For a second I couldn't even talk. I managed to get out a rough a growl. "I hate being shot."

I could feel the hole in my throat already closing. The cells were regenerating and the flesh stitched itself back together. In a few seconds, it'd be scabbed over and then healed.

I cleared my throat.

"We need to talk."

Tara kept struggling, a true fighter.

I shook her a little, flexing my arm to put pressure on her. "Listen to me! I just want to talk."

Tara quieted down. She was still trembling and breathing fast. It was a miracle that she even listened to me.

I let her go and she stumbled over her own legs as she tried to get away. Like a big girl, she spun around to face me.

I glanced up at Ben to see that the gun was still right on me.

I heard footsteps and watched as Lila came running down the cement stairs and out of the unfinished building. Lila wrapped her arms around Tara's side and refused to let go.

Both of the girls looked at me in shock. I guessed what they were looking at and put a finger on my throat where the bullet had come out. The skin was smooth and flawless, not even a scab.

"Yeah," I said, breathing in their surprise. "I don't die easy."

Tara and Lila couldn't take their eyes off me.

I looked up and saw that Ben was gone. I heard him running down the stairwell to join the others. The gun was still in his hand. Tara snatched it away from him as soon as he got close enough.

I expected her to aim it at me, but she didn't. She just kept it loosely in her hand by her side. I think Tara was finally learning. The tears on her cheeks sparkled in the moonlight. In some twisted way she looked beautiful.

"What do you want from us?"

20

What did I want from them? That was the million-dollar question.

I stood there and a thousand things came to mind, but I couldn't say any of them. I'm not usually big on authority. I've seen firsthand what a man with power can be like if he lets it corrupt him. But that night, I had to do things diplomatically. I let Jack run things, but sometimes I had to stop being the reluctant leader and get down to business.

It was time to flex my authoritative muscles.

"This part of South Florida is my territory. I'm in charge of it. You three came down here with a Werepanther and God knows what else chasing after you. Now I don't have a problem with you three looking for your grandmother, but the people after you...them I have a problem with."

"You think we asked for this?" Tara spat at me.

"What you asked for doesn't matter. I don't care what happened or why. All I know is that you've endangered the life I set up here. I risked everything to stop that Werepanther on the beach. Do you know what would've happened if he'd decided to stick around?"

All of their young, naïve eyes stared back at me.

"It would've killed me and then done whatever it wanted to with you three." I started to laugh because I still couldn't believe that I could've died protecting three ungrateful strays.

"I risked my life for you and you just ran from me."

Tara wouldn't look me in the eyes.

"I'm the only person you've got right now. That's just a fact." I looked at Lila and I didn't see a strong Psychic; I saw a scared little girl being hunted by monsters.

"You said you could trust me. *I* didn't, *you* did," I said to Lila.

I looked deep into those green eyes. "Well *I'm* saying it now. You can trust me."

"Why?" Tara asked. "Lila heard your Witch friend say we were going to get you killed. That you should just ditch us."

"Abby's practical. So am I. That doesn't mean she's right."

It didn't necessarily make her wrong either.

"We don't want anyone else dying because of us." Ben finally decided to speak.

I looked at the boy and then to Tara. She seemed to share her younger brother's opinion.

"Listen, you have my word that I'll keep you safe as long as you stay in my territory." As soon as I said the words, I realized I meant it.

I'd never taken anyone under my protection before. It was within my rights as Territory Master to have claim over certain individuals. It meant that anything or anyone who harmed those kids was going to have to deal with me. That meant in so many words, they'd have to die.

I believe you. The words rolled through my head softly.

I nodded at Lila.

"So what do we do?" Ben asked.

Tara looked down at him, surprised. "Ben!"

"What?" Ben waved a hand at me. "He's a Vampire, Tara. Let him be in charge."

Tara looked down at Lila and the little girl nodded in agreement.

"You trust me?" I asked Tara.

Tara wouldn't say.

"She trusts you," Ben answered for her.

"I need to hear it from her." I did. I had to make sure she wasn't going to try and ditch me the first chance she got again.

Tara tucked her gun in the back of her jeans. "What do we do now?"

Good girl. It was finally time to let old Kristopher take the reins. God help everyone.

"You're going to do what I tell you. That means don't shoot me, or steal my car, or run away from me, or do anything else that's stupid." I let out a deep breath and tried coming up with the next step. I was just glad to see that the kids were finally going to listen to me.

"I'm sorry I shot you," Ben said under his breath.

I waved it off. "Don't worry about it, kid. All my friends shoot me at least once."

Ben smiled at that and I think that was the first time I'd seen him do it. I liked seeing those kids smile. What the hell was happening to me?

Sirens started wailing in the distance. Shit.

I focused on the sound and tried judging how far away they were. Turned out not too far. If we hurried, we could still get away without being noticed before more men with guns showed up.

I turned back to the kids. "We need to get out of here."

"What? What is it?" I could hear Tara's heartbeat flaring.

I stared at Ben. "*Somebody* fired a gun on a public beach. Someone who heard the shots must've called the police." I listened to the sirens wailing. Closer and closer they came. I focused and couldn't hear anyone nearby on the beach. Good. Most people tend to run away from gunshots.

"Come on. I drove." I turned to walk away and realized no one was moving.

I couldn't believe it. "What now?"

Tara shook her head and swallowed whatever emotions drifted just beneath the surface of her mind. She grabbed Lila's hand.

"Nothing. Let's go."

"Wait!" Ben shouted. He turned and started running back inside the unfinished building, up the stairs and out of sight.

"What the hell's he doing?" I asked.

"Ben!" Tara called after him.

I could hear the sirens getting louder and louder. "Come on. We have to go."

I started thinking about what I would do if the police showed up and saw us all. Would I have to kill the cops? I didn't want to. But I wouldn't let them see me and I couldn't let them arrest the kids. Oh, to slaughter or not to slaughter? That is the question.

Ben came running back down the stairs with his backpack on his back and the other two in his arms.

"You've got to be kidding me," Tara hissed.

I didn't say a word. If the cops searched the place and found the bags, they would've had evidence. Ben earned some points for being thorough.

Tara tossed her pack over her shoulder while Ben helped Lila into hers.

"We good?" I asked.

Lila nodded happily.

"Alright. Move."

Together we all turned and hurried across the construction site. Tara dashed forward and started scaling the green fence. Once she was holding onto the top, she turned back and held her hand out for the kids.

"Come on," she said.

I rolled my eyes. We didn't have time for that. I lifted Ben and Lila around the waist and held them with one arm each. The second I touched Lila I felt something inside me shatter.

I had forgotten all about Abby's spell. I held onto Lila and I could feel the cord binding us break. It was a relief I hadn't been expecting.

"What are you doing?" Ben asked in my ear, wondering why I'd picked them up and just stood there.

I played it off. No need to tell them that I'd been magically stalking Lila.

"Hold on." I moved and leapt over the fence and Tara. I landed on the other side and set the kids down on their own feet. Ben and Lila were nothing but laughs and odd sounds of excitement. It was fuel for my ego. I usually wasn't appreciated for what I could do.

I crossed my arms and watched Tara climb over the fence and drop down on the other side. She walked up to us, glaring at me.

I smirked at her. "What?"

She walked by me and we all hurried down the beach. The kids broke out into a sprint.

"Slow down," I whisper-shouted at them.

They slowed and the four of us power walked down the beach.

"Be casual," I told them. "Don't draw attention."

"Where did you park?" Tara asked. She was scanning the beach looking around for anyone who might see us.

"Not far."

"Is Kyle at the car?"

"Nope."

"Where is he?"

"On a date," I said.

"Lucky." I caught the sad bitterness in her voice.

We were getting pretty far from the construction site and there still wasn't anyone on the beach that I could see. The police sirens were coming closer, but all they had to go on was the fact that gunshots were heard in the vicinity. I liked our odds of getting away unnoticed.

We slipped off the beach and started walking up along A1A at a regular pace.

Once we reached my car, I drove out of there as fast as possible. The kids must've really started trusting me because Tara actually sat up front. I got off A1A and headed west a little to get away from the beach and the boys in blue.

"Where are we going?" Ben asked from the seat right behind mine. "Back to your house?"

"Nope."

The truth was if they had worse things than a Werepanther after them, then there was no way in hell we were going back to my house. I couldn't risk being followed and someone finding out where I lived during the day. Living forever was high on my list of things to do. Dying would kind of ruin that.

"Where then?" Tara asked.

I drove over the bridge and crossed the Intracoastal, leaving the beach behind.

"I may have a lead on your grandmother."

I looked in the rearview and could tell from the reaction on both Lila and Ben's faces that I'd done good.

"Wait, what do you mean?" Tara sat up in her seat.

"You said you were looking for her. That your dad said she'd be able help you. I thought at first that meant she was a Witch, but she may be a Psychic like Lila."

"But I don't know if Gram's a Psychic," Tara said.

"It doesn't matter. She might not be. There's only one Psychic around here with enough power to be helpful. I got her address from a friend. If we get there and she's your grandma, great, if she's not, we'll think of something else."

"Do you know her name?" Ben asked.

"Portia."

I looked in the rear view and saw Ben and Lila's faces sober up. Tara sat back in her seat and started to stare out the window.

"What?" I asked. "That's not her name?"

She shook her head. "Grams' name is Ruth."

Grandma Ruth…how quaint.

"That doesn't mean anything." I tried being optimistic, apparently a new hobby. "She might be going by a different name. It'd explain why you couldn't find her in the phone book."

Tara didn't even respond.

I thought kids were supposed to be peppy and always looking for the good in things. Maybe normal kids were.

"Well, we're still going to see this Portia lady."

"Can we eat first?" Ben leaned forward and gripped the back of my seat.

"Ben," Tara barked at him.

"What?" he whined. "I'm starving."

I looked over at Tara, wondering if they'd eaten anything since the morning.

The bags under her eyes made her look older. She looked back at me as if she didn't care what I thought. "We've kind of been running for our lives."

I sighed. "Alright, we'll stop somewhere and grab a bite."

Lila started to giggle in the back. I glanced back at her. "What?"

Tara actually smiled; she looked prettier because of it.

"She thinks it's funny that you said, 'grab a bite'."

"Oh," I said dryly. "Because I'm a Vampire…"

Tara shrugged. "Yeah."

"Hilarious."

Lila buried her face in the sleeve of her jacket, trying to snuff her laughter.

"Just so you know, I don't really bite people."

"Why?" Ben asked.

"Too messy."

Tara laughed like I was joking.

I glanced at her.

"Oh, come on." She didn't believe me. "How do you get blood then?"

"Usually with a syringe. I'll use a knife just for a little taste. It's neater and then no one's walking around with bite marks." I said it very matter-of-factly. Lila stopped laughing abruptly.

Tara's smile faded and she looked disgusted. "You're serious?"

"What?"

She made a face as if she'd tasted something rotten. "That's messed up."

I glanced at the rearview. Both Lila and Ben were sitting very still and looking at me as if I'd sprouted a second head.

"Don't judge me."

21

The address that Jack gave me was in West Boca Raton, farther inland than I usually went. I plugged it into my GPS and kept driving west until I reached State Road 7. From there, I headed north.

State Road 7 turns into 441 the further north you drive. It's a busy road and you can find just about every kind of business imaginable on it. There are hotels, auto shops, adult stores, but most importantly, places to eat. I told the kids to pick whatever they wanted that was on the way.

"There's a McDonald's!" Ben shouted from the back seat.

No. I don't like McDonald's. Lila's voice played through all of our heads louder than necessary. I realized that the more excited or stressed Lila was, the less gentle her voice was in my mind. Great.

"There's a Wendy's," Tara suggested.

Ben grunted. "Gross."

Yeah gross.

"Is that a Subway?" Tara asked.

I saw the yellow sign in the plaza. "Yep."

"Come on. Can't we get McDonald's?"

NO! The voice sliced through my head and I flinched, jerking the wheel on accident. The car swerved and people laid on their horns. I almost hit the car next to me before I got back in my lane.

"Alright!" I shouted.

I cut across two lanes of traffic and pulled into a shopping center. I drove towards the small Checkers in the corner of the plaza.

I parked in the lot and turned around in my seat to look at the two kids. "You're getting Checkers. Good?"

Ben started to reply.

"Good!" I shouted first and then got out of the car. I couldn't take any more bickering.

Tara and the others got out and walked around to me. They seemed a little nervous, standing there looking at me like lost puppies.

"What?" I asked.

Tara seemed embarrassed. "We don't have any money."

I looked at Ben and Lila. I remembered the first time I saw them at the hotel and how they got people to give them money.

"What about your little scheme from the hotel?"

Lila looked up at Ben who shrugged. "I threw everything at the manager."

"You never did that anywhere else?"

"Yes." Tara shrugged. "But it was for bus tickets. We're broke."

Of course they were. "Whose idea was it to exploit Lila's abilities like that?"

Ben held up a hand, a little too pleased with himself. "Mine."

"I'm impressed."

He smiled at that and Tara swatted him on the shoulder.

I grabbed my wallet out of my jeans and held up forty dollars. "Go nuts."

"For real?" Tara asked as she took my money.

"For real."

The three kids headed up to the line. I walked over to the outside pavilions they had for people to eat at. I grabbed an empty table. I sat there watching them wait in line and place their orders at the small booth.

I hadn't had a cigarette since I was human. I swapped nicotine for blood. But I could've used a smoke right then. I thought I was done looking after kids after my sister. The fact that I was playing Mr. Nanny was starting to work my nerves. I didn't feel comfortable being anyone's protector and that's what I was essentially doing for Tara, Lila, and Ben. I was keeping them safe from anything that might try to hurt them, at least for that night.

I watched Tara pay for *their* meal with *my* money.

I couldn't look after them forever. I wouldn't. I was really counting on this Portia lady to be their grandmother or someone who could help me. I promised the kids I'd keep them safe; that didn't mean I'd be bringing them back to my house and raising them if we couldn't find them a good home. They would seriously cramp my style.

I was imagining what the house would be like with those three living with Kyle and I when I got this strange feeling in the pit of my stomach. I skimmed the parking lot casually. I don't know why, but I had a funny feeling that someone was watching me.

I sat on the bench with my back to the table. I crossed my legs comfortably and tried to relax. I was usually the one watching people, hunting them, and waiting to lure them in. I didn't like the idea of someone hunting me.

The parking lot was pretty busy. It was only a few minutes before nine so people were still out and about. There was a Target that took up the majority of the plaza and then a few jewelry stores and a couple of small shops. There were a dozen cars other than mine around the Checkers. Most of the cars were empty. Three weren't.

One car was a few spots left of mine and filled with teenagers hanging out and eating their fast food. The other car was an elderly couple and they were getting ready to leave. The third car was farthest away. Its tinted windows were too dark for me to see anyone in the car other than the driver and passenger. I didn't like the vibe I was getting from that car.

It was a dark blue Ford Taurus. It was at least five years old and in need of a paint job. There were two people sitting in the driver and passenger seat. The lights of the lamp poles in the parking lot reflected off the windshield so I couldn't make out what exactly the two men looked like or what they were doing. As for everyone in the back seat, who knew?

Were they parked there already? I couldn't remember. I'm usually paranoid. Paranoia's done a good job of keeping me alive. I'm reckless too sometimes, but hey, I like to improvise. Right then though, waiting for the kids, I sat on that bench wondering if I was just being paranoid or if maybe I was right and the people in that Taurus were watching us.

Tara and the kids came back holding trays of food that smelled like grease drenched in more grease.

Tara sat across from me with Ben by her side. Lila plopped down next to me. She carefully laid her tray on the table as if she didn't trust herself not to spill it. She saw that I was watching her and smiled up at me.

I nodded back at her and then looked over all of the food they bought. I saw burgers wrapped in aluminum, a few boxes of chicken tenders, something that looked like fries covered in what people passed off as cheese and bacon, and some chicken wings. Each of them had a large cup of coke. If the people after the kids didn't kill them, the cholesterol from that dinner would.

And people think drinking blood is disgusting? At least it's organic.

I checked to see if that blue Taurus was still there in my peripherals. It was.

"So…do you eat food, Kris?" Ben asked as he chewed on his burger.

I tried keeping the car in my sight. "Sure."

"You want something?"

I looked over the so-called "food" on the table.

"This doesn't qualify as food. Thanks though."

"Do you need blood?" Tara asked.

God, I really could've gone for a nice pint.

"I'm fine," I lied.

"You sure?" Tara plucked a fry from the pile on her tray.

I looked back at her, smirking. "You offering?"

The look on her face made me laugh and Lila started laughing with me.

"Kris?" Ben swallowed the food in his mouth and sipped at his coke. "Can I ask you a question?"

"Why not."

"How come you didn't bleed when I shot you?"

I love it when people meet a Vampire for the first time. So many questions, so little time…for them at least.

"You didn't know Vampires don't bleed?"

Ben shook his head.

"Why would we know that? We've never met a Vampire before." Tara seemed defensive again.

"I don't know how to explain it. My body is different than yours." I moved on the bench so I could look at all three of them.

I loved playing teacher. "Vampires' bodies need blood to survive. It's like our fuel, our energy source."

Ben thought about it between bites of his burger. "But why didn't you bleed?"

"Because my body absorbs blood, all of it. It doesn't keep any inside me lying around." I grabbed a fry off Lila's tray. "You eat this and your body breaks it down and absorbs it for energy. My body does the same with blood. I cut you and you don't bleed curly fries do you?"

Lila laughed at that.

"That's a really bad example." Tara was grinning.

"Well, alright, humans need water, your bodies absorb it and it keeps you alive. Blood does the same thing for Vamps."

Tara frowned. "So you don't cry blood do you?"

I shook my head. "That's retarded."

"Do you bleed during the day?"

That wasn't a retarded question. "Yes. During the day we're practically human. Our bodies digest food. We have blood circulation and all that good stuff. We're mortal. Just as easy to kill as the next guy."

"My dad said that Vampires were hard to hunt because finding them during the day was tricky. That Vampires can pass for human during the day."

It was true. It also sucked. I hated being so weak and frail during the day. I hated when I was mortal.

"You look different," Tara pointed out. "Why?"

"At night Vampires become immortal. We change and become stronger, faster...better."

Tara was staring at my face, looking for any imperfection she might have seen in the daytime.

Do you have fangs?

I looked at Lila and she was looking at me as if any second I'd perform some magical feat.

"Do I have fangs?" I felt offended. "What kind of Vampire doesn't have fangs?"

"Can we see?" Ben was getting too excited.

Tara nudged him in the arm. "Quit it."

I glanced around the parking lot to make sure no one was looking in our direction.

I leaned across the table so that the kids could see and I opened my mouth. My fangs slid further out of my gums and I felt their pointed tips with my tongue. Tara didn't seem amused and Ben looked thrilled. Lila gasped and dropped her burger on her tray.

"Cool," Ben whispered.

I retracted my fangs. Ben and Lila looked at one another as if they had just witnessed the coolest thing in the world. Maybe they had. Who was I to dissuade them?

"Eat your food," I said as I turned back around.

I crossed my arms and sat there with my head down pretending to be patiently waiting for the kids to eat. My real focus was on that blue Taurus. It hadn't moved an inch. I listened to Tara and the kids eat, and talk, and laugh a little. I don't know why, but it seemed like it had been a long time since they laughed or felt safe enough to laugh. I liked hearing them laugh.

I watched Lila's face light up as Tara reached across the table and wiped the ketchup off her little sister's nose with a napkin. Something so small, so silly, seemed so funny to her. I forgot what it was like to be around children, to hear that pure laugh that everyone loses eventually.

Once the kids finished eating they threw all of their trays and garbage away and we all headed back to the car. I stayed in front of them, taking my time so that I was the last one to crawl into the SUV. I turned the headlights on and we all buckled up.

The blue Taurus still hadn't moved.

I pulled out of the parking lot and turned onto 441. My eyes were glued to the rearview. I was barely looking at the road. I waited for that blue Taurus to pull out of the parking lot and follow us. I waited and waited until I lost sight of the plaza through traffic.

"Kris!" Tara shouted.

I slammed on the breaks and stopped just short of the car in front of me. The traffic light was red and I hadn't been paying attention.

"You alright?" Tara asked.

"I'm fine."

"Not you." She turned around in her seat. "Guys?"

Oh.

"Yeah," Ben mumbled.

Lila nodded to her older sister.

While we were stopped at the light, I kept looking at the rearview. There was still no sign of the car. Good.

The light turned green and I went north with traffic. I kept glancing back and couldn't see any Taurus. Whatever those creeps were doing in that car was none of my business; all I knew is that they weren't following me. Take that, paranoia.

We kept driving for about ten minutes until I saw the street I had to get off on and turned left. The flashy, busy state road disappeared in the rear view mirror as we headed west. The streetlights were few and far between as we passed by offices and plazas and through residential areas. Perfectly trimmed hedges and tall trees covered the cement walls surrounding expensive housing communities and apartment complexes.

It was a two-lane road and I was the only car on it. At least I was for about ten seconds before a pair of headlights flashed in my rear view mirror.

Relax. I forced myself to just stay cool. No reason to jump to conclusions.

I focused on just driving the car. Anyone could have turned onto the same road from State Road 7. It was pointless to start worrying over nothing.

"I hope this lady's Gram," Ben said from the back seat.

"Don't get your hopes up," Tara told him.

I tried to stop looking in the mirror to see the headlights coming closer behind me. I was going the speed limit, they weren't going much faster, probably wouldn't even catch up to me.

The road started to bend and the streetlights vanished. There were a few housing developments on my right and a ditch with a wall on my left. Beyond the wall was a dark forested area.

Damn. I would've preferred a more populated route.

"You think she's our Gram, Kris?" Ben's voice startled me.

I nodded, watching the headlights come around the same curve in the road. "I hope so."

"Kris? You okay?" Tara asked.

I stopped staring in the mirrors and kept my eyes on the road. "Yeah."

I don't think she believed me.

Why are you scared? Lila whispered in my mind.

I gripped the wheel tighter, trying not to think about anything. "We're almost there."

"Are Psychics dangerous?" Tara asked. "In case this isn't our Gram..."

Good question.

I was contemplating an answer when the car behind me suddenly turned its high beams on. The car lurched forward and even with the windows up I could hear the engine roar.

Shit. I hated when I was right.

I sped up on the empty road and my own engine roared louder than the car chasing us.

"What are you doing?" Tara shouted.

I watched the car behind me catching up, switching lanes to come up alongside us.

"Kris!" Tara screamed in my ear.

The car was just coming alongside me on my left.

"Everyone hold on!"

I slammed on the brakes.

The kids all started screaming for their lives. I barely heard them over the screeching of my tires.

I caught a glimpse of the car as it went speeding by. It was a dark blue Taurus, *the* dark blue Taurus. As it rushed past I sensed the excitement from a Were inside the car. It couldn't have been in the car back at the Checkers. I should've sensed it. If it was the same Werepanther from earlier, he must've been keeping his distance.

My SUV stopped abruptly enough to send us all lurching forward and then slamming back into our seats. I had to move. Fast.

I undid my seatbelt and grabbed hold of Tara by the arm. She looked terrified. "Get behind the wheel."

"What?"

"If I tell you to drive, head back the way we came and don't stop." I glanced back at the kids to make sure they were still alive. They were still breathing and not bleeding. That was good enough for me.

I turned back to Tara and I saw her staring at my fangs. I had them out, ready to go.

"Don't get out of the car and don't let those two see what I'm going to do."

"What are you going to do?"

I was going to do what I did best.

I got out of the car and slammed the door shut.

The Taurus' tires screeched as it slammed on its brakes. I watched it swerve into the middle of the road and stop horizontally in both lanes, blocking that route.

I walked right towards them. I let all my frustration about being helpless during the day rise to the surface. It was time to cut loose.

The passenger door behind the driver's seat opened and a man hurried out. He started running at me. He was almost as fast as I was as he sprinted towards me.

I only saw him for a moment before he violently changed.

I watched the man become the beast. I've seen Weres shift before, but I'd never seen one so violent and fast. The man's clothes disintegrated to ash as the flesh beneath them exploded in a cloud of particles. A large familiar panther was running on all fours at me. He let out that vicious roar that only the big cats could do.

I almost got chills.

I charged the beast to meet him head-on.

He was an unstoppable force, sheer strength and speed surging at me. At the last possible second he pounced, his claws ready to tear into me, massive fangs ready to crunch down on my throat.

I stopped dead in my tracks and backhanded the Werepanther as hard as I could.

The force of the blow sounded like thunder in my ears. I only caught a glimpse of the panther flying through the darkness. I heard him hit the cement wall on the other side of the ditch.

I turned my attention to the blue Taurus and rushed it.

The driver was trying to speed away as I rammed my shoulder into the side of the car.

I felt the metal cave in around me like a wave in the ocean. I stayed there and watched the car skid sideways along the street. I went at it again and put one hand under the side of the car. I lifted up and flipped the entire car into the air. I stood there watching gravity work its magic. The dark blue Taurus landed upside down in front of me. Every window exploded outward in a spray of glass.

That took care of them trying to drive away.

I heard the men moving amidst the shattered glass, coughing and shouting at one another. I was about to head to the car when I heard screaming.

I spun around and saw the Werepanther on the roof of my car. The panther's bulky muscular body pressed down on the roof, cracking my windshield and the windows with every move it made. It was slashing through the roof of my SUV as if it were made of butter instead of metal.

Shit.

I sprinted back down the street to the kids and leapt towards the damned Were to tackle it off my car.

The Werepanther saw me coming and the bastard shifted again while I was in mid-air. The particles of his panther form exploded behind him as the naked man reached out for me.

He grabbed hold of my arms and actually used my own momentum to swing and throw me right over the car. The world spun for a moment and then my back hit the street hard enough to dent it. I had tumbled once before the panther was on me.

All I heard was that spine-tingling hiss. All I could see was the pair of massive fangs coming for my face. All I could think was that this asshole had ruined two cars in one day.

I felt the claws slash across my stomach and shoulder as he landed on me. I instinctively reached out with my left hand and grabbed hold of the panther's throat as he came down. My strength alone was enough to keep those fangs from coming down and crushing my skull.

The panther was on his hind legs, choking as I squeezed his throat. One large paw dug its claws into my forearm while the other dug into my chest. I used my free arm to hit the beast in the chest with a punch that would've killed a human.

The Were yelped and hissed, whiskers flaring and spit spewing. I punched him again and again in the chest. I squeezed his throat and threw the panther off me before he could tear me up any more.

I got to my feet as fast as I could and got tackled by the naked man. He had his arms around me and sent us both slamming into the back of my SUV. The whole car nearly toppled over and I heard the kids screaming inside.

I couldn't let the Were get to them.

I kneed the Were in the face hard enough to get his hold off me. He was too slow and I grabbed him by the skinny throat and lifted him up off his feet before moving forward and slamming him down onto the road. The cement gave way under him.

I was snarling at him, wondering if I should rip his throat out, when I heard a growl rise up out of his throat. I knew what was coming next. I let go of his throat and watched the particles of his humanity erupt around him. He'd try to use those claws to eviscerate me.

Screw that.

I looked into those golden cat eyes for a moment before I brought my fist down onto its face.

I felt the cat's skull shatter and go from something solid to mush before my fist hit the solid road. The panther's thrashing body went limp.

I got to my feet and stood over the big cat as its body burst into a cloud of particles. A man was lying at my feet, a pool of blood expanding beneath him. I couldn't even tell you what he looked like. His skull was nothing but blood, bone, brain, and hair all smashed together. That was what happened when I didn't pull my punches. Too bad nobody told him that.

The sound of someone scrambling through glass brought me back.

I looked past my ruined car and saw the driver trying to crawl out of the flipped Taurus.

I dashed away from the Were and over to the survivors.

I grabbed hold of the door, ripped it off its hinges, and tossed it aside. I bent down and watched the man trying to crawl to safety amidst the shards of glass lining the roof of the car. He was middle-aged, bright blond and balding. He was wearing bloodstained black jeans and a shirt. Unlike the Were, this one was all human. I could smell it in his blood.

Blood. There was so much of it. I could almost taste it. The man's blood pouring from his wounds, the Were's blood soaking my hand, and the blood of whoever was in the back of the car. There was so much of it. I wanted to taste some of that blood. I wanted to feed.

But I wanted to quench my anger more. The feeding would have to wait.

I grabbed hold of the man's left arm and started to drag him out, but he wouldn't budge. He screamed in agony so suddenly it caught me by surprise. I gently tugged again and he screamed louder.

"Stop!" He whimpered, "God, my leg. My leg!"

I assumed his leg was pinned under something. Too bad…

I used that supernatural strength of mine to effortlessly yank the man out from under the car. I heard a few bones in his leg snap and the scream from his throat was unpleasant. I hated when people screamed like that when I hadn't even begun to *really* hurt them yet.

He was covered in sweat and blood. Shards of glass stuck out of his forehead and a gash somewhere on his skull brought fresh blood pouring down the side of his face. Fear was the cologne he wore and there was so much of it on him it was suffocating me.

I looked down at his left leg. Blood was spraying from it with every rapid beat of his heart. It was barely attached to the rest of him. Only flesh and threads of tissue kept the leg connected at just above the knee. It was interesting to see what I'd done. I thought I had just broken it, but it turned out I nearly severed it. I wonder what it had been pinned under.

I couldn't ignore his pulse in my ears. I could hear it like a snare drum playing in my head. I breathed in the man's fear, his terror. For a second, I actually forgot about interrogating him. I just wanted to sink my fangs into that soft, tender throat. Forget about syringes, forget about knives and playing it safe. I wanted blood. His blood.

The gunshot rang in my ears and there was a sudden sharp burning sensation in my right shoulder.

I dropped the human and stumbled backwards from the force of the shot. The pain shooting up my arm started to burn. That wasn't good. I could hear the flesh in my shoulder sizzling and crackling.

Shit. Silver. I was hit with a silver bullet.

My legs gave out. I was on my side cradling my injured shoulder when the other human came around the car. He was limping badly and his left arm was hanging at his side.

This human was younger than the other, maybe in his mid-twenties. He was pale and thin, hidden in black jeans and a large black jacket. He had a revolver in his good hand, but he was trembling.

Damn it. I didn't even hear him over the other man's pulse. I deserved to lose. That didn't mean I wanted to.

"Shoot it!" the man I'd crippled screamed from a few feet away.

The younger guy looked confused.

"Do it!"

I watched the human take aim and steady his hand.

I stared into the human's eyes, into the soul of the man who was going to kill me. Silver, unfortunately, is a sure way of making sure most of us monsters stay down. I could heal from most wounds, but silver took time and blood. I didn't seem to have much of either right then.

Stab a Vamp in the throat with a knife and he'll heal. But shoot him with a silver bullet in the chest and he may die just like a human would. Isn't life a bitch?

I heard the gunshot and my eyes instinctively shut.

I waited for the pain. I waited for the bullet that was going to end the game.

I waited...

A body hit the ground and I heard the gun skid along the street.

I opened my eyes and saw the man who would be my death lying in a growing pool of his own blood.

I heard footsteps behind me and then two more gunshots. I put my good arm up to cover my head, but the bullets weren't for me. They flew straight into the blond man I'd dragged from the car. He was screaming and shouting before the bullets hit him in the chest and temple, and then he shut up for good.

I looked over my shoulder and there she was.

Tara was just a few feet away. She had both hands clamped around her dad's revolver. Her slender arms started trembling and shaking. I watched her fall to her knees, her eyes on the two men she'd killed. I knew the look in her eyes. I didn't want her to have that look.

I fought the pain in my shoulder. I dragged my ass over to that kid who saved my life. It hurt like hell, but I did it.

"Tara…"

Her eyes were shimmering with tears. They never broke the surface. She looked furious, as if she wanted to cry, but she just couldn't shed the tears. Her hand was shaking so bad that the barrel of the gun scraped along the street.

I put my hand on hers to keep it steady. She didn't fight me.

Tara just looked up at me and there was so much anger in those eyes. But there was pain, and sorrow, and hatred in there with it. She was turning red as she started to sob, gasping for breath as if she was hyperventilating.

I didn't know what to do for her. I wanted to do something. I really did. But what could I do?

Tara was the one who reached out for me. She fell forward into my chest and wrapped her arms around me. The gun fell to the floor and she held me close, burying her face in my neck. I felt her tears slide down her cheek. They were so warm on my cold skin. I wrapped my left arm around her and we stayed there, the two of us on our knees in the middle of the road. I breathed in her warmth and couldn't remember the last time I'd held someone in my arms for anything other than sex.

I held Tara and let her cry and cry some more.

I wasn't good at stuff like that. Give me something to kill and it'll wind up dead. Give me a traumatized person to comfort and I'm useless.

I stayed there though, the silver bullet in my body burning like a hot poker. I fought the pain to give the kid time to deal with what she had to deal with. She'd killed so that I wasn't. I owed her for that.

I stayed right where I was because it's what *she* needed. Hell, maybe I needed it too.

I looked at Lila and Ben. They were watching us from the SUV. I watched the dark empty road and wondered when the next car would come. I did a lot of things and thought a lot of stuff, but I didn't move just for Tara.

22

The sirens sounded far away. I was getting tired of hearing sirens.

Tara was still in my arms. The sobbing had subsided, but she wouldn't let go of me. We had to get out of there.

"Tara." I wasn't sure if she could even hear me. I tried moving her, but a sharp pain jolted through my shoulder. The silver bullet was lodged in deep. I could still hear it sizzling in my ear.

"Tara. Hey. We gotta go."

I didn't get an answer. Great. I didn't have time for Tara to go comatose on me. I tried moving again and the pain in my shoulder flared up.

"Shit." I really, *really* had to get that bullet out.

Tara released me and noticed my arm. Her eyes were bloodshot and swollen. She looked thinner, more fragile.

"Your shoulder..." Tara's voice was hoarse. "It's not healing."

"Oh, look at that." The joking didn't help the pain. Funny isn't it?

The kid tried to touch the wound, but I stopped her with my free hand. "No."

"Why aren't you healing?"

I hesitated for a second. I had a thing about telling people how to kill me and mine. But Tara had killed for me. That made her okay in my book.

"They shot me with a silver bullet."

"Are you going to die?" The panic was returning to her voice.

"I'll be fine." Hopefully. I had to get the bullet out and then try to heal. If I didn't, then Tara and the kids would be burying their first Vampire tonight.

"We need to get out here before anyone sees us." I winced and forced my legs to get me up off the street. It was just one bullet; it'd take more than that to keep this Vampire down. Tara got up as well, but stayed close to catch me in case I lost my balance. I appreciated the gesture.

"You're driving," I told her, fighting the pain in my arm.

"Okay…"

"You good to drive?" I was worried considering that she had just killed two men. See, who says I don't care about anyone but myself?

Tara nodded at me and hurried to the SUV.

I turned. There were the two fresh corpses. I walked over to them instead of following Tara. I knelt down by the younger body, trying hard not to move my arm. It didn't work out too well. The pain shot through my shoulder, up into my neck and down to my fingers. Biting back the pain, I reached out with my good hand and snatched the handgun loaded with silver ammunition.

I recognized the gun. A Colt Defender with a stainless steel finish that shined in the moonlight. The rubber grip was still warm in my hand as I looked down the three inch-long barrel of the pistol. It was a good gun, reliable and sturdy. I walked over to the corpse and tucked the gun into the belt of my jeans. I crouched down and started checking the body for ammo. I don't have a problem with corpses, considering how many I've made in my life. I also don't have a problem "collecting" things from any asshole that tried to kill me. It wasn't stealing or looting; it was me taking what I'd earned. They tried taking my life and failed. That made me the winner and the spoils were all mine. It's only fair.

"Kris!" Tara called from the SUV.

I waved her over to me. "Bring the car here."

Tara cursed under her breath and got into the car.

I found the man's shoulder holster under his jacket. He had an extra magazine in a clip on his belt. I ran my hand over his legs, down to his ankle and felt something. I rolled up the pant leg and saw another smaller holster with a second clip of ammunition. The kid had been prepared at least.

I took the clip and was about to get up when something caught my attention. There was something black on the back of the body's left wrist. I flipped his palm up so I could get a good look. A black tattoo of a crucifix looked up at me.

"Kris!" Tara shouted again.

I glanced back and saw my SUV idling behind me. Tara had her window down and she looked worried.

I glanced back down at that crucifix on the man's wrist. For some reason I was drawn to that tattoo. I felt like I'd seen it before. But that was stupid. People had tattoos of crosses all the time. It was kind of a popular symbol, the whole crucifix thing.

"What are you doing? Come on," Tara urged.

I didn't have time to think. We had to get out of there before the police came. I got to my feet and walked away from the murder scene with a new Colt Defender and three clips of ammo. Not a bad haul.

I climbed into the passenger seat. It was hard to ignore the damage done to my poor Sandy.

My door creaked as I slammed it shut and the windshield had cracks like miniature fissures running down it from the roof. I looked up and saw large tears in the ceiling from where the panther had clawed through my roof.

If they weren't already dead, I would've killed the Were and the two humans again.

I checked the bullets in the Defender. It had five bullets plus one left in the chamber. The clips had seven bullets a piece in them. I popped out one from a clip and examined the bullet in the dim lighting of the car. I twirled it around in my fingers, watching the silver shimmer off the casing.

Another flare of fire started to burn within my shoulder. "Son of a bitch."

Lila gasped.

I looked back at the little girl. Oh great, I ruined her virgin ears.

"Drive," I growled at Tara.

Tara did as I said and steered the SUV around the wrecked blue Taurus in the middle of the road. We drove off along the dark road leaving behind two dead humans and a Werepanther. I didn't see anyone on the street staring at us. There were no streetlights or cameras. Hopefully there was no evidence that could be traced back to me.

"Where am I driving?"

"Just follow the GPS."

"We're still going to this Portia lady?"

"Why wouldn't we?" I asked. "You got somewhere else to go?"

Tara kept driving, peering through the cracks in the windshield. I was pissed. I didn't want to know how much it was going to cost to get Sandy fixed.

I pulled the Colt out of my jeans and stashed it and the extra rounds in the glove compartment.

"Why did you take the gun?" Ben asked from the back seat.

"It's a thing I do."

"What?"

Twenty questions was my least favorite game and I seemed to be playing it a lot lately.

"I collect the shi…stuff that nearly kills me if it's worth taking. Mostly, it's a good gun."

I turned around in my seat and it hurt like hell. I looked over Lila and Ben.

"You two alright?"

They nodded.

"Good." I turned back around and settled in my seat. "Good. Everybody's alive and well."

"You're not," Ben replied.

It made me smile, which helped with the pain. "Good one."

I stared down at my black long-sleeved shirt. It was ripped to shreds in some parts from the Werepanther using me as a scratching post. I could see the flesh underneath. The deep wounds were almost fully healed. It took a little more time than normal to heal from a scratch or bite from a Were. I don't know why exactly. It's just one of those stupid supernatural rules.

Still, the bullet was the problem. I tore the shirt a bit more in the spot over my shoulder wound. The shirt was just going to get in the way.

"What are you doing now?" Tara was watching me and trying to drive.

"You kids ever play Operation?" I laughed. No one else did. Tough crowd.

Fun fact. If you ever get shot and there's a bullet lodged in your arm, don't try to dig it out with your bare hands. Unless you're a Vampire and it's a silver bullet that could potentially kill you if the silver got into your bloodstream for too long; in that case, by all means, go nuts.

I took a deep breath and held it. This was going to hurt. I expected it. That didn't help much as I dug my thumb and index finger into the gaping hole in my shoulder. I can't begin to describe what it feels like to try and dig your way into an open wound, but it sure as hell doesn't feel good. I felt rough tissue and blotches of things that probably shouldn't be moving as I dug deeper and brought more pain.

Tara made a sound like she was gagging and I heard Lila gasp. I think Ben was leaned over Tara's seat so that he could see what I was doing.

The silver casing of the bullet was preventing my body from healing itself as fast as it normally would. Silver was more or less an inhibiter that pretty much stopped my cells from regenerating. I pressed my fingers deeper and deeper into the wound, grinding my teeth. I had a sudden spasm from the pain and my elbow dented the side of my door.

I'd be pissed about that later.

I hate getting shot. Usually it isn't a big deal. My body just healed and instead of me dying it was usually the person who pulled the trigger that winded up six feet under. I remember a couple months back some psycho who thought he was a one-man Vampire hunting prodigy shot me in the thigh. I still remember sitting in the bathroom on the toilet with a steak knife and a pair of tongs. I had to cut into my own leg and dig the bullet out. I made Kyle watch, forcing him to hold a plastic cup to catch the bullet in. He fainted halfway through. That's why I only let him use plastic.

I felt the casing on the tip of my finger. Finally. I groaned and my anger flared with the pain as I forced my way in deeper, tearing even more tendons and nerves. I had the bullet pinched between my fingers and I pulled it out before I lost my hold on it.

A long piece of ligament came with the bullet. It snapped from the strain and I cursed. I felt calmer when I looked at my hand and saw the tiny bullet covered in my bodily fluids. I could barely see the silver casing.

Silver. I never understood how one little element could wreak such havoc on so many of us supernatural types. Shoot me with a regular bullet or stab me with anything not silver and I don't even really feel it. If the wound's not too serious, the nerves get damaged and heal before your brain can register it as pain. You throw some silver into the mix though and it's a whole different story.

"Cool," Ben muttered.

I glanced back at him and he was leaning so close to me I could count the strands of hair from his bangs hanging in front of his face.

Tara looked sick. "That's so gross."

I dropped the bullet on the floor. It felt so good to get the bullet out I couldn't care about anything else right then. I reclined my seat enough for me to be comfortable and I watched the night pass by my window as Tara drove. I had to relax. My arm wasn't healing by itself yet.

I'd be screwed if I'd kept the bullet in too long and it didn't heal for the rest of the night. I still didn't know what else might pop out after the kids.

"You okay?" Ben sounded worried.

"Leave him alone." Tara glanced at me. She was just as curious.

Are you going to die too? Lila asked.

I kept my eyes shut and tried focusing on healing. I imagined the wound closing up. Sometimes it helped, or at least I think it did. I couldn't let Lila's worry be my own. I'd be fine. I'd heal. I had to heal.

"You can't kill what's already dead," I said softly.

Nobody said anything for a while, but my arm still wasn't healing. Shit.

I opened my eyes and tried thinking happy thoughts. Screw it. I was worried.

Tara turned when the GPS told her to and we were down a more populated side street. I tried keeping cool, watching the GPS, and looking to see where we needed to go next to reach the Psychic's house.

We drove through a few neighborhoods and then out onto another major road. Then we headed north a few miles. The whole time I sat there trying to relax and let my powers heal my body.

We were less than a mile away when I started to feel the pain subside in my shoulder.

I closed my eyes and willed the wound to heal. My shoulder started to numb and tingle as if it had fallen asleep. It always felt like that when my body was combating the silver to heal. I shivered suddenly and propped my seat back up.

Everyone was watching me, even Tara out of the corner of her eye, as I ran my finger along the bullet hole in my shoulder. I could see my dark flesh-colored insides start to stitch back together. It felt good. It was good to be immortal.

I laughed a little. Finally. For once things were working the way I wanted.

Tara was the first to ask it. "Healing?"

"Of course." I smirked at her. "You were worried?"

Tara turned her attention back on the road.

"Would you have died from that shot?" Ben asked. I didn't like the way his voice trembled when he said the word "died".

"Na." I tried moving my arm, but it was too stiff and sore. I'd play it safe and let it heal as best as it could before I overdid it.

"If I left the bullet in there all night then I might've gotten silver poisoning from it. That would've been a real bitch to deal with."

"Silver poisoning?" Tara didn't sound convinced.

"It's what happens when too much silver gets in our system for a long period of time." I moved my hand and flexed my fingers. It didn't hurt that much, and with every second the pain subsided.

"So, Vampires and Weres can be stopped with silver bullets?"

I didn't like where this conversation was going. I didn't want to be the one teaching kids how to kill my own kind. That was frowned upon by the supernatural society. Still, it would probably keep them alive longer if they knew enough to save them one day.

"Silver bullets will keep most of us down. The stronger the Were or Vampire, the faster they'll heal from the wounds. I'm not going to tell you that silver bullets will kill everything because they won't. If nothing else, they'll buy you time to start running."

I had first-hand experience watching a Vampire get his chest torn open from silver shots and keep coming. It slowed him down, but he still managed to kill every single one of the men trying to hunt him. That was a long time ago and I was lucky to be on his side when the shit hit the fan. It's always best to be on the team of the two hundred year-old Vampire if crazy mercenaries in Georgia are ever hunting you.

"Why'd you bring that gun then?" Ben asked.

I glanced back at the kid. "It's a good gun."

"But it can kill you," he said.

I smirked and nodded at Tara. "She's got a gun and it could kill her."

"Oh."

I got a look at the GPS and saw that we were coming up to the address that Jack gave me. Tara saw it too and asked, "Do we just drive right up?"

It was a good question.

I was nursing a silver shot to the shoulder, we were driving a damaged SUV that was anything but inconspicuous, and I had an adolescent telepath in the back seat who was probably reading my mind right that second.

Were we going to just drive right up? Why the hell not?

Maybe I'd even ring the doorbell and shout "Trick or Treat!"

23

The neighborhood was nice. Green freshly trimmed lawns, tall, slender palm trees, and manicured bushes, the works. The houses were huge, modern homes twice the size of mine. They were the kinds of homes where upper class men and women raised their families. I could practically see the dog playing with the children in the front yard, while mom tends to her garden and dad clips the hedges. Then I remembered I was in Boca Raton, so I imagined a group of immigrants doing the yard work instead for dirt-cheap.

The home we stopped in front of looked creamy and pale in the dark. The roof's brown shingles made the white of the house stand out even more. The large, white overpass above the front entrance gave the house a bit more elegance than the other homes.

It was a nice piece of realty. I wouldn't be moving in anytime soon though.

A tall thick palm tree stood up in the center of the front yard with beautiful purple flowers planted around it. There was no car in the brick driveway so Tara pulled up close to the two-car garage. The large white garage door was about a foot away.

I just looked at her from my seat. "You close enough?"

Tara was leaned over the steering wheel trying to see over the front of the truck. "Am I good?"

"Perfect," I told her.

I stared out of my window at the quiet home. We made it. All there was left to do was go in and see if this Psychic was the right Grandmother.

I glanced over my shoulder to Ben. "Hey, is there a jacket somewhere back there?"

I couldn't go up to someone's door wearing a shirt and jeans with giant tears through them. I had more class than that.

Ben unbuckled his seatbelt and started looking under the seat and in the trunk. I usually kept a few spare clothes lying around just in case. I was hoping that Kyle hadn't cleaned the car recently.

"Kris, you're cut." Tara gasped.

I looked down at my chest. The laceration from the Werepanther's claws was just starting to scab over. Tara could see it as clear as day.

"I'm fine." I watched Ben doubled over the back seat rummaging through the trunk.

"You're not going to catch lycanthropy are you?"

I sighed. "No."

"Because you're a Vampire?"

"Yes. Because I'm a Vampire." I whistled at Ben. "How's it coming, kid?"

"I found it." Ben turned back in his seat and tossed a gray hoodie on the center console between Tara and I. Jackpot.

I put the jacket in my lap and noticed that Tara was still unsure about my wounds.

I forget how little most people know about lycanthropy, even these days. In schools they still taught kids that any exposure to a Were meant possible "infection". Oh, progress.

"What do we do if this lady isn't Gram?" Ben asked.

"I don't know." Tara shut the car off and handed me the keys. "You have a plan?"

A plan? Yeah right. "You can't plan genius. I'm better at improvising."

I turned in my seat to get a good look at Lila. "Hey, how you feel?"

Lila shrugged her tiny shoulders. *I'm okay.* She was lying. I don't know if she was doing it on purpose, but I could feel her fear inside of me as if it were my own.

"Can you sense anything inside?" I asked.

No.

"Lila doesn't sense anything," I told Tara.

"What does that mean?"

"It means we go knock on the door." I got out of the car and the cool night air calmed my nerves.

Tara got out and walked around to me, squeezing between the garage door and the car. I didn't even mock her for the terrible parking job. Ben and Lila climbed out of the car and Lila snatched her big brother's hand immediately.

I scanned the street. I didn't see anyone coming after us and I couldn't sense any Weres. Had there only been one car with those three men after us? Doubtful.

I tore my black long-sleeved shirt off with one hand, threw the remains in my car, and shut the door. I stood there in just my beat up black wifebeater and caught Tara staring at me.

"How's your arm?" Tara asked.

I rolled my shoulder and felt a sharp sting. The tendons and ligaments hadn't healed completely yet. I craned my neck to get a good look at the wound. It was beginning to scab over.

"I'll be good." I put on the gray hoodie. I was having trouble getting my arm through the sleeve so Tara helped me. I didn't need her help, but I didn't shirk her away.

"Thanks." I zipped the jacket shut to hide my healing wounds. Wouldn't want to scare whoever opened the door.

I'm scared. Lila's voice whispered in my head.

She stood there looking up at me and she seemed so frail. She was smaller than my sister was. Looking down into those green eyes took me back to a lifetime ago.

I swallowed back the memories and buried them deep. I had work to do. This was business and Lila wasn't my sister. She was Lila. Nothing more.

"You want to wait here?"

Lila nodded and Ben looked disappointed.

"How are you going to know if she's Gram?" Ben asked.

I looked at Tara. She seemed to be wondering the same thing.

"You said her name's...Ruth, right?"

The three nodded.

"Right...piece of cake. I'll take care of this. You three wait here."

I headed up the small beige walkway that curved away from the garage and up to the front door under the overhang of the porch. There were potted plants hanging from the ceiling with vines that almost touched the floor. I could smell lavender in the air, but that was it. What was with people and lavender?

I looked at the white double doors in front of me and knocked three times.

I focused on listening for some kind of movement inside. I couldn't hear anything. I pushed the doorbell. I didn't hear the chimes ringing through the house.

I put my hands in my jacket pockets and stood there trying to figure out what was going on. Something wasn't right.

I examined the doors. I'd missed it before. There were markings carved around the frame. The writing was so small I could barely see it. If you weren't looking for it, you wouldn't ever notice the symbols carved into the woodwork.

I leaned in close to see if I could make it out. The symbols were archaic markings I couldn't understand. All I knew was that it was a spell. I couldn't sense it, couldn't feel its magic, but I knew it was there. A spell that was so discreet that I couldn't sense it had to be powerful enough to keep almost anything out. It must've also cost a fortune to have someone cast it. A Witch in the business would've charged more than most people could afford to have something like that made up. Hell, few Witches in the states had enough juice to even cast the spell in the first place.

Even if this Portia wasn't the kids' Gram, she sure had one hell of a security system. I couldn't afford something like that. Abby might be strong enough to cast such a high level protective spell, but even she wouldn't have been able to discount me what something like that cost in labor alone. Setting up a spell around a home takes a lot of time and a lot of energy.

I was still standing there leaning close to the door and examining the symbols when the front door opened. I tried stepping back casually, my hands deep in my pockets.

"Can I help you?"

The woman stood in the doorway examining me. Her eyes were like dark sapphires in the orange glow of the porch light. Her silver and blond hair fell straight down around her shoulders elegantly. She was taller than I expected. A long, rich blue silk sleeping dress draped over her tanned shoulders and hung down to her calves. The skin that I could see wasn't sickly or pale, but a nice rich tan from bathing in the Florida sun. Her skin was taut and scarcely wrinkled. The only things that hinted at her age were the lines around her eyes and brow. The way the gown curved around her figure, I knew that Portia was in excellent health for her age. I'd have guessed she was in her mid-forties at the oldest. But her eyes told me she was older than that.

I stopped staring at the revealing blue sleeping dress that made the woman more enticing than elderly.

I fumbled to remember what I was doing there on the porch in the middle of the night. "Hello."

"Hello." She smiled, amused.

"I'm looking for a Portia."

The woman raised her brow at me.

"No you're not."

She leaned against the frame of the door. With her arms crossed, the tanned mounds of her breast caught my eye. Her beauty reminded me of an old movie star. She was like Jayne Mansfield and Marilyn Monroe rolled into one. I had to admit, for an older woman, the lady was hot.

Now, I don't have a certain type. I feed off people who are interesting to me, who have a certain quality about them that I admire or intrigues me. I don't just feed off whatever's lying around for easy picking. I have standards. I never ever judged or discriminated. Old, young, or somewhere lost in between; it didn't matter…age was just a number after all. The gleam in those deep blue eyes and the mature, seductive, yet gracefulness resonating from her made me hungrier than I had been around the two humans and the Were I passed up. I wanted to get inside that house and see if I could seduce and feed off her. A two for one would've been a nice deal. After the day I'd had, I could've used a release.

"What?" It took me a second longer to answer than it normally would have. What can I say? The lady was like a fine wine that got better with age.

She smiled at me, as if I was a cute new toy. "You're looking for a Ruth, not a Portia."

Creepy. I took my hands out of my pockets as casually as possible. I wasn't used to dealing with Psychics.

"I dreamt about you last night," she told me.

"Kinky," I answered.

She straightened herself in the doorway. "I suppose. I have to ask you a question."

"Yeah?"

"What do you do when a Vampire comes knocking at your door uninvited?"

Shit.

"Relax." The word drifted from her lips like a soothing breeze. She laughed, but still stayed in her doorway.

"So, you are Psychic," I said.

"Looks like it."

"Is your name Portia?" I asked.

I didn't like the way she was looking at me. I couldn't feel her in my head, but that didn't mean she wasn't up there rooting around.

"Sure. But I've got more than one name."

"How about Ruth?"

The older woman's gentle, elegant appearance shifted for a moment. I watched her eyes widen as they focused on something behind me.

"Gram!" Ben shouted.

I turned and the kid rushed by me. I watched Portia's eyes light up with joy and surprise. Psychic or not, I don't think she saw that coming.

Portia stepped out of the frame of her home and welcomed Ben as he wrapped his arms around her waist. He buried his face in her stomach and she grunted from the force. She looked like she was in shock, staring down at the tuft of hair on Ben's head as if he wasn't real.

"Benjamin?" Portia looked to me for answers.

Tara and Lila came up the walkway and onto the porch. Lila took off for her Gram and joined Ben in tackling the old lady. Tara just stayed back with me.

Portia actually dropped to her knees in the gown to embrace both Lila and Ben.

"My little Nipoti!"

I turned to Tara. She stood there with her arms crossed watching her siblings. I noticed she wasn't running into anybody's arms. Too bad, it looked like fun. I'd run into her.

I watched Portia, Ben, and Lila hold each other so tight that I didn't think they would ever let go. It looked like I'd actually found the kids' long-lost Gram. I'd remember that moment the next time someone called me unreliable.

"Taraya, get over here." Portia pried one hand off Ben and held it out for Tara.

I watched her stare back at the woman and reluctantly walk towards her. Portia got to her feet, both Lila and Ben holding onto her dress like a safety blanket.

Portia embraced Tara, but it wasn't as heart-felt as with Ben and Lila. Portia breathed in Tara and kissed her on the cheek, genuinely overjoyed. Tara looked stiff and awkward, almost hesitant.

"How?" Portia pulled away from Tara and put her hands on Ben and Lila, almost as if she were afraid to lose contact with them.

"How did you find me?"

"Kris helped us." Ben stared right at me.

I smirked and then felt Lila's voice inside my head, too excited and happy to contain it all. I could almost feel her happiness radiating through her as if it were my own.

He's a Vampire. We can trust him.

Portia looked down at her granddaughter.

"It's true," Ben added. "He really is a Vampire. He killed a Werepanther and flipped a car and—"

"What?" Portia turned to me.

She didn't even know the half of it.

I glanced around the front yard, making sure no one was out for a late night stroll. "We should probably take this inside."

Portia nodded. "Of course, you're right. Come in. All of you."

I headed towards the door to follow them in and Portia turned to me. I heard her crisp, sultry voice as easily as if she'd just spoken aloud. Except her mouth didn't move an inch.

I want to know everything, Kristopher Grant. Everything.

24

The inside of Portia's house made the outside look decrepit. The older Psychic was obviously loaded. New, shiny, white tiled floors with light, cream-colored walls. In the large open room near the front door, I saw glass tables and shelves packed with extravagant artifacts from all over the world. There were small jade tokens that looked Chinese and a few framed portraits of Egyptian hieroglyphics. In the living area, there were white leather sofas with a white rug under a glass coffee table. There was a large television in the corner with a complete surround-sound installed around the room. It put mine to shame.

Instead of being in front of the television, we were all huddled in the open kitchen adjoined with the living room. The ceiling was tall and a small crystal chandelier hung down over the glass dining table near the patio doors. The kitchen itself was huge, decked out with black marble counters, stainless steel sinks and fridge, and dark wooden cabinets.

I stood with my arms crossed leaning up against the counter, watching the family reunion.

There was a small island in the center of the kitchen with a flat marble surface and wooden cabinets underneath to match the décor. There were two tall bar stools on one side of the island and Ben and Lila sat there with two oversized mugs of freshly nuked instant hot chocolate.

I watched Lila blow at the steam rising out of her mug, too worried of burning her mouth to take a sip. Ben just kept reaching into the small bag of marshmallows between them and dropping them into his mug, eating the soaked marshmallows, then repeating the process.

Tara sat at the glass table just outside the kitchen. She hadn't been thirsty when Portia had asked if she wanted anything. Tara hadn't been much of anything since we got there. I noticed, but I don't think anyone else did.

Portia stood at the stove pouring some freshly brewed herbal tea she had put on before we'd stopped by. It smelled like jasmine and pomegranate, but I wasn't an expert on teas. If she'd been drinking blood I might've been able to tell if it was A or B positive.

"I'm sorry I don't have anything for you to drink..." Portia sipped at her tea, staring at me over the top of her purple mug.

I watched the old lady and wasn't impressed. I've been in enough pissing contests—even though none of them has been with a middle-aged woman before—to know when I'm being scrutinized. The elegant charm and grace that I'd seen in the doorway had been replaced with the fear and concern of a protective grandmother. Don't you love that maternal instinct?

"It's alright...Ruth...or is it Portia?"

"I'd prefer Portia. It's what I go by down here. It's one of my middle names." Portia sounded as if I should've known better than to ask.

"I didn't know that," Tara said.

"There's a lot you don't know about your Gram, darling."

"Why is that exactly?" I asked.

Portia set her tea down on the counter. "I'm in your debt for bringing my grandchildren to me, Vampire, but I am not obligated to explain myself to you or anyone else."

I raised my eyebrows at that one and forced back a laugh.

Portia turned and scanned the kitchen from Lila to Ben and then finally on Tara. "I would love to know what you three are doing in Florida. Does James know you're all down here?"

I looked at Tara who wasn't meeting anyone's eyes.

Portia looked back at Tara. "How is that stubborn son of mine?"

Ben and Lila stopped fussing with their hot chocolate and kept their heads down.

Portia looked at her three grandchildren and then to me as if I had all the answers. "What's wrong?"

"Dad's dead," Tara whispered the words.

I watched the old lady's grace and composure shrivel down to nothing. The gleam in her blue eyes started to dwindle and her perfectly straight posture sank. She put her hands on the counter to keep from falling to the ground.

"What? No, it…" She turned back to Ben and Lila. "Is this true?"

Ben just nodded his head. Lila refused to look at anything other than her hot chocolate.

"But how?" Portia was fumbling, "When? I should've sensed it. I should've…Tara, what happened?"

Tara couldn't speak. The kid couldn't tell her Grandmother that her only son was dead.

Portia headed for her, frantic. "What happened?"

I stepped away from the counter and she stopped in her tracks.

"Take it easy," I told her, more warning than suggestion.

Portia stared at me for a good long moment before she took a deep breath and visibly attempted to regain her composure. She looked past me to Tara and said softly, "There's a spare bedroom in the back. How about you take your sister and brother and go get cleaned up."

Tara glanced at the both of us and then nodded. I wondered where her fighting spirit went.

I watched the kids get off their stools and follow Tara. She led them out of the kitchen. They stopped only when Lila turned around and ran back to me, wrapping her tiny arms around my leg. I almost flinched. I wasn't around kids enough to be comfortable with one hugging me. It felt wrong and awkward, warm and scary all at once.

I told them you would keep us safe. I knew we could trust you.

I heard the words and put a hand on the head of blond hair. She was so tiny, so fragile yet somehow so strong.

Thank you.

I looked at Ben and Tara. They were standing there watching us. I didn't know what to say.

Lila pulled away and shuffled back to the others.

"Will you say goodbye before you leave?" Ben asked.

"Sure," I said. My throat was hoarse for some reason.

"He's just going to have a talk with me first before he goes." Portia met my eyes.

I shrugged at the kids. "Like she said."

Portia crossed her arms and nodded to the children. "Go on. Get cleaned up."

I watched Tara lead the kids out of the kitchen and down through the halls of the house. I listened to their feet patter on the tile until finally a door shut and all I could hear was the breathing of a very upset old woman.

Portia walked away from me and carefully sat down at the same table Tara had been sitting at. She buried her face in her hands and it looked like she was going to start crying. I hate it when people cry around me. I don't know what to say or do and it just feels awkward.

Portia quickly brought her hands down and straightened her posture as if she were embarrassed by her gesture. Thank God.

"Sit," she ordered.

I leaned against the refrigerator. "I'd rather stand. I'm not staying long."

She didn't seem to like that. "So you just drop them off and leave? You're quite the delivery man."

That made me smirk. I like it when they have some spunk.

"Listen lady, those kids have got a lot of problems after them. I don't need it on me. I brought them to you because they were hell bent on finding you. Besides, from the look of the spells you have protecting this place, they're safer with you than they are with me."

"You mean you're safer without them."

I shrugged. "However you want to look at it."

"I don't even know what they're doing here." She was bitter, upset, and confused.

"Their father...I haven't even spoken with him since I left. I didn't know he was...I haven't even dreamt of him dying."

Dreams meant more to Psychics than to us regular folks. The more powerful mentally gifted ones sometimes see the future in their dreams. As far as I know, they don't have control of the dream and can't consciously look at a specific future. Some had premonitions and visions while they were awake. Most just woke up knowing that tomorrow they were going to get a phone call from a relative or get a flat tire. Very few were talented enough to predict the winning lottery ticket numbers.

What was the point of being psychic if you couldn't even do that?

"I always knew I'd outlive him. From the first time I held him in my arms, I knew." The old lady stared off for a while as if going to some far distant place I couldn't follow her to even if I wanted.

"I need to know everything. I have to. I need to know." Portia got up from the table and headed towards the back of the house.

"Where are you going?" I asked.

"I need Tara to show me what happened."

I grabbed her by the arm and she turned around at once. I let her go, I didn't want to fight, but I didn't think it was a good idea to go force the kid to have her mind read. She'd been through enough for one night.

"Listen."

"Don't you ever put your hands on me again," Portia spat.

I could see where Tara got her personality. It was probably why they didn't get along well.

"Hey, I just don't think now's the best time to go digging through Tara's head."

"I just need to read her. It's easy."

I owed Tara for killing two men to save my life. I wasn't going to let Grammy Ruth Something Portia go messing with her head.

"I saw into Tara's head."

"You what?"

"I'm not going through the details. Just read me and I'll give you everything I know."

The second I said it I wished I hadn't. If Portia was powerful and I allowed her to enter my mind and read my thoughts then she'd be in there and I didn't know what else she could do. I really didn't want some strange grieving woman thumbing through my thoughts like an open book.

Portia considered it for a second. "So, you're strong enough to create a telepathic connection with people?"

I nodded. "I have to keep contact with them, but yeah."

She held out her hand to me. "I've never read a Vampire before."

"Lucky me."

Her face grew very serious then, the lines tightening around the corners of her mouth. "I want to know what happened to my grandchildren."

I contemplated changing my mind and feeding Tara to the Psychic piranha in front of me, but I knew that wasn't an option. I'm not *that* big of an ass.

"What do I do?" I asked.

"Just let me touch you."

"This going to hurt?" I asked. Shit like that always hurt like hell. It's just one of those rules.

Portia shrugged. "We'll find out."

I took a deep breath and let Portia put her dry hands on either side of my face.

It happened so suddenly that it felt like I was falling down a kaleidoscope of memories.

Images flashed through my head from the very time I saw Lila and Ben to just now in the kitchen. They came at me like gunfire, too quick to really make out everything. My mind couldn't process it, couldn't make sense of it. I could feel Portia's presence inside my head like a torch burning in the dark crevices of my mind. She had set out a course and thankfully she didn't deviate. She didn't look anywhere other than my memories and thoughts related to Lila, Ben, and Tara.

Portia's dark blue eyes came flashing into view and I stumbled backwards into the refrigerator. The kitchen was spinning around and around, so I shut my eyes trying to get the spinning to stop.

When I opened them, Portia was holding onto the counter with one hand while the other was cupped to her mouth in shock. The world had stopped spinning so I held out my hand to help support her.

She wrapped her arm through mine and I led her to the table again. She sat down slowly, almost feebly as if she'd aged ten years.

"Are you alright?" I asked her, kneeling down so that I was on eye-level with her while she sat.

She shook her head, keeping her hand to her mouth. "I don't believe it," she mumbled through her fingers. "I don't believe it."

"Did you see everything?" I was worried she had seen too much. I had memories floating around up there that I didn't want anyone to see. I didn't need the old lady to have a heart attack and croak right there in the kitchen because she dug too deep. If that happened, I didn't know what I'd do with the kids.

Portia couldn't speak, her hands were trembling, and her gold bracelet around her wrist rattled on the glass tabletop.

"Take your time," I whispered. "Just relax."

After a few deep breaths, Portia got herself under control. I took it that she hardly ever lost control in the first place. That was good. I liked dealing with people who knew that panicking never got anyone anywhere other than dead.

"Kristopher," Portia kept the tears from breaking the surface, "thank you for keeping my babies alive."

She reached out and put her hand on the side of my face tenderly. There was real gratitude in her eyes then. It had been a long time since anyone looked at me like that. It felt good on some level, and disturbing on another. I wasn't used to helping people like that.

"Thank you so much."

"Quit."

"I owe you."

I shook my head. I didn't care about debt. "Did you see everything you needed to?"

Portia nodded. "Yes. Yes, I saw enough."

"Who's after Lila?"

"I don't know for sure." I tried sniffing out whether or not Portia was lying. She wasn't, not entirely.

"I don't know anyone who would have a Werepanther working for them. But those men that Tara saw kill their da—*my*, James..."

"What about them?"

"They could be...there are many people in the world who deal with Psychics. Some to kill us, and others who want to enslave us." Portia shook her head as she looked at me, disgusted. "Those men could be anybody."

"Well they followed her down here. That's what I think." I got to my feet. "They tried killing me too. It didn't work out for them though."

"I know. I know, I'm sorry." Portia stared up at me. "I know that you think that these people after Lila are connected to the killings up north."

Great. What else did she read of *my* thoughts? "You don't agree?"

Portia seemed to be getting calmer by the second. "It's possible. I saw that you got my address from Jack. What does he think?"

"You don't know?"

"I sincerely tried not to pry into your mind. I've just never read a Vampire before."

"Yeah, I remember. Jack thinks that we should all be careful. I haven't had a chance to tell him about the two humans with silver and the Werepanther I killed."

"I'm worried." Portia was staring down at her hands. They were still shaking a little. "I saw the memories you saw when you...*forced* your way into Tara's mind."

The old lady tried to keep her calm. I knew what she was seeing. I remembered seeing Tara fight off that man. How she felt. What it was like to shoot him and steal his truck.

"Something's not right."

"You're gonna have to be a bit more specific."

"...I haven't heard of any of this in the news."

"Me neither," I said. "So?"

"You're a smart Vampire. Right?"

"I border on intelligent and oblivious."

Portia rolled her eyes. "It means that if these men were following them then they must be influential enough to keep this out of the media. They may even be covering Tara's tracks for her so that she doesn't get found by the police before they can get to Lila."

"You know anyone with that much power backing them who'd be after Lila?"

I watched Portia's eyes grow colder. I knew right then and there that she had an answer for me.

"No," she said.

Liar, liar, if I had a match, I'd light her dress on fire.

I walked over to the table and sat down across from her. She watched me, cautious, worried that I knew she was lying.

It's no secret that most Vampires and Weres can smell when someone's lying. It's a trick you have to be taught. It's all in the chemicals the body releases when it's telling a fib. Once you know the smell, you know what it means when you catch a whiff of it. It has a distinct odor. To me, it smells a lot like bullshit.

I put my hands in front of me on the glass table and looked her in the eyes. I wasn't going to play games. I wanted fact, not fiction.

"I hope I don't have to ask you again. I kept those kids alive for you all day and brought them to your doorstep in one piece. Maybe you should get a phone. Hell, maybe you should leave your address with your family so they can get hold of you when people come to their house and shoot their father in cold blood and leave them alone and homeless, I don't know." I leaned in closer. "You're Psychic, right? Tell me what I'm going to do if you don't give me a straight answer about who's after those kids."

Portia looked more impressed than scared. That was a change. Most people would've started pissing their panties if a Vampire started threatening them. Portia wasn't most people. She sat there, crossed her legs, and smoothed out the front of her nightgown.

"I was approached by a group of Psychics several years ago. They were some of the most talented men and women that I've ever seen. Extremely gifted. One was even a pupil of mine years ago when I still taught."

Good. Facts. "What did they want?"

"They wanted me to join them. To help gather other Psychics so that we could become more united. Something about helping future generations, I don't remember the specifics. I declined of course. I'm too old for politics and little clubs and groups. Besides, the real money's in a solo performance."

I smirked. Portia was a woman after my own heart.

"They didn't like me declining. They tried threatening me. However, threats don't sit well with me. Unfortunately, they ran me out of my business in Philadelphia. I had a fairly large cliental up north doing readings, helping people find things that were lost...simple work. Sadly, some of my clients started dying and word had it that these men were involved. I was forced to move away. It was either that or kill seven other Psychics."

"I would've killed them."

Portia swallowed, and seemed embarrassed. "The truth is that there are at least two Psychics in that group stronger than I am. If they wanted, they could've killed me."

"So you left Lila behind?"

Portia wouldn't look at me. The regret seeped out of her.

"I begged James to let me take her. I tried explaining that she'd be safer with me, but he wouldn't have it. After he lost Lisa, he wouldn't let Tara, Ben, or Lila out of his sight."

"Lisa was his wife?" I asked.

"Yes. She was also one of my pupils. That's how James met her."

"Let's say that these Were and Vampire killings are separate from the people after Lila. Are these Psychics capable of tracking her down here? I was told most Psychics could follow others because of their mental trail or something like that."

Portia seemed impressed. "Almost every one of them is capable of Tracking. It's possible they followed her down here if they were the ones who killed my son."

Great.

"Well, are they safe here with you?" I figured it was time to skip to the important matters.

"You saw the protection I have around the house, but you don't know of the spells set up around the neighborhood. The second you came within a mile of this house Lila's mental trail faded. She can't be tracked here. It's how I keep myself safe as well as practice my psychic abilities."

"Good." I got up from the table.

Portia got up as well. "You're leaving?"

"I only came in to make sure the kids were safe. I've got a feeling I killed the people who were supposed to bring them in. I don't think anyone else is coming after them. At least not tonight."

"I owe you," Portia told me. "You're a better man than most."

I actually laughed at that one.

"What's wrong?" she asked, confused.

I looked at her and wondered if she remembered what I was. "I don't get that a lot."

"I'm sorry."

"Don't be. You saw inside my head, lady. I wasn't keeping the kids safe out of the kindness of my heart."

"No," Portia said. "No, you weren't. Still, you didn't take advantage of them or hurt them. You fed them. You kept them alive. You didn't let them go when you could have."

I shrugged. "Don't go telling people about this. I've got a reputation around here."

"Jack told me about you once, when you first took control of the territory. He said you had potential. I never thought much of it. I tend to stay out of the territory business."

"I might stop by every once in a while. I may need a good Psychic someday."

I meant it more as a joke than anything, but Portia smiled. "Stop by any time you want."

I took a long look at her, trying to see if she was serious.

"I will," I finally said.

I heard footsteps behind me on the tile and I watched Tara and the two kids come back into the kitchen. Ben and Lila were in a fresh pair of clothes that must've come from their backpacks. They smelled a little stale.

Portia gasped. "You don't have to sleep in those filthy rags. Come with me, I'm sure I have a few clean shirts you can throw on."

"You leaving?" Ben asked me.

"Yes," Portia answered. "Yes, it's time Mr. Kristopher left. His night's wasting away while he's here fussing with us."

I looked at the kids and waved awkwardly. I wasn't good at goodbyes. For whatever reason, saying goodbye to the brats was hard to do. That worried me.

"But what if someone else followed us here?" Tara asked.

I looked up at her. She had a point, even though I didn't think there was anyone else following us.

"Can you stay the night?" Ben asked.

"What?" Portia and I asked it at the same time and looked at each other worriedly.

Please. Lila begged, *please don't go yet.*

I stared at Ben and Lila as if I never saw them before. What had I done wrong to make them think that I wanted to spend my night playing bodyguard?

"They feel safe with you," Tara answered my unspoken question.

"Honey," Portia said to Lila, stealing a glance at me, "my home is very safe."

"It's true," I added. "She has a lot of magic protecting this place. You're safer here than with me."

Ben and Lila didn't seem sold.

But you're...

I watched Lila struggle to keep the words coming to me. Her brow wrinkled and her eyes shut tight. She really didn't have perfect control over her abilities.

...We like you.

I turned to Portia. From the look on her face, she'd heard it too. She stared at me as if I had the answers.

Tara looked at me and I saw a glimpse of that girl crying in my arms in the middle of the street. My throat was dry, but not because I was thirsty.

I swallowed every ounce of my pride and checked the clock on the microwave nearby. It was a little after eleven. There was still so much of the night left.

"I'll stay as long as I can," I finally said. "Until I'm sure no one followed us."

Ben and Lila smiled at each other and seeing those smiles made me queasy. I was a Vampire playing watchdog for the night instead of feeding. What had my life come to?

"Are you alright with that?" I asked Portia.

She glanced at the children and then nodded to me. "He can stay as long as he wants."

Lila's face lit up and my heart melted. Her and Ben looked more excited than they should've been.

Portia clapped her hands together. "Come, let's get you some clean clothes and a shower."

The kids all followed their Gram. Tara turned around and glanced at me for a second. She didn't say anything. She didn't have to.

I stood there alone in the kitchen, wondering what the hell I was doing.

Since when did Vampires become family pets?

25

I spent my night sitting in the living room watching movies. Portia had made a big bowl of popcorn that everyone picked at except me. Not that I can't eat food at night, I just don't like popcorn. It gets stuck between my teeth. It's such a pain. *Bird On A Wire* was playing and the kids got through about half of it before they all fell asleep. Lila slept curled in a tight ball with her head resting in Portia's lap. Ben had passed out on the small loveseat in the corner of the room. Tara was on the same couch as me, barely able to keep her eyes open.

"Tara," Portia called. "Honey."

Tara sat up. "Yeah?"

"It's time to go to bed."

Tara reluctantly got up off the sofa. "I'll take them."

I sat there and watched Tara and Portia wake Ben and Lila up to get them to walk to the spare bedroom.

"It's time for bed, sweetie," Portia whispered to Lila as she rubbed a hand through her hair.

Lila sat up slowly and held Tara's hand as they all walked out of the living room.

I got up to stand beside Portia and watch the kids go.

Lila didn't get far before she turned around and hurried over to me. She wrapped her arms around me and I didn't know what to do.

G'night, Krissy. See you later.

I stood there trying not to let the emotions dwelling in the cellar of my heart claw their way up to the surface.

"Goodbye, kid."

Lila looked up at me and she looked so sad, as if she could cry any moment.

Don't say "goodbye".

"Why not?"

Goodbye means I'll never see you. Say "see you later" instead.

I shouldn't have gotten down on my knee to be level with her, but I did. I shouldn't have stared at Lila and imagined my little Erica standing there staring back at me so many lifetimes ago, but I did. I should've just said "goodbye" to the kid and meant it, but I didn't.

"Then I'll see you later," I promised.

Lila smiled and I saw that mouth of imperfectly perfect teeth. She hugged me once more and then hurried back to join Ben and Tara. I got to my feet and Ben and Tara were just looking at me.

"You keep an eye on her." I smirked at Ben.

Ben nodded like a good soldier.

"Thanks," Tara said from across the room. "Thanks for…"

"Don't." I waved it off. "You took care of your family. You did good. Go get some sleep."

Ben and Lila looked up at their big sister and we all saw her eyes starting to swell with tears. "See you later, Kris."

"See you later, guys."

The three of them left the living room and went off to bed.

I stood there trying to ignore the way Portia was looking at me.

"Lila likes you," Portia said.

I sat back down on the sofa even though I wanted to run out of that house and just keep running. I felt cramped. Like I was going to explode if I didn't just start running as fast as I could.

Portia sat down beside me, a thin white jacket over her sleeping gown. "They all like you."

I just focused on the television.

Portia focused on me. "Lila told me all about what you did for them."

"Like scaring her into running away from me?" I realized what Portia had just said. We had all been sitting there all night watching television and just relaxing. Nobody had talked about anything like that. At least not out loud.

"You talked to her telepathically?"

"We weren't really watching the movie. Lila can speak with me easier than she can with others. It takes less concentration because I can enter her mind."

"Good to know."

"She adores you."

205

"Why?"

"She trusts you. Says that she gets a good feeling from you. That you're safe to be around."

"I'm a Vampire."

"That doesn't bother her. She says you flipped a car and Ben thought it was the coolest thing he's ever seen."

Look at that. I had some fans.

"What was going through that mind of yours when you said that to Lila?"

"Said what?"

"The 'see you later' bit."

Oh. That. "She said goodbye was too final."

"That's what her father used to tell her." Portia smiled. I could see her eyes watering in the flashes of light from the television.

I sat there watching Mel Gibson and Goldie Hawn and tried to go back to feeling nothing. Nothing was always better.

"Can I ask you a question?" Portia wasn't interested in the movie.

I looked at her and leaned back in the sofa.

"Why did you stay? You know you didn't have to."

"Are you a psychologist too?"

Portia laughed. "You don't like to be psychoanalyzed?"

"Who does?"

"Good point. Why did you stay though?"

"Because…I don't know. They're weird kids, but…they're good kids."

I thought back to Erica. I looked over at Portia and wondered what else she'd seen when she poked around in my head. I wouldn't let the precious memories I had left of my little sister be dissected and analyzed. I wouldn't let the best and worst moments of my past be anyone's gift or burden but mine.

Portia just watched me. I didn't like it. I was getting uncomfortable and my shoulder was aching. I rotated it a little and the tendons and muscles were still sore. I could've used a drink.

"Lila said the men chasing you shot you with silver." Portia sat forward in her seat. "Is your shoulder okay?"

"It hurts a little. I'll survive."

"Do you need to feed?"

I looked at Portia carefully. I didn't see anything on her face that looked like she was afraid of me. I didn't sense any worry that I'd try to feed off her. She trusted me and was genuinely concerned about me.

I didn't have my syringe and I couldn't just go and feed off someone who trusted me. It threw me off my game. I got performance anxiety if my food actually cared about me.

"I'm fine," I grumbled.

"You really use a syringe to feed?"

Lila must've been quite the Chatty-Telepathic-Cathy. "Yes. No, I don't have it on me. Can we get away from the subject of blood?"

Portia let it go.

I didn't like the silence right then so I decided to let Portia know where I stood. For whatever reason, I felt like it was important to justify myself.

"Lila, Ben, and Tara are all under my protection. As long as they stay in my territory, they're safe."

Portia watched my eyes as I spoke.

"You understand?"

"Yes. Thank you."

"If anything ever happens or you need my help, you call me. Okay?"

Portia leaned closer to me and put a hand on mine. I wanted to flinch but I didn't. Her hand was warm, so very warm.

"Thank you." She gripped my hand gently and smiled.

I turned back to finish watching the movie.

"And if I need a Psychic?"

"You have one of the best at your service."

I nodded. "That's what I like to hear. Now can we please watch something else?"

I climbed into the car just a little after five in the morning. I sat there and took a deep breath to try and clear my head.

"What the hell am I doing?" I asked the reflection staring back at me in the rear view mirror. I ran my hands along my face to try and understand why I let myself get close to those kids. I was doing so well with keeping people out, and now I'd let three in.

I knew I was making a mistake, but a part of me didn't care. Something inside of me looked forward to seeing Lila, Ben, and Tara again. Would it be so bad if I drove up to see them every now and then?

I got a powerful Psychic out of the deal. Not a bad trade-off when you think about it.

I glanced back at the house one last time. Portia had passed out on the sofa around five and I slipped out of the house without anyone hearing. It was getting close to dawn and I was feeling exhausted, physically and emotionally. The emotional part was because I'm an idiot; the physical was because I had to heal my shoulder and hadn't fed all night. Though I guess in retrospect, both fit into the me being an idiot category.

Maybe if I were lucky Kyle would donate some blood. Yeah right. Maybe if I told him what happened he'd try and help me out. I thought about how I had treated him the last time I saw him.

I doubted Kyle would even talk to me, let alone give blood.

I pulled out of the driveway and headed back home.

There was no way in hell I was dumb enough to drive back down the same road that had a flipped car and three corpses in the middle of it. Even if the police and ambulances had already come and gone, I wasn't taking the risk of driving my warped SUV through a crime scene; especially one I'd made. No reason to be nosey.

So, I went north and headed east to I-95 to start the long ride back home.

Morning was coming, and it had been one hell of a night.

26

The sun was coming up over the horizon like a big bright reminder of how bad I was going to feel shortly. My shoulder started aching halfway home and by the time I was on A1A and coming up to the house it was throbbing steadily. I shouldn't have stayed the night. I should've fed. I was stupid.

My eyes were heavy, begging me to shut them for a second. I was tired. Not exhausted, but close. The idea of getting home, rinsing off, and crawling into the sheets naked was the only thing keeping me going. I hated being tired. I hated when I was the one who complicated my life.

I pulled into the driveway and pressed the clicker to open the garage door. Nothing happened. I pressed it again twice and still the garage door didn't budge.

"Perfect."

Kyle must've flicked the switch in the garage. I was too tired to even care. I could feel the sun rising over the horizon. Every second I could feel my power slipping away and the big lead ball of fatigue pulling me down. After a night of getting shot with silver, having to heal the wound and still not feeding, my powers were drained and scrambling into hibernation. It was the price to pay. Vampirism's a balancing act and instead of refueling my energy, I let the tank run low. Stupid little Vampire, I should've just taken Portia's offer and fed off her.

I remembered the gun in the glove compartment. I brought it out and just the weight alone made something in my shoulder tighten and pinch. I hefted it into my lap and looked down at the gun that almost killed me. The Colt Defender…it really was a good gun. I checked the safety again and grabbed the magazines. I put them in my jacket pockets and carried the gun in my left hand to give my shoulder a break.

I got out of the car and headed for the front door. I held the gun loosely at my side. I didn't give a damn about concealing the thing. My neighbors weren't up at six-fifteen in the morning and I really didn't have the energy to give a shit.

Most mornings I was on the back deck watching the sun rise over the Atlantic to see it in all of its power-dampening glory. Right then I didn't care about anything other than my bed.

As I walked onto the porch, I could smell a familiar scent. Kyle's was there too, some cologne he had on, but there was someone else's scent. I swore I knew it. It was only then that I even remembered Kyle said he was bringing someone over last night. I'd somehow forgotten about it…again. Goes to show how important Kyle's personal life is to me.

Still, that scent…I knew it from somewhere.

I thought about it for about a second before I decided I didn't care about that either. I unlocked the door and it felt good to be back in my safe place.

"Honey, I'm home," I called out.

Usually Kyle worked nights and slept all day, so of course I did my best to try and ruin it for him. I don't know why, but it amused me.

I heard footsteps down the hall. I tossed my keys on the small table near the door.

"You better have gotten laid, kid," I shouted again, louder this time. I was admiring the Defender in my hand, checking the weight of it. I'd have to hide it in the gun safe in my closet so that little Kyle didn't accidentally shoot himself with it. Most child-related gun accidents happen because of poor preparation on the parent's part. Well, not in this home.

I looked across the room to the sliding glass doors leading to the porch. I could see the first rays of sunlight coming through as they peaked over the ocean. Just like that I felt the torch burning inside of me snuff out. My heart started its incessant beating.

My legs almost gave out. My shoulder hurt to say the least. My lower back even stung a bit. All I wanted, all I needed, was just to crawl into bed. Even the shower could wait. Yeah, I was exhausted.

I passed by the sofa and headed for the back of the house when I saw her.

I didn't recognize her at first. She was just a thin pale girl with dark hair and dark eyes. She looked like a deer in headlights and I thought it was the gun in my hand, but it wasn't. It was because of me.

I could almost taste her incredible blood on the tip of my tongue. The memory came crashing back like a tidal wave, a surge of uncontrollable need.

Lauren Millar. The last and best person I fed on.

The look in my eyes and the gun must've scared her because she took a few steps back down the hall.

"Kyle," she called, never taking her eyes off me.

She was wearing gray boy-shorts and a baby blue tank top that highlighted her pale skin. In the early morning sunlight and the shadows in the house, she looked spectacular. The exhaustion started to subside. I found energy in my bones I didn't know I had. I looked at her slender pale throat and knew what I wanted. I remembered how she tasted. I needed to taste her again. It was as simple as that. One of the best meals I've had in a long time was standing half-naked in my own house. No one would hear her scream. No one would know.

I walked towards her, unable to talk, unable to trick or charm. I was starving. My body ached, but if I could feed off fresh blood, off the incredibly sweet blood of this Lauren one more time, then I'd be okay. The day could go on. The only problem was that a few vials weren't what I wanted. I wanted to cut her, to let the blood shoot out of her like a faucet of pure life.

I didn't have fangs during the day, but I wanted to bite her still, to feel that flesh and blood in my mouth. I had to.

She turned and ran back into Kyle's room, screaming for him.

He ran out in just a pair of jeans, getting between my meal and me.

"Kris." He saw the gun in my hand. I forgot it was there. "Kris, what are you doing?"

I couldn't answer him. Words were useless. I just needed that woman's blood. That sweet, invigorating, *healthy* blood again. Oh, but I wanted so much more this time.

I tried walking right by him to follow Lauren into the back room, but Kyle shoved me. He shoved me in the chest as hard as he could and I stumbled back.

"What the hell's wrong with you?" He was red, his skin on fire.

I didn't have time for this. The gun was heavy in my hand. I aimed it at his chest. Was the safety on or off? It didn't matter. I'd shoot anyone to get to her. To get to what I craved.

Kyle looked at me as if I were a complete stranger. "You're going to shoot me? What are you doing?"

I kept walking towards him to get around him, but he wouldn't move. I pressed the barrel of the Defender into his bony chest and forced him back a step.

"Move."

"No." Kyle walked into the gun, forcing me back. "Get away from her."

"Move," I growled it this time. It was either he got out of my way or I'd go through him.

"Why are you doing this?"

I didn't have a good answer. But that didn't matter. What mattered was the quality of blood in the other room that I had to get. I just had to. I'd shoot Kyle. I didn't want to, but he wasn't giving me any other choice.

Kyle was faster than I thought he'd be and it was so out of character that I wasn't expecting him to try knocking the gun out of my hand. He went for it and my grip on the pistol disappeared as it went flying.

He tackled me, going for a takedown. He tried picking me up off the ground by lifting my legs out from under me, but I was too tall and he wasn't strong enough. We fought against each other for a moment before I fell backwards. My head smacked into the tile floor and stars exploded in my vision. When I could see again I saw Kyle's fist flying at me.

He punched me in the jaw and my stiff neck cracked in my ear.

That one punch brought me back for a moment.

Kyle hit me across the face again, throwing all of his weight behind the punch. I took it and it hurt like hell.

"Stop," I spat at him, trying to get him off me.

He tried hitting me again, but I grabbed his arm and then lashed out and punched him in the cheek. I'd surprised him and used that surprise to grab him by the throat and squeeze enough to make him gag.

"Quit it," I shouted. "I'm done."

He looked down at me, his hands trying to pry mine off his throat.

I didn't even remember why I was fighting him. The back of my head was already pounding from hitting the floor. "Kyle."

I let go of the kid's throat. I'd crushed enough people's windpipes in my day to know that he'd be okay. He fell back and got to his feet as fast as he could. He was still ready to fight me if I got crazy again.

Crazy didn't even begin to cover it. I was about to kill my human servant to get to the girl he had in the other room. It was the early morning, my abilities were gone, and I had been overwhelmed by bloodlust. Something was very wrong.

I didn't get to my feet. Exhaustion wracked my body again. I just sat up and leaned back against the wall in the hallway. I couldn't move. I couldn't do anything but wonder what the hell was wrong with me.

Kyle stood hovering over me, but he wasn't looking at me.

I looked to my left and saw the Defender lying on the floor a few feet away. I could go for it if I wanted. But I didn't want to. I should've probably told Kyle that.

"You're crazy." He was breathing heavy, his throat raspy with anger.

I just rested my head back on the wall and tried to breathe.

Lauren peaked out of Kyle's bedroom. She was careful not to come out of the frame of the doorway.

The second I saw her again I could taste her blood in my mouth. I was drawn to her. I *needed* her. My mind started to get cloudy. All I wanted was to feed. I wanted every drop of blood inside her.

I looked at the Defender on the ground. I looked up at Kyle.

I knew I could reach the gun first. I'd shoot Kyle. I'd shoot him dead and then it'd be just the girl and me.

No!

I brought my legs up and put my hands behind my head, burying my face in my knees. I stayed balled up there, screaming against the hunger, against the urges. I wouldn't go for the gun. I wouldn't go for the girl. I wouldn't do it. I wouldn't!

"Get her out of here!"

I didn't hear any movement. That meant she was still standing there. It meant I still had a chance to feed.

"NOW!"

Kyle didn't hesitate again. "Alicia, come on."

Alicia?

I looked up. My body was shaking, my muscles clenched to keep from moving.

I watched Lauren run by me with Kyle holding her hand. She had clothes in her hands. I watched them run. I tried not to see her as prey trying to flee, prey that I should chase. They turned the corner; all I could hear was the garage door slam shut.

I tried getting up but I was so tired.

Alicia? He called her Alicia.

Lauren. That's what she'd said her name was. Lauren Millar. She couldn't have lied. It was impossible. She couldn't lie to me.

My head was swimming. I felt nauseas. I let her go. I shouldn't have done that. I forced my legs to work and used the wall to support me. I stumbled down the hall and picked up the gun on the floor. It weighed twice as much as before.

I shouldn't have been so tired. I shouldn't have been craving Lauren…or Alicia's blood like that.

The gun was weighing me down. I made my way into the bedroom and locked the door behind me. My legs were mush. I headed for the nightstand beside my bed. I pulled open the drawer and dropped the gun inside. I tossed the clips of silver ammo alongside it.

I shoved the drawer shut and collapsed onto my bed.

It was heaven.

I didn't want to think. I didn't want to do anything but sleep.

I drifted away before anything else bad could happen.

27

I was standing in the middle of the ocean. The water was calm and peaceful. The moon was full and magnificent in the sky above me. Its brilliant light made the ocean gleam silver. The water was black and I couldn't see beneath it. I knew something was there though, just under the surface, just out of sight. It was a great monstrous thing that made my heart flutter, my skin crawl.

I heard a voice scream out in agony.

I spun around and saw him. Kyle was standing there in the middle of the ocean. He was wearing a tuxedo, with black leather gloves on both hands. His hair was slicked back. He looked good. I saw the pistol in his hand. I could hear the leather of his glove crunching as his grip tightened.

I was naked. I looked down and I was stripped bare for the world to see. I was covered in mud, and dirt, and dried blood. The scar running down my abdomen was fresh and bleeding. The gunshot wound in my shoulder was open again and I felt the silver bullet deep inside it. Warm blood trickled down my back. All of my old scars, the pains of my past, were freshly opened.

"Kyle?"

He didn't answer. He raised his gun in one hand and took aim.

"Kyle, wait." My heart was pounding in my chest. I was scared. I was terrified. I knew I deserved this. I knew I was wrong. I knew that I was the monster. Kyle was human. He was the hero. That's how the stories went.

The hero only said one thing to me. "I'm sorry."

He pulled the trigger and the explosion shattered the silence of the ocean.

There was no bullet.

The gunshot rang out and suddenly the water beneath me exploded upward. I started to fall. The ocean was swallowing me whole. I felt the cold water burn my skin like fire as the undertow pulled me down. Lower than the humans. Down to the depths where all monsters go.

That sensation of falling was what woke me.

I opened my eyes and saw warm rays of sunlight shining in through the curtains of my bedroom window. I was facedown on the bed, my heart trying to break through my chest. The dream was still fresh in my mind. It had rattled me.

I hate dreaming. It's part of the reason I don't sleep much. The more I sleep, the more I dream. Sometimes the dreams were memories, flashbacks to times I wanted to forget. Other times they were just nonsense, like the one I'd just had. I don't know which dreams I hate more.

I pushed myself up with my arms to strain to see the alarm clock on my nightstand. It was already ten in the morning and I still felt like shit.

My heart was beating too hard. That dream really shook me up. I couldn't get back to sleep right away. I sat up and swung my legs over the side of the bed. I ran my rough hands over my face, trying to wake up, trying to forget about that dream. It all felt so real, falling back into that ocean.

The sound of someone gently knocking on my bedroom door almost gave me a heart attack. I jumped, sitting there staring at the door.

I remembered Kyle shooting me in the dream.

I hadn't said anything to him. I hadn't told him what happened with the kids. I hadn't apologized for what happened with…Lauren? Did that even happen or was that part of my same twisted dream? I couldn't remember.

I had to apologize to Kyle. He didn't deserve the shit I put him through. I'd make it up to him for being such a pain in the ass.

It took a lot of effort, but I got to my feet and headed for the door.

I'd gotten a little less than four hours of sleep and I was still exhausted. I tried working the kink out of my shoulder. It was still sore, but definitely better than before. I would've probably felt perfect with just two more hours of sleep.

Kyle knocked on my door again softly.

"I'm coming." I started for the doorknob. "I know you're pissed but—"

A gunshot came from the other side of the door and a bullet exploded through just inches from my face. I instinctively dove to the ground. I scrambled on the floor and crouched behind the wall with the door to my left.

I wasn't hit. Yet.

Another few shots rang out. The bullets burst through my door and into the far wall near my bed. Each of the shots would've hit me in the chest, or maybe the head if I'd stayed in front of the door. If Kyle had lost it and was trying to shoot me, then screw apologizing.

The adrenaline was flowing the second I dove for the ground. I stayed crouched there, waiting. Waiting for the son of a bitch on the other side of that door to come through it. I prayed to whoever was listening that it wasn't going to be Kyle opening that door.

Over the sound of my own pulse in my ears, I listened to see how many men were outside of my room. If it were one, easy; two or more, I'd have a problem.

Whatever was in my hall kicked my door in. I watched the door swing and slam into my wall, barely on its hinges.

I waited and watched as the barrel of the black handgun came through the door. The shooter wore black leather gloves and had both hands on his gun. I watched the man's wrists come into view. I made my move.

The adrenaline overpowered the exhaustion. It was fight or flight time and at that moment, there was only surviving. I'd be tired later once I was safe.

I got up and went for the gun with both hands. I slammed the man's hands into the frame of the door one good time using my momentum and weight. A few shots deafened me, but the bullets filled my bed, not me.

I jabbed my fist into the face of the man screaming at me without even looking.

I broke his nose, got him in his eye, and then jabbed him in the throat before he finally took one hand off his gun. I didn't see anyone else in the hall, just the one man who thankfully wasn't Kyle. I grabbed the man's gun and his wrist with both hands again and used all of my weight to hurl us both back into the room. We hit the ground hard, scrambling.

I held onto his wrist to keep the gun off me. I started kicking him in the face as hard as I could. Once, twice, three times, before his hands went limp and I pulled his gun away. I rolled off him and onto my back, instantly aiming the gun at my attacker. He didn't move.

I was breathing heavy, too heavy. My muscles were pumping with blood and adrenaline.

I didn't have time to sit still. I scrambled to my feet. The man was grunting and moaning, barely able to move. His face was a bloodied mess. He was older than Kyle was with short black hair. He was wearing blue jeans and a gray t-shirt stained with his own blood.

I didn't recognize him. Good.

As hard as I could, I stomped my bare foot down onto his left hand. I felt one or two bones break beneath my heel. He cradled it close to him, but I kicked him in the side harder. I liked the sound he made when I did that.

I knelt down and pushed the barrel of his own gun into his sweaty forehead. I hoped the barrel was still hot.

"Who are you?" I hissed.

He was sobbing, cursing, and moaning like an overgrown child.

My hand was shaking. Every inch of me wanted to pull the trigger, but I needed answers. Like how the hell he'd gotten inside my house.

I heard boots pounding on the tile, coming from the front of the house. I got up and ran to the other side of the bed. I crouched down low and waited, trying to control my breathing. You have to stay calm in times like that. It was the only way you'd get out alive. Easier said than done, I know, but I had years of experience.

"Holy shit," a man shouted as he came into my room. He wasn't Kyle either.

"Where'd it go?" the man screamed.

I popped up over the bed and shot without hesitation.

The guy was tall, over six feet. He was fat too. I shot three times before the gun clicked empty. Shit.

My bullets hit their mark. The man's chest took three bullets and he fell backwards, slamming into the wall and sliding down in the corner of my room. He didn't seem to have a gun on him, but he was definitely dead.

I needed another gun.

I dropped the empty one on the bed and ran to the other side to get the Colt Defender out of the nightstand. It was the closest and was already loaded.

As soon as I rounded the bed, the asshole on the floor grabbed my legs and I hit the ground flat on my face. I rolled and started kicking the man in the face again. He couldn't hold onto me for long. I started to crawl on all fours, scrambling for the nearest loaded gun. I was reaching out for the smaller drawer when I felt someone behind me.

A pair of huge hands grabbed me by the legs and dragged me backwards.

I watched the nightstand go out of my reach before I tried rolling over and kicking whoever had grabbed me. The hands let me go and I could only watch as a giant stood over me and kicked me in the side as hard as he could.

Nothing broke, but that doesn't mean it didn't hurt like hell.

I was curled up in the fetal position when the man grabbed hold of the collar of my hoodie and the waist of my jeans. He hefted me up and swung me around, literally throwing me like a sack of heavy meat just waiting to be beaten.

My back hit the edge of my wooden doorframe.

I hit the ground and was inches away from the first man I'd taken down. It was while I lay there on the ground that I got a good look at the third intruder in my home. It couldn't have lasted more than a few seconds, but I watched him turn around and it sent chills down my spine.

He couldn't have been shorter than six and half feet tall and was nothing but solid muscle. It was as if a professional wrestler had come into my home and decided to kick my ass. He was human, all three of the idiots were human, but this guy…he was big. You didn't have to be superhuman to beat a man to death. You just had to be strong and want it bad enough. I didn't know if this guy wanted it bad enough, but he sure as hell looked strong.

Well, I had tried fight, but it was definitely time for flight.

I fought through the pain in my side and scrambled again on all fours out of the room. I was almost on my feet and down the hall when the big guy came storming out of my room after me.

I managed to get up and sprint through the living room. My instincts said the front door was a bad idea so I tried going through the kitchen and out the back patio. I didn't get far. I glanced over my shoulder and saw a pair of arms trying to grab at me.

I dove to the right, jumping over the back of the leather sofa. I rolled onto the ground, trying to get some distance between the poster child for steroids and me.

I got around the coffee table, putting something between him and I. The big guy was on the other side of the sofa, ready to catch me the second he could.

I used the furniture to keep my distance.

"Come on, freak," the man grunted, his long curly blond hair falling in front of his cold gray eyes. He was huge with me on the ground, but now that we were both standing, I really saw how massive he was. He was closer to seven feet tall and had to weigh at least two-ninety. His dark blue shirt looked like it was going to rip and the veins bulging out of his arms and neck seemed ready to burst.

I had to find a way to get around The Incredible Hulk and onto the beach.

"I'm gonna break your legs, you sonuvabitch." The behemoth stalked around the sofa and grabbed the base of my couch. "Come on!"

He lifted the entire sofa up on one side up to his chest before he pushed out with all of his strength. My seven hundred dollar reclining leather sofa stood upright for a moment before toppling over and crashing into my bookcase on the wall.

I looked at him and then at the small coffee table separating us. Shit.

"Get over here." He came for me.

I grabbed whatever I could on the glass coffee table. I hurled the satellite remote at him as hard as I could and he just covered his face and let the cheap plastic hit him in the torso harmlessly. He started to laugh it off.

I grabbed my marble ashtray next. It had to weigh at least three pounds and I got a good grip on it before I tried rushing by the titan.

He tried to tackle me and I hurled the ashtray as hard as I could at his face.

It hit him right in the forehead. He flinched from the pain and that was my chance.

I made a straight line for the back patio. The glass doors were shut and probably locked. In movies, the big action star would've just burst through the glass and got away to safety. In real life, I'd have to pretty much use more strength than I had to break through the glass, and even then, I'd likely get lacerations and bleed to death on my back deck. Oh, how I envy Hollywood.

I tried frantically pulling the doors open. Locked. Of course.

I had just started to flip that tiny damned metal switch up to unlock the door when a pair of arms the size of tiny trees wrapped around me. I felt my back crack all the way up my spine as the big man trying to kill me lifted me up off my feet and away from the door.

I was kicking and screaming, trying to get free, but there was no way in hell I was getting out of that with sheer strength. Not unless the sun decided to set at ten in the morning that day.

Still, I wasn't going down without a fight.

I braced myself and clenched my jaws before I flung my head back. I felt the back of my skull crash into the front of his face.

There was a sharp pain, a steady throbbing, and a few flashes of lights in my vision. The arms squeezing the life out of me squeezed tighter. I shook my pounding head repeatedly for a moment. Ouch.

I listened to the man groan angrily before he spun me around, away from the sliding glass doors and my freedom.

He jumped back and used the momentum to bring us both crushing down onto my small kitchen table. I felt the wood give out beneath us and I hit the ground hard and couldn't breathe.

The man's arms loosened enough for him to try to get me in a chokehold.

I fought against it. I bit his arm and he punched me upside the head. I swung my head around crazily and he jerked my head back by yanking my hair. I kicked, I tried throwing my weight around, but he wasn't letting go. His legs wrapped around mine and he was proving that he was a much better grappler than I'd ever be.

I felt helpless. Scared. It really pissed me off.

The house phone started to ring and it caught us both off guard. We froze for a moment and looked up, listening to the ringing.

We both resumed the struggle at the same time. I couldn't let him pin me, I couldn't let him choke the life out of me.

The phone kept ringing and ringing. I tried taking a hand and grabbing at some of the ruined remains of my kitchen table. I snatched up a long sliver of chipped wood and tried stabbing it into the man's massive arm trying to get around my throat.

I was too slow though. The big guy had the advantage and rolled us both to the side, putting me directly under his weight. One of my hands was pinned under my leg, but I kept trying to get the asshole off me.

It was too late though.

The answering machine clicked to life. I heard the recording of my voice echo through the kitchen.

"Hey, this is me. I'm not here. You know what to do. Here comes the beep," my voice said, followed by the beep right on queue. Kyle always hated when I recorded the answering machine.

I couldn't stop the big guy from getting his arm around my neck and then pulling us both backwards so that he was sitting on the ground and I was lying up against him.

Those two huge legs wrapped around me again to keep me still. The man brought the bend of his arm up into my throat. He started to squeeze, using his other hand to apply even more pressure.

"Kristopher," Abby's voice yelled from the tiny machine in my kitchen.

I tried punching him in the face, slapping, elbowing, but nothing worked. I couldn't breathe.

"Where the hell are you?"

The man chuckled in my ear. "That your bitch?"

I could feel the pressure behind my eyes building and building. I couldn't pass out. I wouldn't. It was all over if I did.

"I called three times last night. You're not answering your phone. Kyle said you'd be out all night. What the hell are you going to do about my car?"

Her car? I had a little bit of a bigger problem to deal with than her car. Like the American Gladiator trying to kill me.

I tried going for his eyes, but he had his face out of my reach.

"You need to call me as soon as you get this. I'm not paying for what you did to my car."

"Say goodbye, freak." The man's voice buzzed through my ears.

I was starting to see flashes of white light. Little sparks that started to float around my kitchen.

I couldn't pass out. I had to get free.

"I'm serious, Kris. Call me. Have a good morning." The phone clicked and there was silence.

Have a good morning? Yeah...okay.

I felt like my face was going to burst, like my head was just going to pop from the pressure. I stared out at the sliding glass windows and the orange glow of sunlight coming in through the blinds.

I don't remember passing out. It just happened. One second the world was there, the next, it was all gone.

28

I heard tires screeching.

My body felt stiff. I was lying on my side, my head hitting the cold metal. I couldn't move my hands or my feet. I felt every bump in the road.

I tried opening my eyes, but they were on fire. I could barely see. The entire world was blurred and hazy. I saw the figures of people sitting in a van. I was on the floor. It was hard to breathe. All I could smell were chemicals and dirt.

"It's waking up," a man said.

"Put it out then," said another.

The van vibrated from footsteps behind me. I couldn't see anyone. I heard the sound of someone loading a gun.

No!

A muffled shot echoed through the van. Something cold and sharp pierced my right shoulder.

Ouch.

Three more sharp stings in my back and everything started to drift away.

29

When I finally came to, I wished I hadn't.

My head hurt more than any hangover I could ever remember having. I felt groggy. I felt like dying. I was sitting upright, my neck hunched forward. I couldn't even open my eyes I was so tired.

What the hell happened to me?

I remembered the big guy in my house, the truck, and the blackness in between. Oh yeah. I knew exactly what happened to me.

I tried to move and handcuffs bit at my wrists and ankles.

That got me awake. My eyes shot open and in that second I knew I was shit out of luck.

The only clothes I had on were my boxer briefs and I was handcuffed to a straight-backed metal chair. Lovely.

I tried wriggling out of the chair to tip it over or stand, but it was bolted to the floor.

I could taste a lot of blood in my mouth, my blood. Of course it was my blood. Why couldn't it ever be someone else's when I needed it?

I looked up and the sunlight pouring in through the skylight overhead blinded me. I winced and tried seeing just where I was. The splotches in my eyes didn't make the shadows any easier to see through. I was in some kind of condemned building. All the lights were turned off and the windows were boarded up. The only light came from the sun overhead that shined down directly on me like a bright golden spotlight.

For once I didn't want to be in the spotlight.

I knew in the back of my head it was only around four o'clock. Great. There was plenty of sunlight left in the day. Plenty of time left to die.

Most people would've started panicking right then.

Me?

Well, I wouldn't necessarily call it "panicking".

I tried using every ounce of my strength to break free. I rocked the chair, flexed and pulled, and tugged until the cuffs felt like they were going to sever my wrists and ankles. It was pointless. I wasn't getting out. Not in the middle of the day. Not while I was mortal.

I screamed as loud as I could. I had to release all of the frustration inside. Considering my predicament, I didn't care if I looked crazy screaming like an animal.

My voice echoed throughout the entire place. I felt the cold cement beneath my feet. I heard a train off in the distance. I tried focusing, tried to keep thinking. I had to. I couldn't lose it, not if I wanted to live.

I started taking in my surroundings. I had to be in some kind of warehouse. If I could hear trains then I still had to be close to the beach. The trains ran through several industrial communities all along the coast, some of which had warehouses built around them. Pompano, that was closest to my house.

But it was four in the afternoon. I'd been out for close to six hours. In six hours they could've driven me as far north as Gainesville.

Shit.

Well, I gave thinking a shot.

I desperately started pulling at the handcuffs again. I had to get out of there. I couldn't let it end like this. Not like this.

"Take it easy there," a man's voice said from behind me.

My heart nearly jumped out of my throat. I tried turning around to see who was behind me, but I couldn't see shit.

"Who are you?" I shouted.

I heard footsteps and watched the man step into my line of sight. I didn't recognize him at all. His hair was dark and cut close to his scalp. With the light shining down on him, the shadows made it hard to make out his face. He was slim though, wearing dark jeans and a brown leather jacket that clung to his narrow figure. He had on white latex gloves. The seven-inch long hunting knife in his hand gleamed in the sunlight. He stalked around me, keeping his distance like a predator circling its prey. His nice pair of boots echoed with every step in the warehouse.

"We had a bet going that you wouldn't make it," the man said casually. I barely heard him. I was focused on the huge knife in his hand.

"You made me fifty dollars just by waking up," he said with a smile. I finally got to see his face and it was a pleasant one. He needed a shave but he looked like the kind of guy who'd buy you a drink at the bar or hold a cab for you, a nice guy.

Yeah, right.

"You're welcome," I said.

He looked me over, his eyes lingering too long on my crotch. Weird. No, weird didn't quite cover it. Scary was a good word.

"You like what you see?"

The man smirked at me and started laughing as if I'd said something funny.

I heard more footsteps behind me, heavier ones.

I was about to look over my shoulder again when a fist caught me in the jaw. My neck whipped forward and some blood flew out of my busted lip. My jaw felt like it was broken. I opened and closed it, running my tongue along my teeth to see if any were missing.

I spat out the fresh wad of blood in my mouth and watched it hit the ground between my feet, thick and heavy like molasses.

Slowly I looked up and watched my next visitor step in front of me. This one I recognized. It was the giant who had wrestled me back in the house. He was rubbing his left fist with his other hand and grinning like a smug prick.

"So the freak's finally up, huh?" The giant's southern drawl was heavier than it had been back at my house when he was trying to kill me.

"Yes it is," Mr. Smiles replied.

"Want me to take care of that?"

"No. It took too long for him to wake up in the first place." The slim man walked closer to me, watching me carefully. I couldn't take my eyes off that knife. He glanced down at it and smirked even more. "It's silver. In case you were wondering."

Of course it was.

I looked up into those creepy, friendly eyes. I didn't like that he thought he had me scared. I might've been, but he ruined it by thinking he had power over me. No one has power over me. No one.

"If you're going to kill me, you should do it before the sun sets."

The big guy laughed. "You ain't gonna last that long."

I never took my eyes off the little one. He stopped just a foot from me, his eyes wandering all over my body. It made my skin crawl, but I did my best not to show it. Being tied to a chair practically naked with a strange man holding a knife is not the most comfortable social situation, but watching him admire my body just made it downright awkward.

He knelt down so that I didn't have to look up at him. I'm comfortable naked, I'm confident enough with what I'm working with to not care if someone sneaks a peak. But right then, I really wished I had on something more than just my underwear. Maybe some pants. Hell, even socks would've made me feel a bit better.

"We know you die just like any other person during the day. We know what happens when the sun sets for your kind." The man never stopped smiling while he talked. My leg was twitching. I wanted to kick that smile right off his face.

I looked into those eyes and saw that they were black, beady little eyes. I glanced one more time at the knife that he held onto lazily in one hand. If they weren't going to kill me, then they wanted something I had.

"What do you want from me?" I asked.

"Blunt sonuvabitch ain't he?" The Hulk asked.

I glanced over at him. "It's a curse."

The man with the knife laughed. "You're not scared of us? Not even a little?"

I looked down at him and shrugged the best I could. "To be honest, yeah I'm scared. But I'm not giving you two fuck-ups anything you want, so that kinda cheers me up a little."

"I guess that means we'll have to torture you." I watched the tiny man lick his lips as he chuckled. "I love torture."

I heard a chair screech on the floor behind me and heels clicking as someone else approached. Great.

"Warren, stop playing with it," a woman urged.

Warren. I looked at the little guy who was staring past me at the newcomer approaching.

I waited this time for the person to walk into my view.

She was wearing heeled black leather boots that came halfway up her calf. My eyes traveled up the tight blue jeans and the curve of her tight, round ass. The jeans stopped lower than most and I saw the tattoo of a small dark raven on her lower back. It stuck out against the short white vest she had that exposed her smooth, tan back and arms. I didn't take my eyes off the tattoo. I had a weakness for tramp stamps.

She turned to face me once she was side-by-side with the big guy. Her hair was almost pure black and shaved on the sides, giving her a Mohawk. The hair on the top of her head was styled and held in place to curve in front of her forehead. Her eyes looked golden in the sunlight overhead.

I looked at the tight, defined muscles of her abdomen. Her perky breasts looked like they were going to spill out of the white sports bra she wore beneath the white vest. I was surprised to see a small black shoulder holster under the outfit. The butt of a handgun stuck out under her left arm. I hadn't seen it right away. I must've been distracted by the tattoo and the rest of her. She didn't try hiding the gun. In fact, I think she wanted me to know it was there.

"Will somebody please turn the lights on?" she shouted. "Fuck the dramatics. I can't see anything in this shit hole."

The lights flared to life and my eyes didn't have to adjust much from the sunlight shining down on me. The long, thin white light fixtures hanging from the ceiling came to life one after the other.

The place was unfinished. The cold cement walls and floor kept the heat low, even with the sun shining in. Steel rafters lined the ceiling with the occasional light hanging down. I was right. I was being held captive in the middle of the day in an abandoned warehouse. There were a few boxes and mattresses here and there from squatters, or maybe, these people. Other than that, the place was just a big, empty, abandoned warehouse.

How cliché.

With the new lighting, I could see that there were more people in the building other than the creep with the knife, the giant, and the vixen. Two men stood on either side of what looked like an emergency exit. One was holding a steel baseball bat while the other was staring at me with a shotgun in his hands.

Behind the giant was the man whose face I had kicked a dozen times. He must've been hiding in the shadows because I hadn't seen him. His face was swollen and a nasty purple and red. His nose was broken and it didn't look like anyone had set it for him. The hand that I'd stomped on was wrapped in an ace bandage.

Seeing him made me feel a little better. I saw what could have been another door outside but it was boarded shut. *That* didn't make me feel better.

"No more wasting time, Phil," the beauty said to the beast beside her.

Phil, the giant, turned to Warren and ordered, "Get me answers, Warren."

"Oh, my pleasure." Warren held up the knife. "I think I'll start with the fingers."

Crap.

"Oh no you won't," the woman said softly.

Whew. I looked up at Warren. "Yeah, no you won't."

The woman smiled at me. "I think there's something else we could chop off that the little Vampire may care about more."

I looked at Warren and weighed my options.

"Alright, take the fingers. I've got ten."

Warren smirked and looked at my genitals again, licking his lips.

"Hey. Focus, buddy. Fingers. That's spreading the pain around. You know, making it last and—"

"Shut up!" the femme fatale screamed.

"Okay…"

"Where are the children you had with you?" she asked me.

Damn. These people were after Lila? "What kids?"

I only saw the gleam of the knife. Warren slashed at my left leg. I felt the blade cut into my shin, but it didn't sting. It felt numb. No pain was always a bad sign. It meant that it was a deep cut.

I fought against my bindings.

"Where are they?" The woman asked again.

"I got rid of them."

"You killed them?" Phil seemed to be genuinely upset. "You mother—"

"Shut up, sweetie," the woman said.

Phil did as he was told.

"What kind of monster would hurt three children?" Warren seemed upset too. It was hard to sympathize though with my blood running down his blade.

I realized then that I was probably the sanest person in the building. That wasn't a good sign.

"I didn't hurt them." My leg was starting to sting where Mr. Psycho had cut me. I could feel blood running down the hairs on my leg.

"We know the little girl's a Psychic. What did you do with her?" the woman asked me again.

They knew Lila was a Psychic? Were these the lunatics that had been chasing them? They didn't look as professional as the men in Tara's memories had, but they could just be some of the members of a larger group. Great. I knew that helping those kids was going to end up getting me in trouble. I was going to be pissed if I died.

Warren leaned forward and laid the knife against my inner thigh. He pressed the tip against me and held it there. I looked down at the blade; it wasn't near any arteries or my penis. I still didn't like it though.

"Where are they?" he asked, his bottom lip quivering from excitement.

I swallowed back my fear and frustration. "They were too much of a threat. I sent them out of my territory. I don't want any trouble from anyone. I just want to be left alone."

The woman smirked and her dark red lipstick reminded me of blood.

Warren sliced my thigh open. This time I felt the sting and I got a good look at the large laceration on my inner thigh. Blood was already swelling out of the open wound and starting to trickle down my leg. It was a nice shallow cut, nothing that would bleed me out.

I couldn't hide my frustration or my anger anymore. I wanted the asshole to stop cutting me. "I'm telling the truth!"

Everyone remained quiet. They all just kept watching me. Like I was some kind of animal.

I ignored Warren and stared over at the lady in white. "This is my territory. I kicked them out because I didn't want whatever trouble was after them."

It was a long shot, but if these people were only after the kids then I might be able to lie and get out of this. It was all I had to go on.

"Listen to me, I don't know why you want the girl, but she's yours. I can tell you where I last saw them, but that's all I can do. If you find them, do whatever you want with them." I did my best to sound sincere. Lying was something I did well.

Warren got to his feet and before I could say anything he cut me across the chest with the knife. I screamed and cursed. He sliced me up two more times, all across my chest. The first two cuts were shallow, but the third he got carried away and the knife sliced deeper than I think he intended. I could feel blood already sliding down my stomach from that one deep gash while the others kept stinging.

He backed away and the woman stepped forward while I was still cursing and screaming.

She put her hands on my forearms and leaned in close to my face. "We aren't after the girl. We're after you."

I was breathing heavy, trying to fight the pain. She was so close that her eyes looked even brighter in the sunlight. I could smell the stench of her breath on my face, the remnants of cigarettes and whiskey.

I didn't know what to do. I thought these people were the ones after the kids, after Lila. But they weren't. Who the hell were they?

The woman shook her head at me and spit in my face. The warm slimy phlegm hit me and it ran down my cheek and under my chin. I couldn't move to wipe it away no matter how bad I wanted to.

I watched her turn and walk back towards Phil, a sway in her walk.

She wasn't attractive anymore. In fact, I wanted to kill her. I had a thing about people spitting in my face and not being able to wipe it off because I was tied down against my will. Call me old-fashioned, but that was grounds for a good old evisceration.

"Well, you have me. What do you want from me?" I tried steadying my voice.

"You said this is your territory." She turned and looked back at me. "We want the locations of any Were, Witch, Wizard, Vampire, or any other God-forsaken freak that's in the area."

I looked at the group and heard Jack's voice in my ear telling me to be careful. I wished I'd listened to the old grizzly.

"You people have been hunting us down." It wasn't a question. "All along the East Coast."

Everyone suddenly became all smiles, proud of some recognition.

Phil smiling was scarier than him chasing me around my house. "We are on God's mission," he said proudly, "to exterminate those who harm his flock."

Warren wiped my blood off his knife on his jeans. "Our brothers on the West Coast are going to do the same. We're starting a revolution."

Oh great. Religious radicals. My favorite.

The girl held out her hand to me and raised it so that I could see the back of her forearm. Right there was a small black tattoo of a Celtic crucifix. Phil pulled down the neck of his shirt and showed me a similar tattoo over his collarbone. Warren rolled up his jacket and showed me a small cross on both his wrists.

Everyone in the entire warehouse had a cross tattoo somewhere on them and that's when it clicked.

I remembered the tattoo on the man who shot me last night. What the hell was going on? Could they have been with the Were and the two men who tried killing me? If they were, how did they find me? Those three were dead and nobody could've followed me home.

My mind was racing. I had to get answers. "It's only you people starting this…"

"…Revolution," Phil finished.

"Right…it's just you people?" The group didn't look very well equipped or large enough to take down Vamps or anything supernatural.

"We're only a small fraction of God's shepherds," the woman said with more dignity than her outfit portrayed.

"What's your name?" I asked her and it caught her off guard.

"Victoria." Her caution couldn't match her confidence. "Victoria Krauss."

I think she meant for me to recognize the name. I didn't.

"Alright." I looked at the three people in front of me that mattered. Warren, Phil, and Victoria. I'd look for their names in the obituaries tomorrow.

"Well, Victoria, I think it's great that you're all for God's will. But I have one question I'd love for you to answer before you all kill me."

"Oh?" she asked.

"It's a simple one, don't worry. You see if you people kill me before I figure it out, it'll drive me nuts. I just *have* to know. How did you find me?"

It was the burning question of the day. No one in the warehouse was anything, but human. No magic, no psychic talent, nothing but whatever God gave them, which didn't look like much.

"You talk more than other Vamps," Phil stated dryly.

"I hear that a lot."

"Dennis," Victoria called out.

The man by the exit with the steel bat nodded and turned for the door. He stepped out and the sunlight splashed into the warehouse for a moment before the door slammed shut.

"You want to know how we found you?" Victoria asked.

"Yeah. I *really* do."

Victoria smirked. "It's simple. My expertise is finding Vampires. The trick is, you find the Vampire, and you find where all the other vermin are hiding."

Made sense so far. I couldn't argue with logic.

The door opened again and Dennis led two more people into the warehouse.

Victoria's voice sounded far away as I tried seeing just who the two were. "It's not usually this easy. But you seem to have more enemies than friends...Kristopher."

It was the first time I wasn't referred to as "it" or "freak". I glanced at Victoria only to catch her smile before I finally saw the two people they'd brought into the warehouse.

The first was Lauren Millar or Alicia or whatever she called herself. The second I saw that familiar face my blood ran cold.

The next person made my skin start to burn. My throat closed and my heart stopped. I knew the second newcomer too. I knew him very well.

How could I ever forget my human servant?

30

Kyle.

I couldn't believe it. They got him too. From what I could, tell he looked okay. There was no blood on his khaki pants and black button-down shirt. The shirt was open and the wife beater beneath it was drenched in sweat, but that was all. The wound on his forehead looked bruised, but that was from the Were tossing him on the beach. I couldn't see any new injuries. It didn't make me any less pissed.

The anger started to burn in my chest. I was an idiot. I got careless. I'd forgotten all about Kyle. If these morons had managed to get in the house, I should've known they would have gotten him too. I bit my lower lip and watched Kyle follow the thug with the bat over to us. That girl was right by him, Lauren or Alicia, whatever her name was.

She had met Kyle and told him her name was Alicia. She played him to get to me. Lauren, somehow she had found out who and what I was and used Kyle to get to me. That was the only thing that made sense.

Kyle wouldn't look me in the eyes. He was looking at everyone except me. Why wasn't he looking at me?

I just needed him to look me in the eyes so I could promise him that I'd get us out of here. Kyle was *my* human servant, *my* responsibility. It was an accident he even got swept up in my world. He didn't deserve to die just because I got caught. He was a pain in the ass but he was *my* pain in the ass.

I hadn't even thought about him when I woke up. I hadn't considered what it meant for him if I was killed. Was I really so selfish? If I died, he died. Wasn't that important enough to remember?

I wasn't much of a master, but I couldn't let Kyle down. I couldn't let him die with me.

I took that rush of anger and directed it at my captors. What else could I do? Blame myself? It wouldn't solve anything. If I lived, I'd do that later.

I looked at the girl I knew as Lauren and I wished I were the one with the knife. I'm a little territorial when it comes to my slave. I didn't see her and think food. I saw her and thought, gee, I really want to stab her.

I've been around long enough to know when I've been played.

Lauren, that's what she said her name was. I looked at her then and the craving for her blood was gone. She wasn't even as beautiful as she had been that other night. I could barely even remember what she tasted like. It felt like a lifetime ago, a distant dream that never even happened.

"A few familiar faces," Victoria said as tenderly as a rattlesnake.

Kyle still wasn't looking at me so I didn't waste breath on him. Instead, I looked at Lauren. So healthy, so clean with her black hair and smooth pale skin. The pair of jeans she had on hugged her long slender legs and tight thighs. Her black tank top showed those nice firm breasts I remembered so well. She looked at me and she smirked as if she knew some big joke that I didn't. As if I was the fool.

It made me want to kill her a little more.

"Let him go." I tried being direct. I looked straight at Victoria. She shouldn't have dragged Kyle into this.

Phil chuckled at that. "You must be dumber than all shit, freak. We ain't doin' nothin' for nothin'."

Hillbilly logic. Can't argue with that. I caught Lauren looking at me and I got all kinds of curious. "So you're how they found me?"

Lauren didn't look like she wanted to be the center of attention.

Victoria answered my question. "She's the bait."

The bait? I looked at Victoria who had her arms crossed, her breast threatening to spill out of that top a little more.

I turned to Kyle. He still wasn't looking at me.

"Kyle, did your friend Alicia tell you that we met before?" I turned and looked at said two-timing slut, "Oh, I'm sorry, is it Alicia or Lauren?"

Lauren looked at Kyle and I didn't like what I saw. The girl cared about Kyle.

"You just don't get it do you, freak?" Phil asked.

Warren sighed. "I don't think it does."

Phil was all smiles. "Course not. It ain't smart enough."

I kept my anger in check and looked at Kyle. The idiot still wouldn't look at me. I wanted to make sure he knew that I wasn't done yet, that until they killed me there was still a chance I could get us both out of there alive.

I could live with Kyle thinking that I didn't care about him. He could hate me all he wanted, that didn't matter. But I would not let him think I failed him.

"Kyle," my anger deepened my voice, "don't worry. I'll get us out of this."

Victoria started to laugh and then Phil. Even Warren was chuckling, his wrist up to his mouth to hide the mocking laugh.

"Did I say something funny?"

Kyle wasn't laughing. His jaw was clenched so tight that I could see the muscles working in his thin face.

Victoria walked up to Kyle and put a hand gently on his shoulders. That single touch made Kyle shudder a bit. If she hurt him, I'd break her wrist.

"You're slower than the other Vamps we've killed," she said.

"Why's that?"

Victoria's ruby lips curved into a wicked smile. "If you'll notice, Mr. Brody here isn't handcuffed to a chair and bleeding now is he?"

Kyle looked up then. He looked me dead in the eyes.

Victoria's voice sounded far away in my head as I stared back at my human servant. "Who do you think let us in your house?"

In that instant, it hit me. It hit me so hard I forgot how to breathe. I wasn't thinking, I wasn't aware of anything other than the look in Kyle's soft blue eyes. Betrayal always brought out the color in people's eyes.

"You fucking idiot." The words slipped out. "What the hell did you do?"

Victoria ran her hand along Kyle's jaw. He didn't even flinch. I don't think he ever once looked me in the eyes that long. It was as if I were looking at a stranger.

"As I said before, we usually have a simple plan." Victoria looked at my servant as if he were a piece of meat.

Phil chuckled. "We set up the bait."

I turned to Lauren.

"We shoot her up with a nice tonic and some pheromones that draws in your kind," Phil said. "She's the lure. She goes on about her day and eventually any Vampire who comes close enough can't help it. They're drawn to her and they just gotta feed."

I remembered that night. Seeing her at The Hornet. How incredible she looked. How strongly I was attracted to her. I remember how amazing she tasted. How alive. I should've known something was wrong. I should've been smarter.

"Usually the Vampires can't help themselves once they get a taste of our luscious fruit." Warren smirked at Lauren. "See, it drives them insane. They go back to feed the next night, wanting to keep her around. Usually, by the third day they're craving it so much they come looking for her in broad daylight. They don't even care whether they're mortal or not, they just have to get more of that delicious blood. You must be strong to have resisted."

Strong wasn't the word that came to my mind. More like sidetracked with Tara, Lila, and Ben falling into my lap.

Victoria was running her fingers up and down Kyle's shoulder. "Kyle was a blessing from the Lord. He made it even easier to get to you. You see, we drugged you like the others, he kept an eye on you, and let us in the house when the sun's up and you're just like everybody else."

I couldn't believe it. None of it made any sense. I looked at Kyle, really looked at him, and wondered how he could do this to me. Why he would do it. How he could betray me to a bunch of lunatics.

"Don't look at me like that," Kyle said through his teeth.

Don't look at him? He was handing me over to people who were going to kill me and he didn't want me to look at him? Why? Because he couldn't man up and deal with the choice he'd made? Fuck him.

"You're an idiot."

"You ruined my life!" Kyle screamed at me, stepping forward out of Victoria's reach. "You know you did!"

I looked up at him and felt that anger starting to sear through the numbness in my chest like a scolding wave. I tried pushing it back.

"I didn't ruin your life. I tried giving you one."

"Give? You made me your slave. Jesus Christ, you threatened me and forced me to live with you."

"You think I wanted you hanging around? I was stuck with you. What choice did I have? Kill you?"

Kyle wouldn't listen to me.

"I gave you money to spend, a car to drive, a house to live in. I gave you freedom. You just never took it."

"I didn't want it!" I thought Kyle was going to run at me but he didn't. "I never asked for you, or your money, or any of it. You treat me like shit. All you ever did for me was ruin my life."

"What do you think they're going to do with me, Kyle?" I asked.

"Get rid of you." Kyle's voice wavered. "They're going to give me my life back."

"Kyle, listen to me." I was barely in control of my frustration. "They're going to kill me. If I die, you die. Remember?"

Kyle shook his head, "No."

"Yes."

"No!"

It was like looking at a stranger. I didn't recognize the person in Kyle's body. He really believed what he was saying.

"They know how to sever our bond." Kyle was smiling but his eyes looked miserable. "I want my old life back, Kris. That's all I want."

"They're screwing you, kid," I told him. "You got played."

"No." Kyle spun around and looked at Phil and Victoria, and Lauren and Warren. They all were staring at me, none of them smiling or laughing anymore.

"It's true, right?" Kyle asked.

I watched Lauren reach out for Kyle's hand and he took it. She turned to Victoria. It looked like Lauren wanted to know the same thing.

Victoria looked at the couple, amused. "We keep our promises, Kyle. The Lord has ways of releasing you from your curse."

Lauren turned back to Kyle and squeezed his hand tighter. The look in Kyle's eyes said it all, he believed in Lauren. He believed in her more than he did anyone else. Was that love? Was that what I'd never experienced? True, blinding love?

I had to laugh. What else could I do? I started laughing at how absurd it all was.

"What the hell you laughin' at?" Phil yelled.

It was a lost cause. Kyle sold me out because I'd ruined his life. I couldn't blame him for that. I just wished I'd noticed it sooner. I'd been so caught up in my own life, I forgot about the one person I was in charge of. We were both going to die because of his stupidity and my recklessness.

There was no reason to play it safe. No reason to give a damn. If this was it, then this was it. I didn't see a way out. So I continued to laugh. Life's funny isn't it? It's just a game I thought I knew how to play. Too bad it was starting to look like game over.

Phil headed for me, pissed. "I said, why you laughing?"

I shook my head and quieted down enough to talk. "Sorry, I just can't believe this is how I'm going to die. You people are idiots."

"Shut your mouth," Phil warned.

Lauren looked disgusted. "You're nothing but a monster. You understand that? You kill innocent people. You ruin good people's lives by making them your slaves. But you don't even care. How could you? You don't even have a soul."

I smiled then and it made Lauren nervous. "Lady, my soul's fine. It's my conscience that's a little iffy."

Lauren stared at me as if I was a cockroach that needed squashing.

I decided if I was going to die, I wanted answers. I looked to Kyle. "So what? You contacted these people?"

Kyle swallowed as if he were unsure of what to say.

"Answer me!"

"I found him," Lauren said. "I knew Kyle from high school. We kept in touch over the years. I wanted to see him and it had nothing to do with my work."

"Cute."

"Shut up, Kris," Kyle snapped. "Alicia, you don't have to tell him anything. He doesn't even really care."

"Alicia?" I was beyond frustrated. "Why do you keep calling her that, Kyle? Her real name is Lauren. Lauren Millar."

Kyle looked at me like I was the crazy one. "Her name's Alicia Millar, Kris."

I looked at Lauren/Alicia and it didn't make sense. "You told me when I fed from you your name was Lauren."

"I lied," Alicia said. "Part of the cocktail they give me that lures you freaks in helps me resist some of your mind tricks."

"That's not possible."

"It is," Victoria replied.

I wasn't an expert but I didn't know any drug or chemical that could do that to a Vampire. If I lived, I'd have to check it out.

I looked to Alicia. "You told them about me, Kyle?"

Kyle glanced at the strangers in the room.

Phil gave Kyle a dirty look. "We asked around at a few clubs down near the beach if there were any Vamps or Were's they knew about for the big haul. Couldn't get anyone to tell us anything. We left Alicia there at some shithole of a club to lure any Vamp that walked in. You."

"The Hornet…" I couldn't believe it. Gary had called about people asking questions and it was Phil and these lunatics. I had just missed them. If I had only found them that night, I could've prevented everything.

"I still don't get it. If you didn't know what she was doing down here, why did you even tell her about me, Kyle?"

"He didn't," Alicia answered. "Kyle and I ran into each other at a coffee shop last week. One of our brothers smelled Vampire on him."

Smelled?

That's when it clicked.

"The Werepanther?"

Victoria and Phil shared a smile that made me want to vomit.

The entire day I thought the Were was after Lila. I thought those men were there to get the girl and kill anyone in their way. I thought a lot of things that all turned out to be wrong.

"How did you get the Were to listen to you?" I asked Warren coldly.

"Brian," Warren said sharply. He had the knife firm in his grip. "His name was Brian."

"So you know I killed him?" I asked. The look in Warren's eyes cheered me up a bit. "Him and the two guys driving him around?"

Warren's fingers curled into tight fists.

"We know," Phil answered. "If we didn't want nothin' from you, we woulda shot your head off back at your house."

"They attacked me. It was self-defense."

"Brian was trying to rescue the children." Victoria was glaring at me. "He tracked Kyle's scent and found you hunting the children on the beach. He went after them but the excitement was too much. He had trouble controlling his instincts sometimes."

"How'd you control him though?" I asked again. "No Were would help people like you kill his own kind."

"Brian was one of us, not one of you monsters." Warren was showing emotion for the first time all day. That stupid smile was gone and I think I liked him more with it.

"Brian was infected just over a year ago on a hunt." Victoria glanced at Warren, worried.

"He wanted to keep fighting for the cause. He got control of his little problem and was just that much better at huntin'." Phil shrugged. "He was strong and fast as all hell, but you wouldn't catch me becoming like one of you freaks."

"He's a good soldier." Warren gave a cold hard look at Phil. The big man just shrugged it off.

"Was," I corrected. "He *was* a good soldier. He's dead now…just throwing that out there."

That brought everyone's attention to me. I saw Warren's eye start to twitch. I don't think he was attracted to me very much anymore.

Warren took a step towards me, his knife at the ready.

"Warren!" Victoria shouted.

The man stopped, but he looked feral.

Victoria seemed impressed. "Enough of the bullshit. We're wasting time. I want answers. Now."

I looked at the Wicked Bitch of the East and wondered if she really thought she had any leverage on me. She already had my human servant and he was working with them. She didn't have a single thing that would make me betray any of the people I trusted.

"How many other Vampires live in your territory?" Victoria asked.

I tried not to smirk. Good. These people didn't know that Vampires didn't share territories these days. The less they knew, the better.

When I didn't respond Victoria nodded and Warren covered the short distance between us.

"Wait," I started to say but the man slashed out with the knife and sliced me on my right shoulder. I hissed and struggled against the handcuffs as the sharp stinging pain struck. I looked down at my shoulder and saw blood starting to slide down my arm. Shit. It was deep enough that it might even need stitches.

Victoria continued like nothing had happened. "How many Weres live in the territory?"

I looked up at Warren and he had that smug smile on his face again.

"Fuck you," I whispered to him.

The human slowly laid the knife on my left shoulder, the blade pressing down on my trapezium. I clenched my teeth and fought the urge to move as he pulled back on the knife with one quick motion. The blade cut into me and might've nicked my collarbone. I closed my eyes and fought the fire burning from the fresh wound. I heard the sizzling and popping in my ears from the silver blade cutting deep into my flesh. It always reminded me of Peroxide in an open wound. Only the pain is about a trillion times worse.

Warren was nothing but smiles as he stood there waiting to cut me again.

I looked past him to Kyle and saw that he couldn't bring himself to watch. The kid was even a lousy Judas.

Phil looked amused and Alicia's eyes were so wide I thought she was in a trance. Victoria stood there with her arms crossed and a smile on her face. She was thrilled. This was her job and she enjoyed it.

I looked at Victoria and tried lifting my arm but the cuffs prevented it.

"Do you have something to say?" she asked.

I felt the pain in my shoulder subsiding. I took a deep breath.

"No, I just really want to give you the finger, but...these damned cuffs. Would you settle for a 'fuck you'?"

Warren looked back at Victoria, waiting for permission like a loyal knife-wielding dog. I watched her nod.

Uh oh.

"No, now hold on a sec," I said frantically.

Warren knelt down in front of me and he held the blade in front of him like an oversized scalpel. He looked down at my crotch and smirked at me.

"Oh, hell no." I tried moving with everything I had, but it was useless.

Warren looked up at me. "Please...don't tell her anything."

He pressed the tip of the knife against my chest and slowly started sliding that cool blade down my body. He wasn't cutting me, but the chilling silver tip of the blade brushed along my skin going down and down, closer and closer to my groin.

For a second I thought about saying something, anything, but no words were coming to mind. All I could think about was what it would be like to be penisless and how badly I didn't want to find out.

"Tell them about Jack!" Kyle shouted.

Warren stopped with the tip of the knife at the middle of my stomach.

I looked over the man's head at Kyle and tried thinking about what he'd just said. It didn't register at first.

"Who's Jack?" Victoria asked.

Shit. "Kyle, don't you even think about it. You understand me?"

"Who is Jack?" Victoria asked again, the anger seeping into her voice.

Kyle ignored me and turned to her. "He's a Were, I think. He owns some bar. He's Kris' partner."

"Write this down," Victoria said to Alicia.

I watched Alicia reach into her back pocket and pull out an iPhone. She started tapping the screen. I knew she was taking down information, but what the hell happened to pen and paper?

"I thought he didn't tell you much?" Phil asked Kyle.

Kyle was sweating, but he was keeping his composure up. I would've been proud if my life wasn't the one he was killing. "He doesn't."

Phil scoffed and turned to me. "For a three-hundred-year-old Vampire, you ain't got a lot of friends."

I tried not to laugh on account of the knife in front of me, but I couldn't help it.

"What now?" Phil's temper flared.

I couldn't believe it. "Kyle, guess what?"

Kyle was nervous. Good. "What?"

"I'm forty-two, dumbass, not three-hundred. I've only been a Vampire for the last twenty-three years."

Kyle's eyes got a little wider and it made me laugh a little harder. "Jesus. You don't know a damn thing, Kyle. Not a goddamn thing."

Phil looked at Kyle like he didn't trust him. I couldn't blame the big guy. My trust in Kyle was shot to shit too.

"What else do you think you know?" Victoria asked Kyle.

Kyle looked at me and I knew the name that was forming on the tip of his tongue. The most recent person he knew of with supernatural abilities was Abby. If he dragged her into this…I didn't even want to think what I'd do to him.

He seemed to see the anger in my eyes or feel my emotions right then because he got paler. He shook his head slowly. "I don't know anything else."

"Well, Jack's better than nothing." Victoria turned back to me. "Will you elaborate on this, Jack person? If nothing else we'll get a Vampire and a Were out of this trip."

I felt the tip of the knife poke me and I looked down into Warren's deep brown eyes. He was waiting, waiting for a reason to cut me where he really wanted to cut me.

I didn't have many friends. I don't even call most of the people I knew 'friends' because to be my friend meant that I was bound to you with loyalty. Back in my day, friends were people that you loved and who loved you back. People that had your back no matter how much trouble you were in. I haven't had many friends my whole life. Jack was someone I called my friend though. I would choose torture and death over selling him out any day. I was confident he'd do the same.

I looked down at the knife and wished I were a little more selfish. But even if I gave them whatever they wanted, they weren't going to let me live. I was in a lose-lose situation and I didn't plan on dragging anyone down with me. My name wasn't Kyle.

I leaned forward in the chair as close to Warren as I could get, the knife pressing a bit more into my skin. He looked up at me like an expectant dog.

"You should kill me now…because if you don't, I'm going to kill every single one of you." I saw the fear starting to swell up in Warren's eyes, the uncertainty. "Starting with you."

Warren licked his lips nervously again and looked back over his shoulder.

Everyone was watching us. They all heard me.

Victoria stared at me for a good long while.

"What do I do?" Warren asked.

"Shut up," she hissed. "I'm thinking."

Surprise there.

After the longest couple of seconds in my life, Victoria let out the breath she'd been holding.

"I think we can get him to talk." She sounded confident. "Cut it off."

"Done," Warren said, his breath shaky.

I closed my eyes and leaned my head back in the chair. I looked up at the sunlight shining down on me and felt the heat on my face. That was it. Game over.

I waited for the pain. I went into that cool, hard place inside myself that I'd learned to withdraw into. It kept me safe. It made me numb. Still, I knew nothing would keep me safe from the pain that was coming.

I felt the knife slowly start its descent again. The cold blade slid over my stomach. Warren's hand pulled at my briefs and I felt the air as he exposed me. The tip of the blade kept going lower.

I shut my eyes so tight and held my breath.

Here we go.

I heard a loud popping noise, as if the air had been sucked out of the room. The knife didn't cut me. I didn't even feel it on my skin.

I opened my eyes. A dark cloud of smoke started to consume the skylight overhead, smothering the sunlight. In a matter of heartbeats, the warehouse was engulfed in total darkness.

That wasn't a good thing.

My dick was still attached though.

That was a good thing.

31

I don't want to say that I was afraid. Alright, maybe I was a little worked up about someone trying to cut my manhood off, but as I sat up and looked around in the total darkness, fear took on a whole new meaning.

My heart was pounding. And I mean pounding. It felt like it was going to burst any second. I was shivering uncontrollably. I broke out in a cold sweat and it was as if someone had dipped me in a batch of terror and let me stew. I couldn't see anything. The shadow that had flooded the warehouse was total darkness.

I heard screaming, not only inside my head but in the warehouse too. I heard Warren drop his knife and scream wordless, violent screams of sheer horror. Alicia and Victoria's high-pitched shrieks and Phil's deep bellowing and moaning flooded my ears.

It was suddenly cold, too cold. My breath was shaky and I was afraid. Afraid of what was happening, afraid of why I was there. I was afraid of everything and nothing and then I realized it. I was afraid simply because I was afraid.

I could feel the dark energy in the air like a cool fire spreading along my skin. My mind started to rationalize my fear. I dissected the terror that had started to choke the life out of me. I started to see the dark void around me and knew it wasn't real. I knew there was nothing to be afraid of, but still, that fear tightened around my throat and choked me.

It was all a spell. I knew it. I could feel it in my bones.

Vampires are naturally resistant to most spells. This one was so strong that it slipped past my barriers and was affecting me. I was getting a lesser version of the spell than everyone else in the warehouse.

It made me almost feel sorry for the humans trying to kill me. Almost.

I could feel the witchcraft flooding the building. It was familiar.

I tried moving, but I was still cuffed to the chair. I heard people running around, crazily screaming, and crying.

"Help me!" I heard one of the men guarding the door scream.

Victoria was shrieking, "God! Jesus!"

I heard footsteps running towards me and felt massive hands on my shoulders. The strength in those hands was incredible and the fingers dug into my fresh cuts. I screamed because I knew who it was.

"Stop it!" Phil's rancid, sour breath was hot on my face as he screamed at me at the top of his lungs.

He was so close and I still couldn't see him through the darkness. I don't even know how he found me.

One hand unlatched from around my shoulder and a second later a fist hit me in the face. My stiff neck cracked from the blow. A hand wrapped around my throat and started to choke the life out of me.

I couldn't scream, couldn't breathe. I was more afraid of Phil strangling me than the spell. I couldn't do anything to stop him with my hands still cuffed.

It happened fast. One moment there was a hand around my throat and Phil was crying and screaming nonsense and then, nothing.

Everyone stopped screaming and moving. The only sound I heard was my pulse in my ears. I gasped, trying to get in as much oxygen as I could. I wanted to rub my throat, but I still couldn't move. It hurt to swallow and each gulp of air was a painful gasp. A few seconds longer and Phil would've crushed my windpipe.

The darkness started to dissipate. The cloud of smoke became less dense. I started to make out figures on the floor in front of me, bodies littered amidst the dark fog. I saw a huge mound at my feet and knew it was Phil. My eyes were watering, but I forced them to stay open.

Only one figure remained standing in the building.

The person was wearing a long dark coat that nearly touched the floor. It flapped wildly, flailing from the cool supernatural power pouring outward. I would've thought the dark silhouette was Death himself if not for that familiar presence.

My heart and senses knew it was Abby before my eyes could catch up.

The darkness was almost completely gone and sunlight shone down from the skylight above me again.

I looked at Abby standing in front of the entrance to the warehouse. The coat she wore was black leather with shades of scarlet. The sleeves were cut off and it fit her like an unfinished cloak. I noticed her dark crimson tank top and the dark leather pants made from the same material as the coat. Silver charms and bracelets were wrapped around her wrists and a long necklace with strange silver artifacts hung between her breasts. She looked wicked, like a furious dark Goddess seeking revenge.

I'd never been happier to see a Witch.

I tried to speak, but I couldn't. My throat just wouldn't work. It felt bruised and sore. I hoped that Phil hadn't done serious damage. I could breathe, but I wanted to scream.

Abby's leather boots clicked on the cement floor as she hurried towards me. "Kris," her voice cracked a little. "Kris, I'm here."

I looked at the men and women who had caught me and they were all on the floor curled into the fetal position, sobbing and whimpering like children. I looked at Victoria and she was frantically talking to herself. She was praying as hard as she could, praying and praying…for all the good it would do her. The air around each of the humans was dark. A gray cloud hovered around them. Abby had kept the spell concentrated around them individually. She was better than I thought.

I caught movement and noticed Kyle trying to get to his feet. He didn't have the dark veil around him, but he looked shaken up. He must've felt the spell too. Good. The only problem was that he didn't have the spell around him like the others because as far as Abby was concerned he was my servant, one of the team.

Shit.

I tried to say something, anything, but my throat just wheezed and felt too bruised to work.

"Kris," Abby knelt down in front of me, examining the fresh cuts all over me. "What did they do to you?"

Normally being half-naked and handcuffed to a chair in front of Abby was a dream come true, but right then all I wanted was to shout at her. She had her back to the enemy.

Abby turned and Kyle was getting to his feet, wiping his mouth on the back of his hand and staring at her with an unsure, cautious look in his eyes.

"I'm going to break the cuffs, you help me carry him out," Abby ordered Kyle.

I tried shouting. "Ab—"

I started to cough uncontrollably. My throat was too tight and rough. It just wouldn't work. Dammit!

Abby looked at me and I had all the time in the world to watch Kyle scramble for the gun lying next to Victoria. She must've taken it out, to shoot at God knows what, and dropped it when the panic struck.

Kyle scooped the gun up and aimed at Abby's back.

"Kyle," I managed to cough.

Abby turned slowly and saw the barrel of the gun pointed at her chest. "What are you doing?"

Kyle was shaking, his arms trembling. The safety was off and he held the gun with both hands.

"Kyle?" Abby shook her head, the betrayal setting in.

"Don't," Kyle warned her. "Don't move or I swear to God I'll shoot."

Abby kept her hands at her side. She looked back at me and Kyle took a step closer to her.

"Stop!" he screamed. "Turn it off."

"What?" Abby was stalling, trying to think. I hoped she had a plan.

Kyle took a step closer to her and steadied his arms, aiming for her beautiful face. "Whatever you're doing to them. Turn it off!"

The veil around the maniacs started to disappear and I felt Abby's power seep out of the warehouse.

Shit. I couldn't just sit there and watch Abby die and Kyle get played. He was being an idiot because he thought he'd get his life back. He was going to get everyone killed. I couldn't just sit there and let that happen.

Phil got to his feet first, barely able to stand. He looked at Abby and his face turned bright red with rage. Victoria and Warren got up, but Alicia and the man whose face I'd broken stayed sitting on the floor looking terrified.

I glanced to the door and saw that thankfully, the man with the shotgun wasn't getting up. He was alive, but Abby had knocked him out or made him faint with that spell.

While still looking at the man by the door, I caught movement out of the corner of my eye. I looked forward just as Phil charged at Abby and backhanded her across the face as hard as he could.

Abby fell to the ground, raising her hand protectively. That cool aura around her flared for a moment, but she cut it off. She just looked up at Phil, the side of her face already red.

I knew in that moment I was going to kill Phil if it was the last thing I did.

"You fuckin' bitch!" Phil was spitting as he shouted down at her. His eyes were bright red and glossy. Abby's spell had made him so terrified that he'd cried.

I watched him go for her again. He tried to grab her by the hair but Victoria screamed, "No!"

Phil and everyone turned to look at Victoria. Her mascara was running down her cheeks. She looked even more insane. "Don't touch her. She's a Witch."

Phil had to force himself not to go for Abby again. He looked down at her and spat on her. The disgusting wad of phlegm trickled down the side of Abby's face. She wiped the spit off without even batting an eye.

"Dirty little bitch." Phil turned towards me, a hulking figure of testosterone. He looked at me and the only thing I could think about was ripping him in half.

"She is a Witch," Kyle warned. "A strong one."

Victoria looked Abby over.

"A Vampire and a Witch, Vicki," Phil said through his rage. "I say it's enough."

Victoria seemed to think about that. She looked sad, lost in thought. "It's never enough."

"I agree with Philip," Warren said, picking his knife up off the floor. He seemed the most composed. "We're losing daylight. It's time to finish up here."

I closed my eyes and reached out with that part of my senses that always let me tell what time it was. I could feel the sun in the sky. It was closer to five, but that was it. It was too early, too early to live.

Abby turned back to me. I stared into those eyes and wanted her to do something. She used to be a protector; she used to fight to keep her coven safe. I'd never seen her fight before, but she'd told me stories. Combat magic was tough. It took a level of concentration and willpower that few had in them. According to Jack, Abby had been one of the best, one of the most dangerous Witches in the country. I needed *that* Witch now, not the pacifist she'd become.

I watched her eyes grow cold and stubborn. She looked away from me. She knew what I wanted. She knew she couldn't do it.

I would do anything to stay alive, anything. I'd fight to the death if I had to and Abby used to be like that. But she was broken. She refused to kill or even fight back. I couldn't understand it. Abby was going to get herself killed if she didn't do something soon. She was going to let us both die.

I fought against the cuffs. My skin was raw and sore from trying to get out. I looked down at my wrist. It was bleeding from the struggle.

"Victoria." Warren's voice carried through the warehouse. "It will have to be enough."

I looked at Victoria and her eyes looked different. She looked far off, as if she were in some distant place other than the shitty warehouse. I watched her slowly drift back to us.

"Fine."

"Thank God," Phil said. He walked over to the thug named Dennis and snatched the metal bat from his grip. He held it at his side and looked from Abby to me. "Which one should I kill first?"

"Just shoot them," Victoria said.

Phil just shook his head, staring at me like a hungry wolf. "Hell no. I want to enjoy this."

Warren put his knife away in a sheath around his waist.

"Maybe the bitch Witch first." Phil smiled and I didn't like the look in his eyes as he stared at Abby.

I couldn't take it anymore.

"Don't!"

Everyone stared at me, even Kyle who still had the gun aimed at Abby.

My throat was hoarse and it hurt to talk, but it didn't matter. Nothing mattered.

"You listen to me. You all better kill me right now because I swear to whatever God you think exists that I will kill *everyone* in this room if you touch her."

Phil smiled at that, but everyone else in my line of sight looked at me and didn't find it funny. On some level, they could feel how much I meant it. They were all smarter than Phil.

The big man gave me the finger and headed towards Abby.

I tried calling my powers, tried forcing them out, but it was too early. They were like a dream I couldn't remember, a distant thought too far away to grab hold of. It was like trying to catch smoke.

The cuffs cut into my wrists and ankles as I fought with every ounce of strength I had to get free. My veins felt like they were going to burst and my blood was fire.

"Abby!" I begged. "Abby, do something!"

Abby got to her feet slowly and Kyle followed her with the gun. Phil stopped walking towards her and hesitated.

I thought that maybe I'd gotten through to her, that maybe she was going to get me out and keep these people from killing us.

I felt the air around Abby start to grow dense with her rising spiritual aura. She was going to use a spell, and it felt strong.

I held my breath; no one else could feel the magic in the air coming off Abby. They were only human. Kyle might've felt it through his ties with me, but he still had the gun aimed at her.

Come on, Abby. Do it. Do it!

Like a great torch igniting, the energy in the room flared and then disappeared. I felt that power snuff out, my hopes gone with it.

Abby turned back to me with tears in her eyes.

"I'm sorry," she whispered.

Phil closed the gap between them and I watched him raise the bat over his head. I was going to have to watch him crack Abby's skull open. I was going to watch Abby die and there was nothing I could do.

Phil brought the bat down.

Abby snapped her head back towards him. Her power flared to life like an eruption and the steel bat exploded into a cloud of dust in Phil's hands.

Two things happened then at the same time.

The handcuff around my left wrist shattered to pieces and a gunshot rang through my ears.

I screamed louder than the gunshot.

32

I watched the blood spray out of Abby's back. She fell and her head smacked onto the cold cement floor. I tried reaching for her with my only free hand, as if somehow I could've stretched the three yards between us to grab her.

Kyle stood there. He couldn't take his eyes off the horror he'd done.

I looked at the man I'd lived with for the last year and a half and something inside of me broke. I felt the anger that had gotten me through the first fifteen years of my immortal life come burning through me.

I felt all of that rage and hatred deep down inside of me rush to the surface. It clawed, and climbed, and snarled its way up out of the depths of my soul. I didn't do it on purpose. I wouldn't have willingly lost control. None of that mattered though. Nothing mattered right then other than killing.

I've never called my powers out so early. I knew what it was. I knew it was wrong, but I didn't give a damn. It crashed through me like a tidal wave, unstoppable, pure. I screamed, no, I roared, and I could feel the real terror seep into every one of the souls standing around me.

My senses spiked drastically. My body jolted with a surge of energy that couldn't be contained. My immortality was a living, breathing force that I couldn't control, couldn't tame. I didn't want to tame it. I craved blood. I craved it unlike anything I've ever wanted in my life.

A voice inside my head told me this was bad, to focus, to get in control, but that voice was nothing compared to my instincts. There was no wrong, no right, no good or evil, just the hunger, just the craving.

The world couldn't stop me.

There was so much time and so many ways to kill.

I didn't even feel the handcuffs break as I lunged out of my seat. I went for the first person I could get to…Phil.

I rushed into him, grabbed the side of his face in one hand, and lifted him off his feet. I slammed his head down into the cement floor with all my strength. The ground cracked and blood, and bone, and brain burst into the air. I felt it all in my hand and reveled in it.

Everyone was trying to move, but they couldn't move fast enough to save their lives.

I lunged at the man whose nose I'd broken at my house. He was trying to go for the gun in his shoulder holster with his good hand. I grabbed his wrist and felt it shatter like brittle sticks between my fingers. I held onto his wrist and throat as I spun around and hurled him through the warehouse. I only caught a glimpse of his body slamming into one of the cement support beams on the other side of the building.

I blacked out for a second from the rage and hunger.

When I came back, I was holding a spine in my hand and yanking it out of a man's back. It was the man named Dennis and his body was limp as a rag when both halves hit the ground.

I heard screams. I dropped the spine and lunged for Warren. He was going for his knife as Kyle raised his gun to shoot me. I grabbed Warren and he weighed nothing as I spun around. The bullets meant for me hit him in the back. He screamed as I held him there with one hand and grabbed his knife with the other. I silenced the screams as I ran that blade so deep into his throat I nearly severed his head.

Blood sprayed out and I opened my mouth to drink from it. I lunged for that neck and let the blood pour down my throat like a geyser. It was hot, pure life itself and I *needed* it.

I heard people running. I threw Warren into Kyle and knocked him off his feet. Kyle didn't move from under the fresh corpse.

Alicia was running away from the door while Victoria was sprinting for the only exit. I had no thought other than kill. I went for Alicia's healthy figure. I grabbed her by the hair and yanked her back off her feet. I watched her fall, trapped in time like a beautiful dancer, entranced by her grace and beauty. I moved around to the side of her as she fell and locked my jaws around her throat in mid-air.

I kept standing and I tore a chunk of her throat out as gravity took her body to the ground. I spat out the flesh and watched her writhe and choke on her own blood. I looked down at her and saw only a fresh piece of meat. I breathed in and smelled the gorgeous scent of her terror boiling in her blood.

A shot rang out and bullets sprayed towards me. One hit me in the shoulder, another in the thigh.

I stumbled back, almost knocked off my feet, but I didn't go down. I didn't feel the pain of the silver bullets. I didn't hear my flesh sizzling and popping. There was nothing but the thirst, the hunger for death.

Victoria pumped the shotgun and took aim again, walking towards me.

I jumped straight up into the rafters faster than her eyes could see. I heard the explosion of gunshot, but the bullets couldn't catch me.

I ran along the steel rafters as if they were broad streets. I dove down to the ground and landed behind Victoria before she could even turn around.

I locked my arms around her. I crushed the slender hand holding the shotgun.

Her screams were invigorating.

I spun her around as the shotgun fell to the floor.

I saw the terror in her eyes and basked in it. That was the last thing I remembered before I sank my fangs into her throat and felt her hot blood spray down the back of mine.

I fed and the world faded away as I drained that bitch dry.

33

My vision started to clear. I heard heartbeats nearby. I realized I had someone's throat in my mouth. I felt flesh between my fangs and a mouthful of blood.

I dropped the limp body in my arms and spat out the hot blood. I stared down at Victoria. Her eyes were open and void of that spark all living things have. Blood was splashed across the side of her jaw and cheek. It matched her lipstick almost perfectly. Blood streamed out of the gaping hole in the side of her throat.

I knelt down and ripped off Victoria's bloodstained vest. I frantically scrubbed her blood off my face, neck, and chest. I didn't want it on me. I didn't want to even taste her.

It's hard to explain the bloodlust, the hunger. It's like the ocean. The waves come crashing onto the shore. They can't be stopped. You get in their way and they slam into you and drag you under. Then the ocean calls the wave back only to send another wave crashing against the shore again.

I drowned in that hunger. I couldn't fight it. I didn't want to. I called my powers early, earlier than I ever thought I could. It was the price I had to pay.

I looked up at the windows of the skylight overhead. The sunlight wasn't as direct, but it was still bright outside. I stood up and looked at the dark blood covering me. It had been a long time since the hunger took over, but not long enough.

I hate losing control. You black out; you see what your body's doing like an outsider looking in, and when you wake up, everyone around you is dead. All of my strength and speed with no thought guiding it; it was dangerous to say the least.

I was a strong enough Vampire to have perfect control over my own body and my cravings. It's why I didn't force the abilities. To lose control like that even for a few seconds...it scares me.

I examined the massacre that lay around me. Victoria was dead at my feet. Phil's crushed skull and limp bulky figure lay where I left him. Dennis was pulled apart at the abdomen, his spine trailing along the floor. Alicia was farther away, lying in a pool of her own blood with her throat ripped out.

A body lay near the far wall of the warehouse to my right. A huge splash of blood, brain, and clumps of meat clung to the wall where the body had hit. It was the man who had been by the door with the shotgun. I could only assume he ran up on me while I was feeding off Victoria. He should've just run away. His mistake.

I turned to Abby. She wasn't moving.

"Abby," I focused on my hearing, afraid to move if it was too late.

Her pulse whispered in my ear like faint raindrops.

I was by Abby's side before I could even think. I knelt down and held her small hand in mine. She looked at me, breathing as if each breath hurt. Her eyes were drowning in tears of fear and pain.

"You look disgusting," she said.

I didn't like how soft she spoke.

I kept holding her hand, like a scared child who didn't know what to do.

"Don't talk."

She turned her head at me for a moment and then quickly looked away.

"Abby?"

Abby took her hand out of mine. "Put some pants on."

I don't know how she got me to laugh, but she did. I searched for the bullet wound and saw it in her stomach. Blood was welling up through her red tank top. I could see her dark fleshy insides through the small hole.

"I think it went straight through," Abby whispered.

"You've been shot before?" I asked.

"Once or twice." She did her best to smile and I appreciated that. I don't know why, but I did.

I looked over the wound. Abby was losing a lot of blood. There was a chance she wouldn't make it even if I got her to a hospital. I couldn't let her die. That left me with only one option. I had to heal Abby myself.

I've said it before. Vampires don't bleed once their immortality rises. Our bodies absorb blood for nutrients and energy. But there are times though when a Vampire's body *does* bleed. After feeding as much as I did, I had time before my body absorbed all of that blood for itself. That meant I had time to use my powers to heal someone. The trick was pretty simple if I remembered right. You had to drain one person to the point of death, and then take that life and put it into another, focus on healing them and bam, they're as good as new.

There was one problem of course. Healing someone that way was so magically complicated that I didn't do it often. In fact, I hadn't ever really done it before. My nerves started to creep in, but I couldn't let them. I had to try.

"I'm going to heal you, Abby," I promised.

"I'm not drinking your blood." The idea seemed to sicken her.

I leaned in close to her. "You have to. You're going to bleed to death."

She shook her head. "I won't be your servant."

My servant. I looked up and saw Kyle trapped under Warren's body a few yards away. Warren was dead and Kyle still wasn't moving.

I looked back down at Abby and she was staring up at me. "I'm sorry."

I looked her in the eyes. I didn't want to lose her too.

"You won't be my slave. I promise."

I don't make promises I don't intend to keep. My word is my bond, unless I'm lying. I wasn't lying to Abby right then. I hadn't promised her much in the time we knew one another, but for some reason Abby trusted me. It made me want to hold her and go back in time and prevent her from getting shot in the first place. It made me happy and sad all at once.

"Do it. Quick."

I smirked and grabbed the silver bracelet around her wrist. One of them was a sharp silver pendant.

Abby watched me. "Be careful."

I shushed her and snapped the charm free of the band. I stabbed it into my arm and cut it vertically up my wrist. The silver burned and sizzled the moment it punctured my skin.

My blood, or rather Victoria's, started to well up out of my arm. I tossed the bloodied silver charm aside and held my wrist down to Abby's mouth.

"I'm gonna be sick." Abby looked like she was trying to sink into the ground to get away from me.

"Abby. Just drink. Please."

She didn't make the first move, so I did. I put my open wound over her mouth. She resisted at first. She gagged a little and hesitated a bit before finally her tongue glided along the cut. She started to suck at the wound, slowly, and then more vigorously. It felt surprisingly good. I hadn't ever let anyone drink blood out of me before so I started to worry about what side effects there could be if I wasn't careful. I had bitten Kyle and made him my slave on accident. I didn't know if drinking my blood could do the same, but I wasn't going to take that chance with Abby.

I focused my thoughts completely on Abby's wound. I imagined it healing right in front of my eyes like my own body would heal the gunshot. I tried willing my own immortality into her body to stitch the damaged tissues together. I didn't want anything else in the world other than for Abby to heal.

My mind was swirling. I felt dizzy. There was something magical happening between Abby and I. It made my spine shiver and my entire body tremble. My skin radiated with heat. I felt Abby's own supernatural powers swirling around me, enveloping the two of us in some invisible blanket.

I opened my eyes and looked at the bloody hole in her stomach. The flesh was almost a scab. It worked. For once, something finally worked.

I pulled back my arm and Abby grabbed at me to keep it still. She started sucking at the wound as hard as she could, latched onto me like a leech.

"Abby..."

She couldn't hear me, or rather, didn't want to hear me.

"Stop."

She wouldn't.

"Stop!" I used a little strength to get free and I was on my feet out of her reach as fast as I could.

Abby lay there on the ground and I felt her power dance around her. She ran her hands up her body, feeling herself as she swam in the pool of her own cool energy.

The second she realized what she was doing she stopped and looked at me, embarrassed. She sat up and looked at her flat tan stomach. A dark round bit of scar tissue was all that remained of the bullet hole.

"I don't believe it." Abby looked up at me and saw through my briefs that I was somewhat aroused. It made her blush.

It didn't bother me that she was seeing me at half-mast. I'd been half-naked and tortured in front of total strangers and scared shitless. It wasn't my proudest moment, but I wasn't feeling too self-conscious right then.

I did feel physically off though. I was relieved, but the sensation of healing Abby and feeling that connection had made me shaky. I looked at my wrist. I'd cut myself with Abby's silver charm, but the cut was already healing. I remembered Victoria shooting me with the silver bullets in a shotgun while I was going berserk. I checked my body, but I couldn't see any wounds. It had to have been from all of the blood I'd taken, not only from Victoria, but from Warren and Alicia as well.

I couldn't remember the last time I had so much blood at one time.

I looked down at Abby. "How do you feel?"

"Good. I could feel you willing yourself to heal me." She tried getting up and I helped her to her feet. "I felt you channeling your powers. I didn't know Vampires had to focus so hard."

I shrugged. Maybe Vampires didn't. I knew I did.

I didn't know how the magic worked enough to explain it to Abby and I didn't want to admit that I was practically winging it when I tried healing her. I'd only focused on healing her because I really didn't need to turn her into my human servant. One unwilling slave was one too many for me.

I heard movement nearby. Kyle.

"Stay here," I told Abby.

"Kris…"

I looked back at her and I don't know what she saw in my eyes, but she just nodded.

"I drove here. I'll get the car." Abby turned and headed for the only exit. She made sure to walk around the pools of blood and the corpses on the ground.

I heard the door shut behind her as I reached Kyle. He was barely conscious and squirming under Warren's dead weight.

I grabbed the back of Warren's jacket and lifted him off Kyle with one hand. I tossed the corpse aside like the garbage it was. Kyle was covered in Warren's blood. I stared at the kid for what felt like an eternity.

I got down on my knees and I didn't know what to do at first. Kyle was just a body lying there in front of me. His familiar face seemed foreign. I'd lived with him for over a year. So much time and I didn't see any of it coming. I was filled with too many emotions to understand half of them. I didn't want to feel anything anymore.

I slowly went to touch Kyle's hand. I was afraid. A part of me wanted answers. Another part of me wanted to run away. I couldn't do that though. I had to know what Kyle was thinking. I needed to connect the dots.

I wrapped my hand around his. The memories flooded my mind. They were intense, but clearer than what I was used to. I blamed it on all the blood I'd taken, but maybe it was my bond with Kyle.

I was sitting in a coffee shop.

Alicia was right beside me. She was so pretty in high school. She had grown even more beautiful.

I was so nervous. We had kept in touch over the years until last year. I couldn't believe it when she called and said she was in town.

Alicia told me how good I looked. How proud she was of me.

She never finished college. She dropped out of art school. She was always such a good artist.

She told me about some church she was involved in. How she was trying to make the world a better, safer place.

I barely heard her. All I could think of was how soft her lips looked. How lovely she smelled. I had spent nights thinking about her. Remembering the first girl I ever loved.

265

I didn't know what was happening. A giant sat down beside me at our table with a gorgeous woman and a thin man.

The thin man didn't sit down. He just kept staring at me. I think he was growling.

"Brian smells Vampire on him," the big man told Alicia.

I couldn't believe it. How could they have known about Kris?

Alicia didn't believe it. She kept saying no and when I tried to answer her the big man put a hand on my shoulder.

"Don't move." he warned.

I was scared. If Kris was there he would've known what to do, but I wasn't Kris and I didn't have a clue.

I told Alicia I didn't know what was going on. She just kept staring at me, tears welling in her eyes.

The woman with the big man leaned in close to me. She smelled amazing too, but she was too beautiful, too intimidating.

"Tell me why you have a Vampire's scent on you." the woman asked.

I didn't know what to do. I started to panic. I didn't know what Kris would do to me if I talked. He told me to never tell anyone about us. That it put us both in danger.

The man growling at me started to tremble and the big man told him to go outside and get some air. I watched him go and Alicia put a hand on mine.

"You're in trouble aren't you?" she asked.

I looked at Alicia, at the only face that's ever cared about me.

"We can help you," Alicia said.

She turned to the older woman.

"We can help him. Please." I couldn't tell if Alicia was asking or begging.

The woman nodded slowly. "We can help."

I trusted her with my life. I had missed her so much.

The woman promised she could help. Victoria was her name. Phil was the large man with her.

They promised me. I told them I needed time.

I was in a hotel room.

I skipped work at the hospital for Alicia.

I ran my hands along her breasts and kissed her neck. She was so warm. She was so safe. She told me she loved me and she was sorry that I was trapped.

I told her about Kris. I told her how he treated me.

Alicia said he deserved to die. I wasn't sure. Kris wasn't a monster...not the way Alicia described other Vampires. He just had me trapped. He just treated me like shit. My life wasn't my own, it was his, and it came second.

I was sitting in my room looking at old yearbooks and notes from when Alicia and I dated. The old shoebox I kept them in was on the edge of my bed. I should've thrown them out, but I never did.

I was terrified Kris was going to find out about what I'd done. It had been three days. Three days of hoping he wouldn't sense something. That he wouldn't just somehow know that I'd made my decision. He'd stop me if he found out. He'd do whatever he had to do to save himself.

I got out of bed feeling better than normal that morning. Last night Kris said I could have the house to myself. Alicia would spend it with me. Our last night together just in case things went bad tomorrow when Phil and the others came for Kris.

I didn't even really register how weird it was that Kris was using the spare bathroom to shower. I wasn't thinking that early. I went to take a piss and saw the girl pull the curtain aside. She was naked and dripping wet. I only got a glance before she fired the gun in her hand.

My heart was racing. I was in my room getting dressed. Everything was falling apart. Three kids. Kris had brought home kids, one of them maybe even a Witch. Kris had said we were all going out. I didn't have a choice. I never did.

I texted Alicia about what was happening. Phil wanted us followed. Brian the Werepanther and two others were tailing us as I drove to Abby's. Kris didn't notice. Thank God he didn't notice.

We were driving back home. My whole body hurt from Brian throwing me across the beach. He had lost control and chased after the kids to save them. I couldn't believe that Kris had driven Abby's car into him.

I hoped Brian was okay. I hoped more that Kris wouldn't sense what was going on in my head. I kept asking about the Were, just kept talking to mask it all. It would be dark soon. I wouldn't have to worry about anything once Kris left.

Please, God. Help me.

I was crying in my hallway. I couldn't help it. I was so angry.

I had never hated Kris so much. He was going after the kids. I didn't think he'd hurt them, but I wasn't sure. He was just a monster after all. Alicia was right. He had to be stopped. He deserved what was coming.

Alicia and I made love in my bed and it was the most intense sex I've ever had.

I fell asleep next to her; she was promising me that tomorrow I'd be free and we could be together.

I would do anything just to have my life back so I could start a new one with Alicia.

Anything.

I couldn't take anymore. I got out of his head and would never go back there again. I'd never read someone's thoughts so smoothly, so detailed. Had I drank that much blood?

Kyle started to wake up.

I held his head up so that I was the first thing he'd see when he came to.

Kyle's eyes fluttered and fixed on me and I knew he was mine. He wasn't afraid. He wasn't afraid because I told him not to be.

I held his hand tighter and looked into those dark blue eyes.

He smiled up at me.

I smiled down at him.

"I fucked up didn't I?" he asked.

I nodded, keeping my smile. "Yeah."

I could feel his fear boiling under the surface of his mind, but I kept it back. I didn't want him to be afraid of me anymore.

"What do we do now?" he asked.

I shrugged.

"I'm not sorry." Kyle meant it.

"I know you're not," I told him. "I am though."

Kyle nodded and his hand squeezed mine. His eyes grew wider. "If I die, you die...right?

My smile faded. I couldn't pretend anymore.

I leaned just a fraction closer to Kyle so that I could see every speck of blue in his iris. So he could see my eyes just the same.

"No," I whispered. "You die...and that's all."

I felt Kyle's fear start to rush to the surface. I pushed it so far down that he actually felt happy for a moment. Happier than he'd felt since I came into his life and ruined it over a year ago.

He felt happiness before I snapped his neck.

The connection that bound us together shattered. It simply disappeared and the bond I had with him vanished. It was as if it was never there.

I stayed there on my knees, holding him for a little while. I just watched him finally find the peace I hadn't been able to give him. The peace I didn't want to give him.

Kyle died with no fear or regrets; just positive, happy emotions in his mind and heart.

It was my final favor to Kyle, my apology for ruining his life.

34

I sat on the edge of Kyle's bed. The shades were drawn and the room felt cold, even to me.

I held one of the yearbooks he had lying on the floor. It was from his senior year. I ran my fingers across the golden letters on the front.

I had taken a shower and scrubbed the blood off me, but I still felt dirty. I could smell Kyle and Alicia's scent in his room and it bothered me.

Two hours ago the sun was just setting when the warehouse went up in flames.

Abby had found a couple of trucks that apparently Victoria and the others owned. There were a few gallons of gasoline and lighter fluid in the bed of one truck and matches in another. They had planned on killing us and then burning the warehouse down to begin with. I don't think they imagined that I'd park *their* trucks inside with *their* dead bodies and burn the place down for them.

Just goes to show life never turns out as you plan.

I'd been forced to put on pants that were in a duffle bag in one of the trucks. I think they were Warren's because they were a little too tight. We left the scene of the burning corpses in the rental car Abby had gotten that morning, with me wearing a dead man's spare jeans.

The drive back was silent. I didn't feel like talking. I didn't really feel like doing anything. Abby respected that so she talked enough for both of us.

It turns out that Abby had been calling and calling the house to yell at me about her car. When I never picked up and Kyle didn't either she got worried and drove to the house herself. She saw the mess that Phil and the other douches made of my home and went looking for me.

She used a similar locator spell to find Kyle like the one I used to find Lila. The spell wouldn't work on me, but she found Kyle just fine.

Abby had dropped me off at the house and I kissed her because I didn't know what else to do. She kissed me back. I wasn't expecting it and I don't think she was either.

For one moment, I felt warm again, close to someone. I needed that. Maybe the reason Abby kissed me back was that she knew I needed it too.

I headed inside and Abby promised she'd check in on me tomorrow.

I opened Kyle's high-school yearbook to skim through it when a picture fell out. It landed facedown at my feet.

I picked it up and turned the photo over. It took me a second to realize I'd seen the same picture before. A frozen moment of four friends standing in front of lockers, smiling about their senior year of high school. The boy and girl up front had their arms wrapped around one another. Big smiles chiseled into their young faces. The girl was an Alicia. The boy was a Kyle.

I heard a tapping on the bedroom door.

Jack was standing there watching me. "Abby called me up."

I couldn't stop staring at the picture. I saw the twin copy of that photograph inside of Alicia's apartment the night I fed from her. The very same picture and I didn't even notice that it was Kyle holding her.

How could I have missed it? Did I really care so little about Kyle?

"How'd you get inside?" I asked.

Jack came in and stood beside Kyle's bed. No, it wasn't *his* bed anymore. He was gone. It was just *a* bed. It didn't belong to anyone. Just me.

"Abby told me how to get past it. She said if you want, she'd work out a new spell for free. You trust me though don't you?"

"Trust. If you can't even trust your own slave, who can you trust?" Even I didn't think the joke was funny.

Jack put a hand on my shoulder. "You going to hold up okay?"

I kept holding the photograph, staring at how young, and naïve, and happy Alicia and Kyle looked.

"I'll live."

"Yes you will. There anything you need?"

I ran my thumb over the picture, over Kyle's face. I never saw him smile like that in all the time I knew him.

I closed my eyes and burned that image of him smiling in the back of my head. That's how I wanted to remember Kyle. That's what I wanted to see when I thought of my first human servant.

The photograph fell out of my hand.

I looked up at Jack and didn't know what to say. I felt cramped. I needed to burn off energy. I had to get out of the house for a while. I had to get away.

"You want to go for a run?" I asked.

Jack frowned. "A run?"

"A run." I took a nice deep breath and sighed it out. "I could go for a long run right about now."

The old Werebear grinned. "Well, let's do it then."

It took a lot to get up to my feet and actually walk out of that room.

Jack and I walked out onto the back deck and took off our shoes and socks.

"You think you can keep up, old man?" I asked. I had to keep it light. I had to stay away from all of the thoughts swimming in my head.

Jack rolled up his jeans a bit and then straightened up and ran a hand over his stomach. "I think you need to go to hell."

"Someday," I said it and it meant more than I wanted it to.

Jack walked up to me and made sure I could see his eyes. "Kris, I don't know what's going on in that head of yours. I never really do. I just don't want you to think that this was your fault. You were the innocent in all this for once. You got played."

"I should've treated the kid better."

"Maybe. You want to know what I think?"

"No. Sure."

"I think you treated Kyle the only way you knew how to."

"Shitty?"

Jack sighed. "At times maybe. But there's one difference between you and Kyle. You don't betray your friends. In your own fucked-up, retarded way, you're loyal. You'd kill to protect yours."

"Is that a compliment?"

Jack put both hands on my shoulders and narrowed his gaze on mine.

"Kris, you are without a doubt one of the worst Vampires that I have ever met in my entire life."

"That was the compliment."

"No. You may be a bad Vampire, but you're a good man. *That* is the compliment."

I didn't know what to say. Jack meant what he was telling me and I wanted to believe him. I really did. Maybe one day I would.

My skin started to crawl. I wanted to get moving. I wanted to clear my head and stop feeling. I wanted things to get back to normal.

I swatted Jack in the gut and stepped off my back deck. "We running or what? I've got a whole night to kill."

Jack watched me for a few moments and didn't say a word. He looked worried.

I felt the cool sand between my toes and it invigorated me. I had to run.

"Come on, Jack." I really needed him to stop talking and just start running with me.

Jack grinned and stepped down onto the beach. He smacked me hard enough on the back to rattle me a bit.

"You think you can keep up with a Were as old as I am?"

"You think you can keep running without having a heart attack?"

Jack went to hit me again, but I took off running out of his reach.

"You little shit," Jack called, laughing.

We both started our jog along the beach. Jack might've been over one hundred years old, but he kept up with me the entire night without breaking a sweat. You gotta love lycanthropy.

We ran and ran and ran some more until my home and all the memories inside it were miles away. We ran along the beach until the sun came up and my immortality faded.

Jack and I went out into the ocean and watched the sun rise up over the horizon.

It had been a long time since I did that with anyone.

35

Not much has really changed since that day. Sure, I was down a roommate, but there was some good to come from everything. Abby and I have gotten closer. I got her car fixed up for her cheap at the auto shop that Al the bartender works at during the day. I think she feels a bit more protective of me now; I know I do of her. We saved each other's life.

Technically, I saved her life twice, so I still had one up on her. But who's counting?

Jack stops by more frequently to drink and talk. It's not all business all the time. Abby comes and visits me too. We go out for lunch and hang out during the day a few times a week. It's nice to have the company.

As far as Tara and the kids go, they're doing well. They all live with Portia, so I drive up there during the day sometimes to visit. Portia's trying her best to patch up her family. She's teaching Lila how to control her abilities and grow as a gifted Psychic. Ben and Lila are going to be homeschooled and Tara is trying to find a part-time job and go to a Community College next fall.

The men who killed the kids' father weren't ever in Florida as far as I know. They haven't come for Lila yet, but that doesn't mean they won't one day. Portia won't let me forget that I promised the children my protection in my territory. I wish I didn't open my big mouth sometimes. Still, I'm around for those kids whenever they need my help.

My immortal life seems to be going good considering I nearly lost it all. Even though I normally collect the things that almost kill me, I left Kyle's body to burn in that warehouse. It was a day that doesn't need remembering and a keepsake I don't want. I emptied out his room and donated everything to the Salvation Army. The only thing I did keep was the photograph of him and Alicia. I put it in the gun safe in my closet.

Jack is on high alert since I told him about the God-loving, monster-hating lunatics that were behind the killings along the

East Coast. He spread the word to any contacts he had out of state about the movement this group of humans were trying to start. It feels good to know who to keep our eyes on and who to take down to prevent more needless killings.

As for little old me, I'm trying to make the best of what I've got. I'm playing it even safer during the day and ignoring any and all little Psychic children that are just waiting to pounce.

I'd like to say that I learned a valuable lesson, but to be honest I'm a slow learner. Sure, I feel bad about Kyle and I regret that I wasn't a better master. Unfortunately, I love the open buffet that is South Florida too much to let one bad day burden me for too long. You only get one immortal life after all. You've got to make the most of it, or else, what's the point?

Oh, that reminds me.

I've started the search for a new human servant.

I'd prefer a woman this time, with a good head on her shoulders and a nice body to match. Someone who doesn't complain and who won't betray me and almost get me killed.

What? Is that too much to ask for?

Come on, it'll be fun. I promise.

I don't bite.

ABOUT THE AUTHOR

Jon Kershner is twenty-three years old with a Bachelor's Degree in English from Florida Atlantic University. Jon currently lives in South Florida where he writes constantly.